LOOSE HEAD

A DEX REED RUGBY THRILLER

BY JEFF KEITHLY

Loose Head is a work of fiction. Names, characters, places and incidents either are the product of the author's imagination or are used fictitiously. Any resemblance to actual persons, living or dead, events or locales is entirely coincidental.

ACKNOWLEDGMENTS

I would like to take this opportunity to thank Detective Chief Inspectors Charlie McMurdie and Alan Bostock for their insights into the inner workings of the Metropolitan Police Service. Thanks to the Portland Rugby Club and Portland Old Boars: to Dennis Fernandes, always there in support; to Peter Carmine and Craig Olson, who taught me what I needed to know both on and off the field; to Andy Fraser, a tower of generosity in both friendship and hospitality; and especially to the real Dex Reed, for allowing me to borrow his name and best qualities.

For Mara, who has shown me worlds I never knew existed.

This book is dedicated to my grandmother, Elizabeth Osterhaus Bobbitt, and to my daughters, Lilli and Elise, who have always believed in the power of a good story.

PROLOGUE

On those rare occasions when I have contemplated my own death, I always assumed it would be in some noble cause: dismembered by a train as I tossed a wayward child to its mother; killed by a stray bullet as I dragged a police comrade out of harm's way; entombed in rubble while shielding civilians from a terrorist's blast. But not like this. Not like this.

The rusted chain clamped round my ankles was as hard as a divorce solicitor's heart, and as warm. The other end of the chain passed through the ruined hulk of an engine block – it appeared to be an old Ford V-6 – grating moodily back and forth across the teak decking. I stood, arms bound behind my back, in the stern of a 30-foot motor launch, heaving at idle somewhere off the foggy coast of Dover. The night was moonless, and black waves slapped the sides of the boat as it rolled sickeningly in the chop. Below me lay 50 fathoms of icy, lightless brine. All my life I have feared deep water, and now my soul throbbed with dread.

Any moment, as soon as the four big men in the wheelhouse had consumed sufficient whisky to steel themselves for the deed, the engine block would be heaved to the rail and dropped overboard. I would have little choice but to follow, plummeting through Stygian darkness, pulled down by 400 pounds of steel, my brain pleading for air, my eardrums rupturing from the pressure, until I could resist no more and icy seawater filled my lungs...

With luck, I would be dead before I hit the seafloor. Short of being introduced to a wolverine with a taste for testicles, I could think of no worse way to die.

The empty bottle went overboard with a splash. "Time to do what we came for, boys. Let's get it over with."

Artemis Paul. Not a shred of human emotion in that voice – not that I expected any. Paul was a clinical sociopath, but one who had turned an otherwise-crippling malady to his advantage in a very successful criminal career. Loan-sharking. Pimping. Maybe murder as well, though I had no hard evidence. Not until tonight.

"Mr. Paul. He's SCD. They won't rest until they find who killed him."

"You let me worry about that." Paul's voice was hammer-head hard. "All you should be thinking is what you won't owe me after tonight."

So he was forgiving their undoubtedly substantial debts in exchange for this little night's work – clever. Knowing how much Artemis Paul loved money, I realized just how desperately he wanted me dead.

They came for me now, the rough seas and the whisky keeping their movements slow and careful. The two I didn't know seized one side of the greasy engine block, somewhat squeamishly, I thought, not looking at me, concentrated on preserving their digits as the boat rolled. The two I did know – Artemis Paul and Mick Ryan – took the other side of the wallowing hulk of steel, and made ready to feed me to the sea.

The evening had just gone from bad to worse.

1

A storm was coming, and my only consolation was that it would wet the virtuous and vice-ridden alike. As the wind waltzed with a weary whirl of withered leaves and the first sheets of rain began to fall, my partner, Brian Abbott, and I made a brisk circuit of the secluded, shrubbery-screened nooks and crannies of Soho Square. I jammed my fists deeper into the pockets of my mac and hissed in annoyance. The bell of St. Patrick's church on the east side of the square tolled somewhat mockingly, I thought. Our quarry was nowhere in sight. Time to check the chalet.

We were looking for Mick Ryan, a leg-breaker in the service of one Artemis Paul. Paul was a particularly loathsome specimen of London loan shark – or, to be more accurate, all-around turd-snapper – a man with the lifestyle of a lord and the pitiless soul of a Thames estuary seagull. Mick Ryan was one of Paul's debt collectors, a curly-haired, cheerful-looking thug famous for his ability to inflict agony without leaving a mark. More than one delinquent Paul client had soiled himself under Ryan's sympathetic ministrations, and afterward, we had never been able to prove a thing. But for all his proficiency, Ryan was no sadist; to him, dislocating digits and traumatizing tissues was just a job, one he could leave at the office when his long day's toil was done.

In fact, by the standards of the day, Mick Ryan was a virtuous man in a brutal profession. Quiet and surprisingly abstemious in his personal habits, he didn't do drugs or lash out in random violence. Oh, he would take a pint or two of Sam Smith's Sovereign Best Bitter after indulging in his twin passions: playing flanker for the London Celtic rugby union football club, and the Uilleann pipes in a traditional Celtic band called Poteen. But he was just a social drinker, not a pro.

This is not to say that, despite a face better suited to a Renaissance cherub than a loan shark's enforcer, Mick Ryan led an entirely seraphic life. He did enjoy an occasional wager. And then one day, his brother introduced him to Shane McMurdo.

Shane was a jockey, one of the best – five feet and eight stone of red-haired, whip-wielding dynamite. Ryan's brother, Timothy, had done McMurdo an unspecified service, and in return, a grateful McMurdo laid bare the secrets of his guild. Specifically, he told the brothers Ryan which horse to bet in one race of a given meet, in return for half of the resulting swag.

And so Mick Ryan made the transition from casual gambler to major player. At first all went gloriously according to plan, and McMurdo's tips proved to be pure gold. But there came a day when both the Ryans' ever-increasing winnings and their clandestine chats with the diminutive McMurdo came to the notice of the wrong element. At the jockey's direction, the brothers put £50,000 on a filly called Cucaracha in the fourth race at Epsom Downs. Cucaracha pulled up lame, and McMurdo vanished from the jockey's lounge and was never seen again.

Alas for Mick Ryan, 25,000 of those pounds had been the sum total of his and his brother's ill-gotten gains from their earlier wagers. The other £25,000 he had borrowed, in certainty of quick repayment, from his boss, Artie Paul. And in two minutes flat, Ryan made the transition from valued employee to deadbeat customer.

Time passed, and accumulated interest triggered an automatic response. Ryan found himself on the receiving end of the same treatment he had so often meted out. But with no source of income other than his weekly pay envelope, Ryan had no hope of paying what he owed. Then, ogling Ryan's too-pretty features and rugby-hardened body, Artemis Paul offered a diabolical choice: die, or join the legion of rent-boys plying their trade in his service. To sweeten the pot, Paul said he would credit Ryan's account with double the going rate for each sexual act.

And so it was that I approached the ancient, half-timbered chalet in the centre of Soho Square. I saw that the decrepit padlock on one of the doors had been torn off. Nodding to Brian, I nudged the door open with my toe. As my eyes adjusted to the gloom within, I beheld Mick Ryan, kneeling in fellationic worship before a chubby, red-faced Dutch tourist. At my entrance, both looked up, with the startled eyes of guilty pets; I flourished my warrant-card and the tourist, fumbling with his fly, fled.

"Still sucking peter to pay Paul," said I, sadly. "A shame you aren't as good on the bagpipes as you are on the skin flute. A few gigs with the Chieftains and you'd be laughing."

"What d'you mean, barging in here like that and chasing away me customers?" Ryan snarled, rising menacingly to his feet.

"It's my job. And I didn't see you return his money. Anyway, at least you didn't have to…"

"Ahh. What d'you want, Reed, ya Cockney bloodsucker?"

"Hah. Better a Cockney bloodsucker than a bloody coc…"

"Yes, yes, most amusin'. Why're ya bustin' me balls?"

"I need a small favour – and it's not your balls I'm out to squeeze. In fact, you may come to think of me as your avenging angel."

Ryan's scowl didn't change, but something kindled in his eyes, a sort of hopeful ferocity, the kind of look I had often seen when the rugby ball suddenly popped loose after a tackle. Ryan was a very good flanker, one of the best I've ever played against, strong, agile and ferocious. Only a slight lack of ambition, an inability to commit unreservedly to the game, had held him back from true greatness.

"So what is it, then?"

"Simple. I want you to introduce me to your boss."

And it had all gone so smoothly. SCD – Specialist Crime Directorate – were interested in Paul because of his pimping and loan-sharking, obviously. There was also the matter of Martin Wallace. Wallace was a small-time drugs dealer who, my sources told me, was looking to make a reputation as a man who feared no one. He borrowed £10,000 from Paul, then ostentatiously refused to repay the debt.

One night Wallace staggered forth from his local, fairly foaming at the ears from the beer he'd consumed. A few minutes later, the denizens of the neighbourhood were startled from their beds by a flaming apparition, caroming from car to car down the middle of Redchurch Street and uttering ghastly, window-rattling shrieks. At last he collapsed, and the horrified neighbours rushed out to smother the flames with blankets. Someone had doused Wallace with petrol and set him aflame. He died an hour later, in agony. We at Hendon SCD had a strong suspicion who that someone might be, but there was the small matter of proving it – hence my visit to Mick Ryan.

On the strength of Ryan's good word – he told his boss I was a rugby mate who needed the money for a dead-cert stock tip – I borrowed £5,000 from Artemis Paul that night, promising to repay him within two weeks at 30 percent a week interest. Paul had even credited Ryan's account with a 10 percent commission. It was now two weeks later. A bit early to pay Paul a return visit, but then, leaving work, I suddenly thought of Mick Ryan, and his degrading new career. A few minutes later, almost without intervention of conscious thought, I alighted from a taxi in front of Paul's nightclub, a surprisingly tasteful and jazzy enclave called Blue Hour 'round the corner from the Kilburn tube station.

My inner voice, which I long ago learned to ignore at my peril, told me I was being stupid. It's completely against Metropolitan Police Service policy to deliberately seek out a suspect on your own – you always take a colleague along, both for safety and to corroborate evidence. Still, I told myself, this was merely a visit of reassurance, to let Paul know I'd have his money soon, to keep the investigation ticking along. As I pulled open the door, I prayed my supervisors – and my partner – would understand.

I had hardly licked the cream from my Irish coffee when I felt a hand on my elbow. He wasn't a tall man, but he was a hard man, his neck threatening to burst his collar like ice from a frozen pipe, his shoulders and biceps straining the fine wool of his black cashmere turtleneck. "Mr. Paul would like a word," he said pleasantly, and shepherded me firmly toward the back.

Paul's office was surprisingly spacious, given the rents in this corner of London. A series of CCTV monitors on the opposite wall displayed views of the club: the bar, the dance floor, the booths, the kitchen, the cellar, the toilets, the bins out back. In the women's loo, a willowy blond was just settling her knickers as I entered, and I paused for an appreciative ogle. I caught sight of myself in the office monitor – a head taller than the bloke who had me by the arm, thick-necked, slope-shouldered, skin the colour of café-au-lait, a legacy from my Bahamian father, nasty scar over the left eye, ears like rawhide dog-chews from my years in the forward pack, a flash of watchful green eyes beneath close-cropped black hair.

The hand on my elbow became a clamp, and I moved along. Nothing to see here.

Paul sat motionless behind a laptop computer atop an ornate and respectable Victorian desk. He was a pious-looking man, tall, gaunt and smooth-cheeked, who took great pains to hide his reptilian nature behind a facade of genteel opulence: elegant dark-grey suit, tasteful tie, high-tech German spectacles. A stockbroker, perhaps – or a mortician.

Paul regarded me without expression for what he considered an appropriately unsettling length of time. "You're late," he said at length.

I feigned craven fear. "Mr. Paul, you've got to believe me. I've been trying – I really have."

"You owe me £9,950. Do you have it?"

"Not yet, Mr. Paul, but It's only been a week. I'll have it for you on Friday, without fail."

"But you don't have it tonight." He sighed and looked aggrieved. "Obviously you fail to appreciate the seriousness of your commitment. Dean." He gestured to the leg-breaker at my elbow. "Impress it upon him. Don't leave any marks."

Instantly the grip on my elbow became an unbearable pressure as my hand was forced up between my shoulder-blades. In seconds, ligaments would tear. I made an executive decision. With my free hand, I took possession of Dean's manly bundle and gave it a friendly squeeze. "I wouldn't," I said conversationally. "Just let go my arm, and you might have children yet, if anything female will have you." Dean let go, staring on confusion at his boss. This wasn't the way things were supposed to go.

The door opened behind me, and I heard heavy breathing from multiple sources. Paul had pressed a button. "Don't even think about it," I told Paul. "I'm DI Dexter Reed from Hendon SCD. I know about the loan sharking, I know about the rent-boys, I know about your offshore accounts, and I know you made £3 million last year and declared £200,000 to Inland Revenue. I'm afraid you can kiss that knighthood goodbye, mate. We're rolling up your operation like one of your delicious tandoori wraps."

In the tense silence that enveloped the room, Paul suddenly looked up. "We? Where's your support, DI Reed?" he asked gently. "They should be here by now."

I shook my head pityingly, and began the caution. "You do not have to say anything, but it may harm your defense if you do not mention when questioned something that..." Then something hard and heavy dented the back of my skull, and I knew no more.

And now I stood on the deck of Paul's boat, the *Compound Interest*, wearing an iron ankle bracelet. Would Artemis Paul kill me to protect his ill-gotten gains? Does a hobby-horse have a teak todger?

For a moment, Mick Ryan glanced up, and I managed to arch one quizzical eyebrow before he looked away. I had one last shot, and licking my parched lips, I took it. "If he's crazy enough to kill a copper, you'll be next. Toss *him* overboard, instead."

"Heave away, boys," Paul growled, and with a sickening swoop of despair, I saw the engine block leave the deck.

Then Ryan lost his grip, and the anchor dropped with a deck-denting crash. The Irishman bent over, groaning as if he'd ruptured something, and when he straightened up again, there was something in his hand. A piston-rod. Two soggy thuds, and the two nameless hooligans hit the deck.

Paul, face contorted in rage, plunged a hand inside his overcoat and came out with a blade. With the swiftness of thought it was flickering toward Ryan's throat. The Irishman jerked his head back; the blade sliced his cheek. Then his makeshift cosh caught Paul on the ear, and he went down like the sack of shite he was.

It had started to rain. I let out a long, shuddering breath and tasted its sweetness. Fresh water, not salt. "Thank you, Mick. I truly thought that was the end of a most promising career."

"For that matter, so did I. But think nothin' of it."

He picked up Paul's knife and cut the ropes binding my arms. "What changed your mind?" I asked, desperately rubbing my wrists to restore the flow of blood, suddenly shivering uncontrollably in the deathly-chill deluge.

He had squatted to unfasten the chain from around my legs, and gazed thoughtfully out over the sea, toward the lights of Calais, the rain and the blood trickling unnoticed down his face. "D'you remember that match at Spitalfields, in '98? It was just before you retired from the Hastewicke first XV. I thought you were well past it then, that you were the weak link in the pack. We were pushing for the winning try, and one of our props – Tommy Gallagher, biggish lad, about twenty stone – picked up the ball and found some space. I thought he'd score for sure, but you caught him from behind and put him down – hell of a tackle, by the way. There was a ruck, and we had an overlap, but you just wouldn't let the ball come out until your support was there. The boots were flashin', and when you got up, your jersey was bloody tatters, man. And somehow the ball came back your side, the scrum-half booted it away, and that was the match."

"You saved my life because of rugby?"

"It's the greatest game in the world. You earned my respect that day. I thought you were past it but I was wrong. You had one more game left in ya."

"But then I met you in Soho Square."

"Ah. But you never looked at me the way *he* did, did you?" He gestured disdainfully at Paul's crumpled form. "When he looked at me, there was nothing but... contempt. Disgust. And cold amusement." He suddenly raised the piston-rod overhead, on the verge of bashing Paul's brains in.

"Don't!" I cried.

He thought the better of it, and drew a shuddering breath. Then he continued as if there had been no near-homicidal inter-ruption. "Oh, you ragged me a bit. But when I looked in your eyes, I saw... compassion. Anyway, Paul would've killed me sure, sooner or later. It was only a matter of time and convenience."

He disappeared below, returned with a fresh bottle of whisky. "Here. You look like you could do with a drink. Then we'll see if we can drive this boat."

2

It was far too early the next morning when I stood before my guv'nor, Detective Superintendent Peter Wicks, for the bollocking I so richly deserved. It had taken the night crew at SCD until 3 a.m. to take my statement, and it had taken more than half of Artemis Paul's bottle of Bushmill's to calm my shattered nerves. Now, a scant four hours later, I surveyed DS Wicks through the yellow eyes of a sick ferret.

At 5'5", 10 stone and 71 years of age, DS Wicks looked more like Mr. Burns from *The Simpsons* than Martin Johnson. I knew well, however, that what he lacked in brawn he made up for in brutal intellect and a God-given talent for invective. When things went wrong – and make no mistake, the events of last night were very wrong indeed – Peter Wicks' venomous tongue could make an SAS drill instructor stick his fingers in his ears and run away, singing "La la la la...".

"Of all the Uruguayan cluster-fucks I've seen in my 50 years with the MPS, this one takes the prize! You amateurish bungler! Is the only purpose of your life to serve as a cautionary tale to others? Have I taught you nothing of proper investigative procedure in your 17 years on the force? Is there a single rule of good policework you failed to violate?"

He was in good form today. I adopted an expression of stoic repentance.

"It didn't go quite as I expected, sir."

He paused in his restless pacing and glared at me, eyes bulging, yellow teeth bared, like a bull mandrill about to charge. "Do you mock me, DI Reed?"

"Definitely not, sir."

"By the hairy scrotum of Satan, man, whatever possessed you? Too many blows to the head on the rugby pitch?"

A shadowy figure detached itself from the window, where it had been gazing out over the suburban maze that was Hendon: Detective Chief Inspector George Oakhurst, recently-appointed senior investigating officer for Hendon Specialist Crime Directorate and my immediate supervisor. He had a handsome, pock-marked visage and a cold blue gaze; his once-flat belly now strained unpleasantly against the fine pearl-grey wool of his suit jacket as if someone had shoved an air compressor-hose up his bottom. Too much good living, I thought – and too much bad intent.

DCI Oakhurst and I had a lengthy and unpleasant history; I could think of few members of the Metropolitan Police I would less rather have present as Wicks so eloquently catalogued my deficiencies. Still, I had only myself to blame.

"Sir, it was a miscalculation. It was meant to be a routine check-in – it was at least a week too early for him to resort to violence." I was on shaky ground there. Paul's volatile temperament was well-known – just ask Martin Wallace. So why *had* I put myself into his hands last night, against departmental policy, on a whim, if I was honest with myself, with no planning, no support, not a word to anyone? I thought I knew.

It was the same impulse that had impelled me, on dozens of occasions on the rugby pitch, to engage in violent physical confrontations. To redress a wrong done to a helpless teammate at the bottom of a ruck, a gratuitous stamping, a deliberate attempt to injure, unwarranted off-the-ball aggro. It was my own grandiose sense of fair play. Because in that grimy chalet in Soho Square, Mick Ryan had become my teammate. Artemis Paul had clocked him big-time. And I simply couldn't stand by and let that happen.

I also couldn't give DS Wicks or DCI Oakhurst the slightest inkling of that fact, or I was finished as a detective. I may have been stupid, but I wasn't professionally suicidal. "As I say, sir, it was a miscalculation. It was meant to be a routine check-in, to reassure Paul that I was good for the dosh. He overreacted."

"*He* overreacted?" Oakhurst asked, injecting himself into the conversation for the first time. "What about you?"

"Are you suggesting I should've taken the beating, sir?"

"You richly deserved one!" Wicks cried. "I daresay you've taken worse, and cheerfully, many times on the rugby pitch! I can't believe you went to see him without support! You jeopardized the entire investigation! The man's a lunatic!"

I managed a sickly grin. "I appreciate that now, sir."

"Wipe that smirk off your face, DI Reed!" Wicks bellowed. "Give me one good reason why I shouldn't put you on suspension!"

"Because Artemis Paul is going to prison for the rest of his life, sir. And I'd like to do whatever I can to make it two lifetimes."

Wicks glared at me for a full 30 seconds, parrot's eyes gleaming with malevolent intelligence. Finally he made an inarticulate sound, half phlegm-hawk, half-whinny. "Get out of my sight."

"Sir?" I asked hopefully.

"Start with the list of clients from his computer. Get me names, dates, amounts owed, persuasions inflicted, then go see them all. And his rent-boys. I want enough evidence to bury Artemis Paul for not two, but ten lifetimes. And Reed." His voice was almost gentle now.

"Yes, Detective Superintendent?"

"If you put one toe out of line from here on out, my boot will be so far up your bunghole, so quickly, you'll think your tongue has grown laces!" DCI Oakhurst's eyes fairly glowed in pleasure at the prospect.

II

The delectable Emma Kwan, Chief of the Metropolitan Police Service computer crime lab at Wellington House, was waiting, shapely ankles crossed on my desk, when I returned to my cube. She uncoiled sinuously as I entered and gave me a long, searching look. "All right, Dex?"

"No thanks to me, as DS Wicks has just explained in vivid detail. Thought I was fish bait last night."

"One of Paul's little elves just happened to be an old rugby mate?"

"Bit more complex than that, Em. Still, it was a lucky break that Paul decided to include him in the party." I shivered involuntarily, remembering the black void that had so nearly claimed me.

"I've always thought of you as so big and indestructible." There was a curious look in her hazel-green eyes, not unalloyed with sympathy. "Are you sure you're OK?"

I wasn't, but I nodded anyway. I wanted Emma Kwan to pull me to her spectacular breasts and stroke my rugby-gnarled ears. Instead, I heaved a businesslike sigh. "Any luck with Paul's laptop?"

"Luck's got nothing to do with it," she scoffed. "You can't hide anything from my boys. He's got interesting taste in porn, your Mr. Paul. Ever heard of 'bugging?'"

"Oh, that is so yesterday. I'm into shaved Chihuahuas, myself. Find a client list?"

"It's on your desk. I'll ring you if we turn up anything else of interest." She turned to go. "And Dex?"

"Yes?"

"Your partner. He's not best pleased with you."

I sighed again. "I know. He's sulking. He'll come around."

III

It took several hours before Brian could master his emotions sufficiently to join me in our shared cubicle. I'd just set aside Paul's client spreadsheet, mind boggling at the sheer numbers involved, when I heard – or felt, rather – his unmistakably ponderous tread.

Brian Abbott makes me look small. And at 6'4" and 18 stone, I'm not exactly Frodo Baggins. Brian is three inches taller than me and large enough to qualify for his own postal code. He's the best partner I've ever had – tough, dogged, never gives up. Observant, with a near-photographic memory. A brilliant and omnivorously wide-ranging intellect, capable of prodigious leaps of intuitive logic. Speaks four languages fluently. Competent at all sorts of arcane skills, from picking locks to gourmet cooking. Excellent darts player – just leans over the line with his ape-like arm extended, until his hand's about a yard from the board. You hardly ever have to buy a pint when Brian's around.

The thing about Brian, though – despite his mountainous physical presence, he's also the most tender-hearted bloke I've ever known. He's not always capable of the emotional detachment that armours the souls of most policemen. Blubs at the drop of a hat. And he looked close to tears now as he leaned on the door-frame of our shared cubicle, arms like baulks of timber crossed over his chest.

I held up a placating hand. "I know, I know, I'm an ass."

"What were you thinking, you stupid, stupid twat? How could you go see Paul without me?"

"I know. Look – it was just an impulse. I should've called you."

He eyed me shrewdly. "It was Ryan, wasn't it? You wanted to put an end to his...indenture."

Prodigious leaps of intuitive logic indeed. Brian knew me too well. I could've lied, but it would have been a waste of breath. "Yes. Maybe. I don't know. I wasn't planning any aggro. It just happened."

"Look – we're partners! We're mates! If you had a feeling... I should've been there, all right?"

"No argument. I was wrong."

Brian seemed mollified, but I wasn't fooled. He was hurt, and it was going to take time. He squeezed past me and sat down at his desk, managing a sour grin. "So you're a wanker, as if we didn't know that already. Now, what've you found out?"

"I'm just amazed at the sums involved. We'll contact every-one, of course, but there is one name sticks out. Timothy Bernard Plantagenet."

"What, Lord Delvemere? Don't you play rugger with him?"

"That's right. Old Bernie. Plays hooker. He was on our recent tour to Vegas. I'll see him tonight, in fact. The Charlie Chalmers memorial bash."

"Ah. Perhaps the opportunity will arise for a quiet chat."

"Perhaps." I felt a prickling of unease, as if a tarantula was crawling up my leg. "Hate to mix business and rugby, though."

"I thought he was rich – thought all of the Hastewicke Gentlemen were rich, except for you."

"So did I – it's a mystery."

3

In the end, curiosity got the better of me, and I left work early so that I could dart home, slip into the old dinner jacket, and head over to Bernie's Belgrave Square digs for a private chat before the festivities. Why had Lord Delvemere, whose Devonshire estates yielded a startlingly large annual income, needed to borrow £100,000 from the most vicious loan-shark in England?

As anyone who has ever played or watched a match will tell you, the game of rugby is governed by a most intricate set of laws. However, one of rugby's most sacred rules isn't set down in any manual. This unwritten law is simple and inviolable: what happens on tour, stays on tour.

Even at the amateur level, touring is central to the life of any rugby team, a blissful, intoxicating, much-anticipated interlude of sport, beer and travel, in the company of two dozen or so congenial mates, to exotic locales, where you will meet – and often, appall – people you will most likely never encounter again. It's a sort of turbocharged holiday, a delirious, testosterone-drenched escape from the harrowing banality of the everyday, filled with merry companionship, pranks, laughs and the sort of behaviour you'd never get away with at home.

Populated as it was with, myself excepted, the scions of wealthy and privileged English society, the Hastewicke Gentlemen Rugby Club toured more than most. During my tenure alone, the club had been to Italy, South Africa, Canada, Australia and New Zealand twice, Argentina, Texas, and, most recently, Las Vegas. On those tours, I had witnessed all sorts of reprehensible behaviour – drunken buffoonery, sexual misadventures, cattle tipping, the frequent theft of small boats and electric golf carts, and one particularly repulsive incident involving a marsupial. Any especially flamboyant infringements were dealt with by the team, primarily via the kangaroo court held at the close of each tour. But because protecting the guilty is one of the most sacred tenets of rugby life, such incidents were never, on pain of excommunication, revealed to those outside the team – wives, girlfriends, co-workers. We all knew one another's darkest secrets – and held them in sacred trust.

It was with a certain heaviness of heart, then, that I approached Bernie's house in Belgrave Square. I didn't know that his sudden and clandestine need for funds had anything to do with what had happened on our recent Vegas tour, though the timing, at least, was suggestive. What I did know was that, if my professional duties compelled me to shine the bright light of official inquiry into the tour activities of my teammates, it would be an unforgivable violation of my sacred rugby oath. I fervently hoped that wouldn't be necessary.

Bernie was in his study when the housemaid showed me in. An aromatic fire of split oak logs crackled merrily on the Georgian hearth, keeping the autumnal at bay. The flickering firelight burnished a room of privileged wealth and good taste. Bernie stood by the mantel, struggling to do up his tie. "Here," I said, "let me – you were always hopeless."

"Dex! Yes, thanks – never have gotten the hang of these bloody things."

"You never had to – you even had a valet at school."

"Yes, that was my mother's doing, bless her soul. Whisky?"

"Yes, please."

He handed me a heavy tumbler half-full of nut-brown spirit. There was a wary pause. "So – to what do I owe this honour? You'll be at John's later?"

"I will." I took a warming sip; this *was* awkward. "I'm afraid this visit has a bit of an official tinge, and wanted to speak to you privately. Do you know a man called Artemis Paul?"

Bernie looked away, considering. He was still the same old Bernie, physically; still a compact, strong-looking 5'10" and 15 stone. But there was more grey than I remembered in his thinning sandy hair; while he was still reasonably fit, the skin of his face suddenly looked loose, like a badly-fitted slipcover. "Rings a bell," he said noncommittally. "Should I know him?"

"He tried to kill me last night."

Bernie put down his glass. "Yes, I heard – it was on the telly. Bloody maniac!"

"The reason I'm here... look, this is awkward. But I was poking 'round the client list on his computer, and there you were. A hundred thousand pounds is a lot of money. But not, I would've thought, to you."

"Look, Dex." He set down his glass, then picked it up again and drained it. "When I heard what Paul had done, I thought you might be coming to see me. You and I have known each other a long time. We've been mates for over 30 years. In some ways, we're closer than brothers – you certainly know things about me my brother doesn't, and never will. If I tell you, in confidence, why I went to Paul, can you keep it confidential?"

I thought about that. There were plenty of other names on Paul's client list. But I owed Bernie an honest answer, at least. "Assuming you haven't committed a crime...have his collectors been to see you?" He shook his head. "Then there's a chance you'll be asked to testify against him, but I doubt it. We'll be more interested in the clients he's roughed up. Certainly your reasons for borrowing the money shouldn't be an issue in court, even if you are called to testify. But there's always a chance it could come out on cross."

He sighed and poured himself another stiff drink. "But you're curious?"

"Not curious enough to get out the thumbscrews. But Bernie, if you're in trouble..."

"Tell me, Dex. When we were on tour in Vegas, did you take advantage of Suite 455?"

"Suite 455?" I searched my somewhat clouded memory; after a moment, the light came on. "Ah... our anonymous benefactor." During our stay in Vegas, a note had been slipped under each of our doors. It read: "An anonymous benefactor wishes it to be known that Suite 455 has been booked through the weekend for the discreet use of any Hastewicke Gentleman. Time is available in four-hour blocks. Please book in advance with the tour secretary."

I shook my head. "No. What about it?"

Bernie looked up then, and in his eyes I saw infinite regret. "Ask John," was all he would say.

II

A few minutes later I stood outside Bernie's house, still pondering this enigmatic reply. A black cab approached the kerb, and I absent-mindedly hailed it. Then the cab door opened, and as the passenger stepped out, all thoughts of the mysterious Suite 455 were driven from my head.

I thought, as I always did, that the years had been extraordinarily gentle with her – the same slim figure, the same lustrous, curly, honey-coloured hair, the same perfect skin, the colour of warm desert sand. Rarer still, the weary weight of time had failed to dim the ethereal intelligence and earthy good humour that shone from her face like the halo 'round a Botticelli Madonna.

I had seen her many times in the 15 years since our brief sintimacy – after all, she had been Bernie's wife all that time. But I felt the old familiar pain all the same. When she saw me, her eyes kindled with pleasure. "Dex! What brings you to darken our doorway?"

"Lady Delvemere! What an unexpected pleasure! Just wanted a quick chat with Bernie before the party."

"What's he done this time? Aren't you going to arrest him?"

"Nah, let him off with a caution for impersonating a lord, and criminal abuse of a tie."

Her eyes sparkled gaily. "Really pathetic, isn't it? Are you coming to the party? Of course you are – black tie, you look smashing."

"Just my usual Wednesday night attire, Jane. Look, I won't keep you – I know you need to get ready. I'll see you later."

"Right, see you at John's, then." And with that heartbreak smile and an airy flutter of her fingers, she was gone from my life. Again.

III

Ten years ago tonight, on a stormy autumn afternoon, Charlie Chalmers, the charismatic captain of the Hastewicke Gentlemen, boarded his twin-engine Cessna at Gatwick for a routine business trip to Paris. Instead, he had joined Glenn Miller's choir invisible. Early the next morning, his business partner, awaiting his arrival, reported him overdue. Two days later, the plane's tail section was found floating in the Channel. The main wreckage, and Charlie's body, were never recovered.

The team were shattered. For a time, we considered never playing again. How can you overcome the loss of such a man? Charlie was the heart and soul of the team – our unquestioned leader, on and off the field, a rugby player of consummate skill and ferocity, the most charming and loyal of companions off the pitch, the ringleader of a thousand merry pranks, dating back to a time when we were all kids together. He seemed to lead a charmed life – born wealthy and noble, lucky in love and business, unfailingly generous, tall, strong and unfairly handsome, with a charmingly self-effacing sense of humour. And then, one day, he was gone.

For many months afterwards, the team struggled to come to grips with his death. And then, late one night in the venerable bar of the Hastewicke Gentlemen's Hampstead clubhouse, John Weathersby, Lord Southampton, our loose-head prop and newly-elected skipper, rose to his feet. "Here's to Charlie – best of teammates, better friend."

We somberly raised our glasses and drank the toast. John remained standing. "Listen. We can't replace Charlie. But we can remember him, as long as one of us has the strength to raise a glass. I propose that we gather together each year on the anniversary of his death, and tell stories about the old bugger. My house, my treat."

And so it came to pass that I stood in the sumptuous, candlelit main hall of Penthorne House, John Weathersby's posh Notting

Hill address, on the night of October 11, with my arms around two of my teammates, clutching a flute of Veuve Cliquot and fighting back the tears. For some reason, I found myself harkening back to the first time I laid eyes on the man who would have such a profound effect on my life.

Hastewicke, in Devon, is one of the oldest public schools in England, an academic hothouse which, for more than two centuries, has nurtured some of the most exotic blooms of British society: poets and Prime Ministers, saints, scientists and scoundrels, explorers, big-game hunters, and an impressive roster of the mightiest names in Debrett's Peerage.

Each year, Hastewicke also admits a handful of scholarship students of humbler means. In the fall of 1978, having attracted the favourable attention of the masters of my neighborhood school, I received the Sir Arthur Nichols Scholarship, and found myself, a skinny little sprog nine years of age, enrolled at Hastewicke.

I'll spare you the gory details; suffice to say that life among the sons of the mighty and privileged wasn't always easy for a mixed-race publican's son from East London. There was a series of ugly and humiliating incidents involving the scholarship boys, which culminated in the expulsion of my best mate, a gentle and studious lad named Bill Tanner, when a valuable watch, stolen from another boy in our house, was found under Bill's mattress.

The next day, I was in the changing-room, miserably donning my gear for our afternoon cross-country run, when I heard Colin, son of Lord Westbrook and the ringleader of the gang of bullies who were making our lives so miserable, laughing to his cronies that it was he who had stolen the watch, planted it in Bill's room, and told the headmaster where to find it.

We Cockneys regard swearing as a Shakespearean art-form, and some of my dad's customers, sailors and stevedores from the splintery end of the London docks, were true virtuosos. They would have wept with quiet pride if they could've heard my frank appraisal of Colin's character and ancestry. Our little chat swiftly escalated into an epic fistfight, which culminated with my pushing Colin's head into a toilet and pulling the chain.

When he arose, bloodied, dripping and murderous, two of his minions had me by the arms. He drew back his fist. "You're dead meat, Reed, you little Cockney pile of shit. It's your word against mine. The headmaster will never believe you."

Then a heavy hand fell on Colin's shoulder. "No – but I will." Looking up, my wondering eyes beheld a towering fourth year who looked familiar, in some sort of vaguely heroic context. "Now go piss your beds, you pathetic firsties, while I decide your punishment." Colin opened his mouth to bray forth an indignant reply, but a swift kick to the backside sent him and his swarm of sycophants stampeding for the exit.

My benefactor bent down and studied my battered face critically; then he broke into a radiant grin. "No permanent damage. I say – I like your style! Ever think of coming out for rugger?"

That was the first time I met Charlie Chalmers.

IV

"D'you remember that night in Melbourne?" cried Richard Devilliers, our dapper, silver-haired fullback, raising his voice to be heard over the noisy throng near the bar. He had been Charlie's best mate on the team, and the Chalmers memorial was especially hard on him. "The Aussie Rules football match? It was Charlie's turn to buy the beer, and as he staggered toward the aisle, he caught the eye of a buxom sheila the next row up. She whispered something to her husband, who suddenly bellowed...."

"Hey, mate! If you drop your pants, she'll bite your arse!'" laughed Dr. Vince Maitland, chief of oral surgery at the Royal College of Medicine and my counterpart at flanker on the Hastewicke Gentlemen.

"Don't interrupt, Vince! Charlie thought about it for a moment, then fwp! Down came his trousers and he assumed the position. He was expecting a friendly nip; instead, she lunged at him like a snake from a drainpipe and sank her teeth into his right buttock. He let out a bloodcurdling falsetto scream – 'Eeeyaaaagh!'– that echoed from one end of the stadium to the other. Everyone in the bloody place turned to look, even the players on the field! Mums were covering their kids' eyes... absolute bedlam! Charlie pulled up his pants and tried to lose himself in the throng, but when security arrived, what were we chanting?"

"Throw 'im out! Thrown 'im out! Throw 'im out!" we all roared delightedly.

The evening had reached the stage of mellow hilarity, the better to mask the essential melancholy of the occasion. John's magnificent hospitality – oceans of drink, a groaning sideboard and the classical opulence of Penhurst House itself – had worked its annual magic.

The big room held a splendidly-dressed throng of players, wives, girlfriends, club officials and hangers-on; the old rafters rang with laughter, animated conversation, and, from one corner, the strains of "Swing Low, Sweet Chariot." These were men I had known almost all my life – men I had grown up with, spilled blood with, traveled to the far corners of the earth with, drunk far too much with, shared triumph, despair and imbecility with, in equal measures. Many were men I admired, for their skill on the pitch, their wit and intelligence, their companionship. A few I held in lower esteem – the braggarts and the cheats, the stuck-up bastards. Some had always regarded me fondly; others, with supercilious distaste. But tonight, clashing egos and past injustices were forgotten. We were everything a rugby team should be.

Off to one side, near the French doors, sat Sir Percival Henry St. John Barlowe, our burly, bearded tight-head prop, sipping soda and lime under the watchful eye of his wife Sarah, a formidable raven-haired woman in scarlet silk. A year or two older than I, Harry had promised his wife that he would quit drinking; she had allowed him to join the Vegas tour, his first in two years, only on the condition that he stay on the wagon. To the best of my knowledge, he had manfully stuck to his pledge. He was talking to Roger Seagrave, the slim, elegant winger, nearly 55 now, who stood with his arm encircling the newly-svelte waist of his wife, Catherine. Over the past two years, Catherine had shed almost 15 stone – over 200 pounds – a triumph of self-discipline that had left her glowing with pride and good health.

I saw Bernie Plantagenet over by the gigantic fireplace; he was talking animatedly to Sir Chester Atkinson, "Jester" to his mates, the towering and eccentric electronics entrepreneur who had replaced Charlie as our number 8. Evidently Bernie hadn't let our earlier conversation spoil his evening. My traitorous thoughts turned naturally to Jane, and when I turned, there she was at my elbow, as if summoned by telepathy.

"You miss Charlie terribly, don't you?" she asked sympathetically. "You look done in."

I replied truthfully. "He was unfailingly kind and generous. He didn't have to be. He was a happy soul, and he wanted everyone he cared about to be happy too. And one day he was there, and the next he was gone. So yeah, I miss him."

"Buy a girl a drink?" she asked, taking my arm.

I walked with her to the bar, ordered her a Bellini. Since she appeared to be in no hurry to be rid of me, we strolled out onto the terrace; we leant on the stone balustrade and looked out over the landscaped common that separated the two rows of houses, bathing in the ravishing fragrance of roses. The sounds of the party washed over us through the open French doors. I turned to look at her; an unseasonably balmy breeze stirred her shoulder-length hair.

"Why did you come to see Bernie tonight?" she asked, without turning her head. "Is he in trouble?"

I wasn't best sure how to reply to that. On the one hand, I would cheerfully have committed murder to keep Jane from being hurt, yet all my professional instincts were whispering that hurt was lurking just around the corner, like a mugger in a doorway. On the other hand, Bernie's transgression, whatever it was, was not yet part of our official inquiry, and at least for now, I felt bound to respect his confidence. I decided to stall for time. "Why do you ask?"

"I don't know... he hasn't really been himself since you came back from tour. You know Bernie – not a care in the world. But he's been... snappish. Off his feed. The other night I got up for a pee, and he was gone. I found him sitting in his study, just staring into the fire. He always sleeps like the dead. It's not like him."

"If he's in trouble, he hasn't confided in me. You know I like Bernie – you can't help but like him. If he needs help, I'll do whatever I can." I glanced ostentatiously at my watch. "Christ, it's late. Early meeting tomorrow. I'd best find John and say my goodbyes." I patted her arm awkwardly. "Try not to worry. And if anything's wrong, tell Bernie to ring me. Any hour, day or night."

"I will." Her face was wintry and bleak. "Bernie told me you were almost killed last night. Is it true?"

I thought about lying. But I couldn't – she was the one person I had never truly lied to. For, but not to. "Yes. I made a mistake. But it was a mistake I would make again, I'm afraid."

"You've always been reckless, Dex. It's one of the things I've always loved about you. And one of the reasons I chose Bernie."

There was nothing to say to that; I turned to go. A small voice, almost a whisper, held me back. "Can I tell you something, Dex? That night, when we met at the Park Hotel. That wasn't just chance, you know – I knew you'd be there." And with a maddeningly enigmatic glance over her shoulder, she turned back to the moonlight.

V

Re-entering the great hall, I cast about the vast, oak-paneled room, but our host had disappeared. I set out to find him, down Persian-carpeted hallways, past Impressionist oils and Renaissance tapestries. Outside Weathersby's study, I paused to admire a fine, floodlit marble bust of Caligula, reputedly almost two thousand years old.

Abruptly the door to the study flew open, and Robert Leicester, Lord Palmerston, the famed philanthropist and Hastewicke Gentlemen outside centre, stalked forth. Rather out of keeping with the general mood of the gathering, his brow was furrowed, and he looked decidedly pissed off about something. He started as he saw me and his expression changed at once to one of fond sadness. "Dex! Your turn next, is it?"

"Actually, I was just looking for John. My turn for what?"

For a moment, Bob looked flustered, but he recovered well. "Oh, you know John. Loves to bore the socks off of you, gabbing on about his latest acquisition. He's in his study, fondling it as we speak. Thought you were his next victim."

"Right – I'll just say my goodbyes then. See you next week at training."

Leicester strode off down the hall without another word, evidently preoccupied, or swollen of bladder. I knocked at the doorframe and entered at John's cheery "Come!"

Weathersby stood in the centre of the room, cradling an immense double-bore rifle, a blissful smile on his broad, sable-bearded face. The loose-head prop's mule-broad shoulders and massive girth strained the seams of his white dress shirt. His tie was undone, and he held a frosty and ample G&T in his free hand, which he raised in salute as I entered. "Dex! Sorry we haven't had much of a chance to chat tonight. How are you! Come see my latest prize!"

I took the rifle from him, amazed at its weight. It was an old Holland & Holland .450/.500 side-by-side, and had obviously seen an amplitude of both hard knocks and tender care. Its magnificently-burled walnut stock was scratched and dented, but lovingly-oiled; the bluing on its engraved barrels was worn down to bare metal in places. But when I opened the breech, the action worked soundlessly, without a trace of play. I examined the inscription on the intricately-engraved breech-plate: "D. Finch-Hatton, Nairobi, Kenya."

"H&H Nitro Royal Express hammerless sidelock double, calibre .450/.500, vintage 1904 – a true elephant gun, so powerful it once killed two Cape buffalo with a single shot," John said. "You recognize the original owner?"

"Denys Finch-Hatton. Immortalized by Isak Dineson in *Out of Africa*, and badly impersonated by Robert Redford in the film version."

"Spot on. Had my eye on this gun for years – knew it was out there, for the right price. It'll be the centrepiece of my collection."

John's enthusiasm for Victorian collectibles, and the safari age in particular, was legendary. He owned one of the finest collections of African memorabilia in England – guns, photographs, camp equipment, ivory, skins and other trophies, native art and other artifacts. "Still in working order?" I asked.

"Fired it myself only yesterday, at the Holland & Holland range." He pulled open his shirt, to reveal a deep purple bruise, in the shape of a rifle-butt, on his heavily-muscled shoulder. "Amazingly accurate, but it kicks like a bloody mule. Have a look at the cartridges." He gestured toward his desk; I opened one of the boxes and whistled as I pulled out a gleaming, cigar-sized cylinder of brass, tipped with an immense nickel-plated bullet. "Over an ounce of lead there, with enough powder behind it to shove it clean through an elephant and out the other side."

"Congratulations, John – it's a beautiful piece. Must've cost a bloody fortune, with a pedigree like that."

"Two bloody fortunes," he grinned. "But it's only money. Had a bit of luck on the futures market last week, and I thought, what better way to spend it?"

"Well." A delicate pause. "Another year gone by. Thanks for another lovely party. Most generous of you, as always."

"You're not going? But the night is young!"

"Duty calls. Some of us, unfortunately, have to work for a living."

"Come on, Dex – one for the road, while I call you a taxi." He gestured toward a well-stocked drinks cabinet and reached for the phone; I helped myself to a generous Springbank while he rang the taxi company. "Ten minutes, he says."

"Ta." I gazed into the fire for a moment, marshaling my thoughts. "You played well in Vegas, for an old fat bastard. What's your secret, then?"

"Avoid training like the plague, but eat a hearty breakfast an hour before game-time. Sex with multiple partners the night before. That, and silk jock-straps. No chafing."

"Ah, for the life of a lord." I raised my glass.

John laughed. "It was quite a good tournament, though. I particularly enjoyed the final – always relish a chance to trample the Yanks into the dust."

"You don't like Americans?"

He shook his head. "Too full of themselves – treat you like they've known you for years and shagged your sister besides on the strength of a few minutes' acquaintance." He looked at me with evident amusement. "You don't agree?"

"I find them refreshing, myself. Unpretentious, and good for a laugh. You have to admit that there's good fun to be had in Vegas."

"No argument there. You just have to be prepared to pay for it."

"Speaking of which, I hear we have you to thank for Suite 455. That was uncharacteristically generous of you."

He fixed me with a bright stare; for just a moment, some of the hearty good humour left his eyes. "And who told you that?"

"Sorry, I can't reveal my sources. But really, that was above and beyond the call."

"Yet you chose not to take advantage of the opportunity."

"No need – I was rooming with The Gland."

"Ah." His face cleared, as if a mystery had been resolved. "He left not a strip club or blackjack table untried, I suppose?"

I nodded. "And you? Did Suite 455 feel your mighty presence?"

"Indeed it did!" John laughed, eyes twinkling. "The wife of the Sonoma Rugby Club's captain practically dragged me there – said there was nothing like an English accent to charm her knickers off."

I winced at the imagery, but said nothing. John, however, noticed. "I see you don't approve," he said, smile fading. "I suppose you wouldn't stoop so low as to shag an opponent's wife. And yet you had no compunctions about shagging the wife of a teammate. Curious."

I kept the shock off my face with an effort. I was suddenly and forcefully reminded that Weathersby was one of those who had not favoured my selection to the First XV, or my presence as a member of the Hastewicke Gentlemen. "Who the hell would tell you a thing like that?" I asked conversationally.

"Ah, laddy." That feral grin was back. "I have my sources, just as you do. But don't worry." He leant forward to whisper conspiratorially. "Your secret is safe with me."

4

My affair with Jane began one night in Belgravia, 14 years ago; it lasted just seven days. I had gone to the Park Hotel for a colleague's retirement dinner. The Hastewicke Gentlemen were off touring Argentina, but I had been unable to accompany them, my finances being unequal to a South American holiday that year. The testimonial dinner was winding down, and I went to the bar for a final pint. I saw a familiar face and breathtaking body, lovingly encased in a sheath of deep-blue velvet. "Jane! What a surprise! You look smashing!"

"So do you, Dex. What brings you here?"

"Oh, a retirement party. Nearly over, thank God. Bernie's in South America?"

"He is." Her eyes shone in the dim light of the bar. I'd had just enough to drink to facilitate impure thoughts, but tried manfully to suppress them. "I was bored sitting at home – can't find anything to read. So I decided to dress up a bit and go for a drink." She leant forward conspiratorially; her hand rested gently on my forearm. "You won't tell Bernie, will you?" she whispered.

"Absolutely not – what happens when the boys are on tour stays on tour."

"So I've heard!" she said with mock outrage. "I've always wanted to know what really goes on on those tours of yours! All sorts of deliciously bad behaviour, I'd wager! Come on, Dex, I could use a good gossip! Got any scandalous stories about Bernie?"

"No, no, absolutely not! I'd be betraying my sacred rugby oath! Besides, you'd fall off your barstool in shock if I told you a quarter of what he's done."

There was amused fascination in her eyes now. "Really?"

"Nah. Bernie's actually one of the most boring guys on the team. In fact, before he married you, we were sure he was gay."

She laughed throatily, deliciously. "Ah, Dex. You've always been able to make me laugh. That's a most attractive quality in a man, did you know that? Bernie's just lucky he met me before I met you."

In the awkward silence that followed we both rose slowly to our feet. "Well, I should be going," she said, blushing fetchingly. "It was lovely to see you, Dex."

I touched her lightly on the arm as she turned to go. "I'd feel better if I walked you home," I said. "Belgravia can be pretty rough this time of night."

"Belgravia?" Her eyes twinkled.

"You'd be taking your life in your hands if you walked home alone. Trust me – I'm a policeman."

She eyed me speculatively for a moment, still smiling. "You know, funnily enough, I do trust you. All right, then." A sudden thought occurred to her. "But what about your girlfriend?"

"I'm without one at the moment, I'm afraid – came stag. Let me just say a quick goodbye, and I'll meet you in the lobby."

Five minutes later we were walking down a quiet Belgrave Street, toward Belgrave Square. Jane took my arm, and we strolled in companionable silence for awhile. "Sorry you missed the tour?" she asked at length.

"Nah. Pretty boring, really – nothing but exotic scenery, oceans of beer, the odd rugby game, total lack of responsibility..."

"...and chasing beautiful Argentinian girls?" she asked, arching a knowing eyebrow.

"Most of them have moustaches, and a fondness for riding crops, or so I've heard. Not my type, really."

We had reached the square. We strolled past the Bahraini embassy, the Spiritualist Society of Great Britain. A full moon ghosted through the clouds above the leafy oasis of the square itself. We were nearly to her door when she asked, "And what is your type, then?"

Good question, that, I had to admit. "I'm still working that out. Sometimes it seems as if all of the good ones are already taken."

We were at her gate, now; beyond the delicate wrought iron, the gardens lay silvered by moonlight. She took my hand, then stood on tiptoe to kiss my cheek. "You're sweet, Dex." I felt my heart beating unreasonably fast, despite my best intentions. She drew back and looked at me, still holding my hand, a slow smile on her face. "But so serious. Now what are you thinking?"

I decided to be honest. "What a shame it was that Bernie met you before I did."

She came closer then. What was my arm doing around her waist? Then she tilted up her face, and I kissed her. Her arm was around my neck; her fingers tangled in my hair. She opened her mouth and her tongue brushed mine, like an electric shock. Then she broke away.

"Jane, I'm..." She touched a cautioning finger to my lips, turned and punched in the code to open the gate, then took my hand and drew me inside, into the deep shadows beneath an ancient elm. I took her in my arms and kissed her again, as if I meant it this time. Her hands caressed the small of my back, then ventured lower. I touched her bare shoulders gently, like one in a trance, then moved more purposefully. As I cupped her buttocks, she gave a small moan. Her hands found my zipper; I felt her breath, warm and sweet, on my ear as she freed my rock-hard shaft. I allowed my hands to travel lower, under her dress, slowly slid her panties down to mid-thigh. Her breathing came harder; she shoved me back against the elm and unbuckled my belt. Her knickers slithered silkily down her calves; my trousers soon joined them on the ground. She hopped up and wrapped her legs around my waist, and now it was her back to the tree. I felt her shaking. "Why are you laughing?" I whispered.

"Try not to give me splinters," she breathed, and reached down to guide me into her silken warmth.

We were together every night for a week, and every night was like Christmas when you're a kid. Every night, she showed another facet of herself to me, another endearing quirk, another surprising appetite, another unexpected gentleness. And then finally, on the seventh night, as we lay abed in my flat in Barklay Mews, absolutely knackered with sex, she gently touched my cheek. "Dex," she said.

I looked up, and in her face, I saw my doom. "What is it, my love?" I asked, awed by the sadness I saw there.

"I'll never forget the time we've had. But I can't go on like this. It's tearing me apart."

"But..." I began.

"Dex." There were tears in her eyes now; I couldn't stand that. "We must stop."

And that was that. Except for several hours of pathetic begging on my part, of course. She had gone back to Bernie; I'd gone back to the job, and to my intermittent brief and unsatisfying encounters with the opposite sex. Brief, because there was something within me that I always held back. Unsatisfying, because none of them were her.

Sometimes it was torture, seeing Jane as often as I did. But I had gradually come to accept it as a reality I couldn't change. To be sure, she still possessed me, and every so often, when I caught her eye at some rugby do, I flattered myself that I saw a longing there. Better to have loved and lost than never loved at all? Perhaps, at least for the masochistically-inclined.

II

I was in the midst of an interesting dream involving Kylie Minogue and the gigantic inflatable castle I had rented for my niece's birthday party when I suddenly became conscious that a telephone was ringing somewhere nearby. I cracked open an eyelid that felt as if it had been dipped in sand; the glowing digits of my bedside alarm showed 3:17.

No hope for it; Kylie was gone for good. I groped for the phone. "Reed," I rasped resentfully.

"Dex. Wake up, you, lazy bastard." It was my partner, on his mobile.

"Brian. What's on?"

"There's been a murder. Get dressed and come down."

"Where are you?"

"Five minutes away – I'll pick you up."

"Right. Where are we going?"

There was a pause. "Penhurst House."

My sleep-addled brain took a moment to absorb this. "Penhurst House. I've just come from there."

"Yes, I know. It's Weathersby. Lord Southampton."

"What happened?"

Brian sighed. He didn't like delivering bad news. "Somebody blew his head off. With an elephant gun."

III

By the time we arrived, Penhurst House had been transformed from a quiet urban oasis into a circus – police cars, forensic vans, half a dozen TV crews, lights blazing – with the neighbourhood for an audience. It isn't every day that the quiet predawn of Notting Hill is shattered by the thunderous blast of an elephant gun. John's neighbors stood about in nervous herds, like sheep when there's a horny Scotsman about, their faces reflecting the lively mix of horror and fascination that generally accompanies a good murder.

The on-call crime scene manager, Dr. Michael Uduk, met us at the door, looking as shell-shocked as I've ever seen him. Which was saying something, given the fact that he had come to us from the Soweto coroner's office, and had performed post-mortems on many of the worst victims of the ferocious racial and tribal violence that rocked South Africa in the '80s and '90s. Normally Dr. Mike was a cheerful soul, who took the gruesome nature of his duties philosophically. This morning he shook hands with us solemnly, all trace of his habitually sanguine demeanor gone. "Brian, Dex. We're in the study."

We followed him through the entryway, past the great hall, so recently ablaze with light and laughter, now dark and quiet as the tomb. Arriving at the study door, I gave old Caligula a pat on the head, then pulled on a pair of blue latex gloves, ducked under the crime scene tape sealing the doorway, and steeled myself for what lay ahead.

John Weathersby was the centre of attention in death as he so often was in life, surrounded by a half-dozen forensic technicians, all busily photographing, measuring, sketching and dusting for fingerprints. Lord Southampton was a man of tremendous appetites, a throwback to previous generations of English nobility, always larger than life. He seemed smaller now – about 10 inches smaller, to be precise.

Weathersby lay on his back, near the other door in the center of the opposite wall. All except his head – that was in the corner, some 10 or 12 feet away. Coagulating blood dripped with syrupy languor from the frame of a fine old Constable landscape on the wall above, and drenched the lush Persian carpet beneath the body in a ghastly halo three or four feet in circumference. The position of the body suggested that someone had shot him as soon as he came through the door. The instrument of death, Finch-Hatton's .450/.500, leaned against John's desk. A white cashmere scarf lay beside it on the floor.

A couple of the forensic boys were minutely examining the French doors leading out to the common garden behind the desk; I could see that the lock had already been dusted for fingerprints. Other techs were checking the carpets for shoe-prints and soil residue, while yet another team scanned the desk, where the shot had come from, for any stray bits of DNA. It was worth checking; if the killer had been a passionate sort, and delivered a premortem soliloquy, he might have left traces of spittle, hair or fibre behind.

I moved forward for a better look at the body, careful not to touch anything. John still wore his white shirt from last night;

it was open at the neck and his black tie lay next to him on the carpet. Both were drenched in blood. His neck now ended abruptly in a ragged plateau of splintered bone and torn muscle. The elephant gun's gargantuan slug had taken him on the point of the chin and completely torn his head off. I turned away, ostensibly to study the fist-sized bullet-hole in the plaster of the wall, but actually to grope for the professional detachment this savage crime demanded. I hadn't always liked John, and we hadn't parted on the best of terms. But this was ferocity on a prehistoric scale. Who could have hated him enough for this?

I sensed Brian's mammoth and comforting presence beside me; for such a large man, he moves very quietly when he wants to. "All right?" he murmured. "He was a friend?"

I took a calming breath, focused. "A teammate. What do you have?"

He consulted his notebook, but we both knew it was for form only – all of the relevant facts were already filed away behind Brian's capacious forehead. "The staff heard the shot at 3:01. Thought a bloody bomb had gone off. They searched the house, and the housekeeper, a Mrs. Chatham, found him here. They touched nothing in the room. Housekeeper says the French doors were open. Forensic say the alarm was bypassed – quite a professional job of it, too – and the lock was forced from the outside. The bullet went through at least two walls – the FSS boys're still looking for it. Housekeeper says Weathersby had gone up to his room after seeing off the last of his guests around 1:30 a.m., but she heard him come downstairs again just before the... hullo, this is interesting."

Brian went to the desk, peered around it, then squeezed underneath. He emerged clutching a pair of cables. "Power supply and ethernet cable. But where's the computer?" I joined him in his careful search of the desk and room. No luck; there was no computer to be found. Brian disappeared for a minute, then returned. "Mrs. Chatham says he had a state-of-the-art MacBook Pro. But I don't see it here."

I considered briefly. There had been a slim silver laptop on his desk next to the boxes of cartridges when I had been here earlier in the evening. I told Brian as much and suggested that we check his room – perhaps Weathersby had been working in bed.

We looked, but the computer wasn't in his bedroom. Brian shrugged. "I'll have forensic search the house and his car. Did he have an office?"

"I think he worked from home. But I'll check."

A young detective constable, whose ruddy cheeks had earned him the nickname "Vesta," after Swan Vesta matches, leaned against the wall in the corridor, breathing carefully. "Ah – DC Talbot – just the man I wanted to see," Brian said. "All right?"

"Vesta" focused his blue eyes on us. "Yes, sir," he said. "My first decapitation. Bit of a shock, I'm afraid."

Brian nodded sympathetically. "I've an important job for you, lad. You're on CCTV patrol. Get the videos from any camera with a view of the house, both street-side and garden-side, and see what's on them from last night."

It is a little-known fact that London is perhaps the most extensively-surveilled major city in the world. Virtually every square foot of the greater metropolitan area is under the unwinking gaze of a closed-circuit television camera; on the platforms of Euston Station alone, more than 250 CCTV cameras record every incident that occurs. There are even cameras inside and outside most London Transport buses. In recent years, this vast automated surveillance network had made life incalculably easier for the MPS. Though, as Brian and I were keenly aware, CCTV evidence was far from a sure bet.

DC Talbot, glad to have something to do, scurried off to begin collecting the videos. Brian and I returned to the study. Nothing had changed; the lads and lasses from forensic were taking it slowly and methodically. John Weathersby was a member of the House of Lords and had a lot of influential friends. Although it would run counter to MPS policy to treat this crime differently from any other – even a suggestion that we were giving preferential treatment to an upper-class victim was taboo – there was nevertheless going to be intense pressure to get this one right, and to slap the steel bracelets on John's killer, straightaway.

The first rays of the rising sun had found John's head, still lying in the corner where it had come to rest. His eyes bulged in horror; his lower jaw was gone, atomized by 480 grains – just over an ounce – of lead, moving at 2,000 feet per second. There were no powder burns on the face; obviously the shot had come from some distance away. That, and the position of the rifle against the desk, made any thought that he might have committed suicide a non-starter.

Looking at John's terrible wound, something suddenly occurred to me. I beckoned Brian over to the torso and gingerly pulled open the shirt. The purplish recoil bruise stood out lividly against his chalky skin. "What's this?" Brian asked.

"Recoil bruise. Showed it to me earlier tonight – he fired the rifle two days ago."

A sudden avaricious light gleamed in Brian's eyes. "Ah. And when we find our murderer, chances are he'll be wearing its twin."

"Possibly." I looked over at the scarf, crumpled on the floor next to the gun, as if seeing it for the first time. "But it looks as though he may have had the sense to use a pad."

Brian whistled. "Clever boy. But would that be enough to absorb the recoil?"

I smiled mirthlessly. "Only one way to find out. Flip you for it."

5

ere's a soul-chilling thought. Or perhaps, in some cases, a comforting one. If, as you inevitably will, you form a bond of affection with even one other person in this world – a parent, child, friend, sibling, lover or spouse – no matter how passionate, indelible, constant or all-consuming your feelings may be, there will come a day when you will see that person for the very last time. Even your spouse, if you are so blessed, of 30 years or more. Think about that. Someone you've seen every day, or every week, for decades, and of a sudden, that cheerful morning conversation, that midnight caress, that weekly "How are you, mate?" phone call is the last you'll ever receive.

If you're lucky, you'll die first. Or if, God forbid, that person acquires a terminal illness, you might at least have time to say goodbye properly. If you're unlucky, they might simply vanish from your life. If you're very unlucky, like my friend Jerry Stewart, whose father died in a fiery car crash, you'll have a huge, screaming row with the person you care about most in the world, and the last thing you'll ever have said to him or her will be "I hate you, you miserable prick/cunt, and I hope you die!"

My conscience was only slightly clearer, in this regard, with respect to John Weathersby. True, we had parted on less-than-gracious terms. But it had been at his instigation, not mine. Or had it? After all, I had hypocritically allowed my disapproval of his philandering to show. But the nagging question remained: how had he known of my affair with Jane, give the fact that he had been 4,000 miles away at the time it occurred?

We didn't have to wait for the Crown pathologist's report to know that John Weathersby had died by violence. The obvious question then became: who had wanted him so thoroughly dead?

Contemplating his untimely end, I thought back over my own complicated relationship with John. He was a year older, a distinction that made no difference later, but at school, had been a gulf to be exploited and emphasized. Even as a boy, John had possessed a bull-like strength and, perhaps even more valuable from a rugby standpoint, a finely-calculated recklessness. Despite his bulk – upwards of 19 stone, nearly 270 pounds – he retained, to the end, a surprising nimbleness and turn of speed. To encounter the quintessential fat prop, who canters forward a few yards, then gratefully accepts the tackle, goes to ground and presents the ball, is a rugby cliche. To encounter John on the pitch was to meet a rugby Range Rover, fast, agile and elegant in all sorts of terrain.

Though outwardly jovial, there were steely depths to John I had never been able to plumb, even after 30 years of acquaintance. One thing that had been obvious from the beginning was his absolute need to have the upper hand – some trick, some strategy, some information that gave him an advantage in everything he did.

In 2001, the Hastewicke Gentlemen had toured South Africa. In our final match, against the Transvaal Baboons, their tighthead prop, a gigantic Zulu named Jama Buthelizi, had manhandled John throughout the game – lifting him, pulling him down, shoving him off-balance. He was a physical prodigy, so strong that I could feel John yawing and stumbling as I leaned against him in the scrum. Despite everything I and the second row could do to steady and support him, he was jerked about like a small child wrestling his father. We lost the match, and afterward, in an unforgivable breach of rugby etiquette, John had refused to shake Jama's hand. For me he reserved a look of bitter scorn, and turned wordlessly away from my proffered pint of beer.

Returning to Hendon, I thought about that side of Weathersby as Brian and I discussed motive. It seemed that whoever had killed John had wanted to utterly obliviate him, although we couldn't rule out the possibility that it had simply been a crime of convenience – a panicked burglar who had seen the rifle and used it. It seemed unlikely though. After all, whoever had killed John had had to load the gun first.

I knew that Weathersby was well-off, divorced, and had derived his income primarily from an invested inheritance. An only child, he had come into Penhurst House and a tidy stack of cash when his mother, Lady Southampton, died in 1982. There was a country house as well, somewhere in Kent. John's teenaged children, a boy and a girl, stood to inherit his estate. Of course, his ex-wife, Tess, would have the use of it until they reached 21. "Shall we pay her a visit?" Brian asked.

Tess Weathersby lived in Reading, in a semidetached house that seemed, like the rest of the neighborhood, to have been stamped from a mold. It was solid and respectable, and the small garden out front had obviously been tended with loving care. But given John's circumstances, I was surprised at its modesty.

I had always liked Tess, but I hadn't seen her since the divorce nine years ago. She appeared promptly at our knock, a short, angular woman, fit and comfortably dressed in blue jeans and t-shirt, her greying chestnut hair confined in a French braid, and gazed up at me in surprise. "Dex! I didn't think it would be you! Come in!"

"You've heard, then? Tess, I'm so sorry."

"I'm not." And she led the way inside.

"Sorry, I didn't mean to shock you," she said, as we settled ourselves around the pleasantly-sunny iron table in the back garden. "I know you liked... I know John was your teammate. But he was such a massive prick to me and the children that I can't pretend to be sorry he's dead."

"How do you mean?"

She frowned toward a nearby azalea as if it needed pruning. "The first few years we were married, it was magic. He was kind, romantic, faithful, a good father. He made me feel like a fairy-tale princess. But then, about 10 years ago, something changed."

"What changed?"

She thought about that. "I don't know. I suppose he started to show me who he truly was. It was as if we had crossed a border, somehow. I found that he despised me. Do you know what that's like, to live with someone for 11 years, and then to discover, quite by accident, that they wouldn't scratch their arse to save you from a burning house?"

I nodded. I had seen that side of John. "What about the children? How was his relationship with them?"

"That was the worst. They're 14 and 16 now. But their monthly support – he was always behind. I've had to call and remind him almost every month, and it's been excruciating. Wizened, blood-sucking harpy, relentless bitch, housecow – those were some of the kinder things he called me." She shook her head bitterly and unconsciously slipped into the present tense. "He never calls them. He never even remembers their birthdays. Sophie – she's 16 now. Applying to university. Do you know what John told me last month? That he wasn't going to pay for her schooling. He was a slag."

"Nice friends you've got," Brian smiled at me. "But the reason we're here, Mrs. Weathersby, is to ask whether John had any enemies. The kind who might want to blow his head off with an elephant gun."

Tess managed a rueful smile of her own. "You probably think it was me. And the thought has occurred, believe me. But it wasn't me – the children are both down with the flu right now, and I was up and down with them all night. You can check."

Brian shook his head. "Can you think of anyone else? Someone John had a business relationship with? A lover?"

"I don't know who John was seeing romantically, at least not now. He knew lots of people through his work in Parliament, of course, but the only real friends John had were his rugby mates. And the people he knew through his collecting. He was obsessed. Do you know, he paid £200,000 for a rifle, just last week?" She flicked her fingers contemptuously. "He still owes me £6,000 in back support."

"So he had money troubles?"

"Only of his own making. His trust paid him £50,000 per month. He owned Penhurst House outright, and he wasn't supposed to touch the principal of the inheritance. But he fancied himself a speculator, and he was always looking for what he called the super-deal." She looked bleakly off into the distance. "There were times, when we were married, that he worried about money. In fact, just a year or so before we were divorced, he was really frantic about it – he'd invested a goodish chunk in some stock Charlie Chalmers tipped him on, and it turned out to be a real dog. John was furious. But then, a couple of months later, another investment came in and he was laughing. Took us all to Portugal for a month."

"Thank you, Tess. If you think of anything else, will you call me?"

"Sure. And Dex?"

"Yes?"

"When you catch John's killer, be sure to thank him for me, will you?"

II

Back in our cube, I found a note on my desk: "Dex: ballistics are ready." I fished out a pound coin. "Flip you for it."

Brian grinned. "How about a game of darts instead?"

"No, thanks. I want to win."

I flipped the coin. Heads – I lost.

We drove south through the city, across Lambeth Bridge to Forensic Science Services headquarters. Simon Vickery, the diminutive, bearded FSS Chief of Ballistics, met us at the door to his lab. Finch-Hatton's rifle was almost as tall as he was.

"Right," he grinned. "Who's the lucky one?"

The ballistics tank was a water-filled metal cube four feet square and 10 feet long, painted drab tan, with a rubber port to receive the weapon. Brian handed me the white scarf we had found on the floor of John's study; I wordlessly folded it and tucked it inside my shirt. I took the rifle and opened the breech; Simon handed me a cartridge and stood back, smiling, to watch. I slipped the round in, inserted the barrel of the rifle into the port, snugged it to my shoulder and, grimacing with apprehension, fired.

There was an apocalyptic boom! like a subterranean clap of thunder; at the same instant, my shoulder felt as if it had received a right cross from Manny Pacquiao. I rubbed it while Simon opened the tank and, with a long-handled net, retrieved the slug. "All right, you great baby?" asked Brian smugly. I opened my shirt. The shoulder was sore, but the scarf had absorbed most of the recoil. In my estimation, based upon my lifelong experience with rugby, there would be little or no bruising. "No joy," I said.

Brian looked troubled on the drive back to the office, and not just at the failure of Finch-Hatton's rifle to produce a livid bruise on my shoulder. "I think we're missing something. Was Weathersby a photographer?"

"I've seen him taking photos and videos on tour. He seemed moderately obsessed with it. Why do you ask?"

"His missing computer. It was a MacBook Pro. Do you know what they're known for?"

"No."

"Graphics. Photos, video. You can make your own movies on them, store and edit a feature-length film. I can't help but think that the fact that it's gone missing has something to do with why he was killed. Without it, we're working in the dark."

"No question about that." We had arrived at our cube; there was another note on my desk. "Wicks wants to see me. What shall we tell him?"

"That we're pursuing a promising lead. Of course, he'll know you're lying through your teeth."

III

"You're off the case." DS Wicks stood with his back to me, ostensibly admiring a photo of himself with Tony Blair at the Lord Mayor's ball.

"Sir, there's no need..." I began, but he cut me off with a wave of the hand.

"You're too close to this. You had a personal relationship with the victim. You've played rugby and swilled beer out of the same trough with him since you were both kids. Can't help but cloud your judgment."

"Yes, I knew Weathersby. But we weren't exactly mates. Sir, I can bring an objective view to the case."

Wicks turned; surprisingly, his expression was almost sympathetic. "And what if, as is extremely likely, the killer turns out to be someone you both knew? A rugby mate, or wife, or girlfriend?"

"Sir, I want to find John's killer as much as you do. Perhaps more."

"I know, Dex. You're a fine detective, when you stop and think. But you're off this case. Brian can handle it. God knows you've enough on your plate already, with this Artemis Paul business."

I clenched my fists in frustration. In my heart I knew Wicks might be right. But John Weathersby had been a teammate. "Sir, please. I'm aware of your concerns. But I know I can do this properly. It's true I knew Weathersby. But we weren't close enough to compromise my objectivity."

"And yet here you sit, arguing, when my decision has already been made. Why?"

I chose my words with care. "I suppose it's because I feel it's my duty to him, sir."

"Your duty, DI Reed, is to me, and to the Metropolitan Police Service – not to your teammates. No –" he held up a cautioning hand "– not another word. I've made my decision."

Seething with a fury I dared not express, I returned to my cubicle. Brian only had to glance at me, and his large features sagged in dismay. "You're off the case."

"Yes." I sighed bitterly. "Apparently our boss has less confidence in my professional judgment than you thought."

"Now, now, Dex. I know he thinks highly of you. Just the other day, he told me your work on that Notting Hill drive-by was absolutely top-shelf."

"He did?"

Brian looked away, a grin lurking in the corners of his eyes. "Well, not in so many words. He did say your report had rather less shit about it than most of the rubbish he has to sort through."

I managed a sour grin of my own. "Once more my life has purpose. Just do me one favour, Brian."

"Name it."

"Delicacy. The light touch, to the greatest extent possible. Weathersby wasn't exactly my closest mate on the team. But some of the others you may have cause to investigate... let's just say I've seen them in action on tour, and I'd hate to see anyone get hurt who isn't essential to the case. I don't know that this had anything to do with rugby. But if it does, promise me you'll be discreet?"

"Oh, absolutely, lad. The soul of discretion. You have my word."

IV

Sir Steven Barnes, CVO, OBE, removed his white wig and set it carefully on the bust of the Duke of Wellington atop the marble mantlepiece. Everything about him – the Greys Inn office where Charles Dickens once toiled as an apprentice, with its walls of well-loved, leather-bound books, the tailored suit of fog-coloured grey wool, the cup of Earl Grey steaming on the gleaming expanse of his inlaid desk – bespoke wealth and solidity. Even this morning's Times had been ironed to a voluptuous crispness by his clerk.

He picked it up now, a frown creasing his fleshy brow. There, just below the fold, was the headline he didn't want to read: "House of Lords Member Found Dead; Murder Suspected." His eyes, surrounded by pouchy folds of skin like a tortoise's, flicked over the lead: "A peer of the realm as well-known for his prowess on the rugby pitch as he was for his Conservative political views died of gunshot at his Notting Hill home early Thursday morning.

"John Weathersby, Lord Southampton, 45, who was once invited to try out for the England rugby team, was slain by a single shot from a large-bore hunting rifle. A Metropolitan Police spokeswoman described the violence of Lord Southampton's wounds as 'savage in the extreme.' A coroner's inquest is scheduled for later this afternoon.

"The police were called to the Penhurst House in Notting Hill by Lord Southampton's housekeeper, Edith Chatham, 57, who was awakened by the sound of a single gunshot about 3 a.m. A search of the house revealed Lord Southampton's body. The house's security system had been disabled, and sources say police found evidence of forced entry at the scene.

"Lord Southampton, who had served in the House of Lords since 1989, was a well-known collector of antique sporting firearms. The apparent murder weapon was a Holland & Holland elephant rifle once owned by the legendary African sportsman Denys Finch-Hatton..."

Sir Steven let the newspaper fall to the polished surface of his desk with a disgusted "fwap!" It was always a bad business when one's client met an untimely end, but murder? What *had* Weathersby been mixed up in?

After a moment's thought, Sir Steven arose ponderously and made his way to the heavy safe that crouched in one corner of his office, opened it. He rummaged for a moment among the safe's contents – heavy parchment envelopes bound with silk ribbon, case-files, ledgers, a World War II-vintage Webley service revolver – before he found what he sought.

The object of his search was a single envelope, sealed, inscribed "To be opened in the event of my death – John Weathersby." Sir Steven re-crossed the room, set the envelope in the geometric centre of his desk, and sat looking at it for some minutes, long, steepled fingers tapping his chin.

Not for the first time, he wondered what it contained. Some sort of small lumpy object – that much, a blind man could deduce. But what was really inside?

Plucking an ivory-handled letter opener from his desk drawer, Sir Steven slit the envelope open. An object clattered to the desktop – the key to a left-luggage locker, number 182. There was a single sheet of note-paper inside. "Euston Station," was all it said. Something – perhaps nothing more than instinct ingrained by more than 40 years of reading law – warned him that whoever received the locker's contents would find no joy in the experience.

It had seemed an eccentric codicil when Weathersby had come to see him three weeks ago. But there was no doubt about Lord Southampton's instructions; the wording was unambiguous. The locker key was to be used if Weathersby died, under any circumstances, before August 11, 2017, and the instructions contained in the locker followed to the letter.

Sir Steven sighed. It was a bad business. But after all, when you were called to the bar, how often were you so blessed as to be the bearer of good tidings? Too bloody rarely.

He knew he should dispatch his clerk to Euston Station without delay. Perhaps he was wrong – perhaps the locker contained a trove of riches, to be distributed to Weathersby's heirs with philanthropic largesse. Having known Lord Southampton for more than two decades, Sir Steven snorted derisively at the thought.

Glancing at his watch, Sir Steven decided he had done enough for one day. Whatever pain lurked in the locker at Euston Station had waited this long to ooze forth. It could wait another day.

6

For the next couple of days I moped about the office, prowling the electronic corridors of Artemis Paul's laptop, filling a legal pad with the names and contact information for the miscreant's enforcers, clients and, shall we say, "service professionals." By the time I'd finished, I was staring at a list only slightly shorter than the MPS telephone directory. With the help of Detective Constables Burnett and Goodspeed of the Hendon SCD outside inquiry team, I spent the rest of the week doggedly calling each entry, making appointments and interviewing. By Friday, we'd made it about a third of the way through the list of names, without much of substance to show for our efforts.

In the course of my research, I came across one interesting tidbit I had failed to notice the first time I had seen Bernie's name on Paul's client-list. I started to reproach myself for the oversight, then realized that it was because the list I'd seen had been a Computer Crime-lab compilation, not the information on the lap-top itself. The missing item consisted of a single Christian name appended to the end of Bernie's entry: "Boris."

Brian appeared only intermittently in the course of the week; he was devoting the initial stage of his investigation to a meticulous examination of the house and crime scene, and of Weathersby's personal and business affairs.

Late Friday afternoon, I returned from an interview with a singularly uncooperative but wonderfully-named male prosti-tute called Crevice Delver to discover Brian, morosely overflow-ing his chair. He consulted his watch. "I believe The Chandos is serving Sam Smith's Museum Ale from the oak," he said. "Care to join me for a pint?"

Half an hour later we sat in one of the old leather couches in the quiet upstairs bar of the Chandos, just up the street from the National Portrait Gallery, hands wrapped around cool, gently-carbonated pints of the working man's friend. The malty elixir slid down my throat with marvelous ease. Brian set his empty glass down with a thud and a satisfied smacking of his meaty lips.

"How's it going with Paul?" he asked. "The case proceeds?"

"At its current rate, I hope to bring Paul to trial before he dies of old age. He's not talking – refuses to answer the simplest question on the grounds that it might incriminate him. His loan-sharking clients won't admit they know him. His rent-boys are as closed-mouth with me as they're open-mouthed in their daily duties; his kneecappers all claim to be bouncers at Blue Hour. And no one's ever heard of Martin Wallace, naturally. Still, I don't think he'll wriggle out of it entirely." I finished my pint. "What about you – any sign of John's laptop?"

"Not a sniff of it." He arose and fetched us two more of the same. "And not a sniff of motive, either. Although we did find his will."

"And?"

"There was one rather suggestive codicil, added two moths ago. His solicitor was to use the key Weathersby had entrusted to his care to open a locker in Euston Station, and follow the instructions it contained to the letter."

"What instructions?"

"We don't know what's in the locker, do we? More to the point, we have no idea which locker it is."

I gulped meditatively. "Anything else?"

Brian scratched his short-cropped beard thoughtfully before downing another half-pint at a gulp. "I've been going over Weathersby's financials. One thing doesn't add up. His wife told us he'd paid £200,000, only last week, for the rifle that killed him. Yet over the last year or so, the markets have given his trust a walloping – his income was down, not up. And I don't see a pay-out of that magnitude from any of his accounts."

"He told me he'd scored on the futures market. But maybe it was cash – maybe he had a run of luck in Vegas. Funny he didn't mention it, though – that was just the sort of thing John would crow about."

"Her Majesty's Customs would've had some probing questions if he'd tried to bring a wad of cash that large into the country without declaring it, though from all we know, Weathersby was far from risk-averse."

"There's another possibility. You've heard what his relationship with Tess was like. If I know John, he had assets squirreled away where Tess' lawyers would never find them."

"Offshore accounts, you mean – BVI/Caymans stuff?" He nodded slowly. "Could be. No paper statements – all wire transfers. All of the information would've been on his computer. I've a call in to the man who sold him the rifle – apparently he made a profit, because he's been on holiday in Turkey since two days after the sale. When he gets back, maybe we can back-trace the source of the funds."

"We?" I asked bitterly.

"Figure of speech, lad. But don't worry. The situation is only temporary."

II

In my 22 years as a policeman, first as a bobby, then as a detective constable, now as a detective inspector in Specialist Crime Directorate, a sort of catch-all for the nastiest crimes no other MPS division wants to touch, I've discovered one surprising fact about the criminal mind: no one is completely bad, just as no one is completely good. No miscreant, no matter how twisted, how sociopathic, how indifferent to the misery he has caused, is utterly without redeeming virtue. Even Jack the Ripper probably visited his frail, wizened gran on occasion. I've known violent muggers who were volunteer Big Brothers; drugs dealers who were very active church members; I knew a pædophile once who was very kind to his elderly grandparents-in-law. And sometimes, for an experienced investigator, such information can provide a crucial advantage.

So it proved with Artemis Paul, though in his case, as with all genuine sociopaths, self-interest lay at the heart of his actions. There was only one other person he loved nearly as much as he fancied himself – his wife. Paul's own mother had been a cruel and distant alcoholic. But he had found the ideal substitute in his wife, Debra, by all accounts a woman of rare steadfastness, warmth and solicitude. To her he was as devoted as it is possible for one in his mental condition to be, and her good opinion, as I was shortly to learn, meant a great deal to him.

As I sat at my desk on Monday morning, the buzz of the intercom suddenly rent the air. "There's a Debra Paul on line 2," said Jade, the department secretary. "Says she's Artie Paul's wife."

"DI Reed," she said when I picked up. She took a deep breath. "I know I shouldn't be speaking to you without my solicitor present. And I know you can't discuss the case against my husband. But I just want to know..." I could hear her voice catch as she struggled to master her emotions; then out it spilled in a rush. "Is he... is he being treated well? I know he tried to hurt you, but you have to understand that it was my fault. Whatever stupid thing he's done, he did to protect me. And the children. I shouldn't be talking to you, I know that. It's just that I've heard..." and now came the choking sobs, "...what happens to people who try to hurt policemen."

"Mrs. Paul, please," I purred. "Your husband got a knot on his head during the altercation on the boat. Beyond that, he's fine."

"You must hate him," she sobbed. "But he's a good man, you must believe me. A good husband. A good father. He didn't tell me about his business. I thought he owned a club! I... I just can't believe it's come to this!"

"Mrs. Paul. I don't hate your husband." I wouldn't be inviting him 'round for drinks anytime soon, but that was beside the point. "But you're quite right when you say you shouldn't be talking to me without your barrister."

"I know, she told me not to call you, but I'm so worried! I haven't even been allowed to see him!"

"Haven't you." I had a small brainwave. "You know his bail hearing's this afternoon."

She sobbed again. "Yes."

"It's against regulation but... perhaps I can arrange for you to see him. Just to set your mind at ease. But only for a moment, mind. Of course, things would go easier for everyone, wouldn't they, if your husband was a bit more cooperative. You'd be able to see him a bit more often, for one thing. But I'll arrange for you to see him this afternoon – have a private word with him. See for yourself how he's doing, tell him how you and the children are holding up."

"You'd... you'd do that, for me?"

"Yes. But don't tell anyone it was me, all right?"

"I won't. Bless you, DI Reed."

And blessed I was. A scant few hours later, I found myself sitting across a steel table from Artemis Paul and his solicitor, a competent terrier of a man named Tom Jenkins, in a grimy ground-floor interview room at Hendon Station. Apparently my little gambit with Debra Paul had had the desired effect, and she had reminded him of his domestic responsibilities. "My client requested this meeting," Vickery growled. "Against my advice."

Artie Paul leaned across the table. The recorder was turning, and a uniformed officer stood silently against the door. Gone was the steely facade he had shown me at Blue Hour and aboard the *Compound Interest*; he looked as if he'd spent an hour in a paint-shaker, rather than a few minutes with his wife. "I only want to know one thing," Paul said, and I noted with professional satisfaction the slight tremor in his voice. "If I'm a good boy, and I play the game, will it have an effect at my sentencing?"

I considered. "Without consulting the Crown prosecutor, I can't make any promises. But if you cooperate, based on my experience, I'd say offhand that you're looking at 15 years and out. You'd have to be a model prisoner, mind. Not try to, say, collect any outstanding debts."

For a moment, Paul closed his eyes behind his lozenge-shaped spectacles. Then he nodded. "Done."

Vickery fairly blanched in horror. "Artie, no!"

Paul removed his restraining hand. "This way there's a chance I'll see Debra and the girls again. And they can be a part of my life. Now." He addressed me. "What d'you want to know?"

We spoke for two hours, and Paul never looked up from his hands where they rested on the table. He told me as little as he decently could, and volunteered nothing, but when I asked a question, he told me the truth. Except about Martin Wallace – he steadfastly denied any involvement in his murder. I let it slide for now, knowing that, if we were able to prove Paul's involvement in that crime, all bets, in terms of my estimate of his likely sentence, were off.

Having shown him that this was the most advantageous course, given his present circumstances, for him, the person nearest and dearest to his own heart, at least Paul was talking to me. "One last question," I said, as the interview wound down "– Lord Delvemere. He came to see you."

"Yes."

"Why?"

"He needed money. Quickly. I lent it to him, at 10 percent a month."

"Ten? You charged me 30. Why 10?"

"Because I knew he was good for it."

"How?"

"Because he was a customer. A regular."

My brain, knackered by the length and intensity of the interview, suddenly ticked over. "Boris."

"Yes. Once a month, for the past three years. Like clock-work. Boris was a dead ringer for someone he knew at school, apparently."

I trembled inwardly at the ramifications of this information. "Did he tell you why he needed the money?"

"No. He did say he didn't want his wife to know." Paul looked up at last. "Would you like my professional opinion?"

I already knew what that would be, but he told me any-way. "He was being blackmailed. Seen it before – I know the symptoms."

III

Each Monday evening, I have a standing invitation to join Brian and his wife, Fiona, and their daughters, Rose, 10, and Kate, seven, for dinner. Fiona, tall, well-fleshed, with sharp, laugh-ing brown eyes enlivening a sculpted oval face, met me at the door of their Southwark row-house; I handed her three bottles of Oddbins' best and gave her a wet one on the cheek. "Sorry to be such a bachelor," I said. "Is there enough for me?"

"Need you ask?" she said wryly "– Brian's cooking."

My partner was sweating over the stove when I arrived, a well-splattered "Shag the Cook" apron straining to protect his ample girth. "Smells lovely," I observed. "What's on the menu tonight, then?"

"Roast loin of pork with apples and cream, Potatoes Anna and veggies, with a greengage cocagne and cream for a sweet." He wiped the sweat from his massive brow. "I forgot to get wine. Did you bring some?"

Dinner was a great success, as always; the pork was roasted to a sweet aromatic perfection, crisp and fatty outside, tender and juicy within. Brian harbors a deep distrust of anyone else in his kitchen; he fervently believes that if you love to eat, as he does, you'd better learn to cook yourself. He's a brilliant cook, and has often avowed his intent to open an unpretentious but hideously expensive restaurant, specializing in the cuisine of Normandy, when he tires of policework.

As always, I felt a familiar pang as we sat around the scragged-up old pine dinner table, a part of their merry and contented domesticity, but an outsider as well. Brian adored his girls, and the feeling was obviously mutual. Tonight, Fiona was wonderfully sarcastic, as always, and Katie and Rose were in rare form as well.

"Uncle Dex, have you and daddy ever arrested a cat burglar?" Rose asked me, as Fiona served up the cocagne, still warm from the oven and drowning in cream custard.

"Matter of fact I have – bloke by the name of Peter McCaffery. He was ever so clever, and robbed lots of posh houses while the people inside were sleeping. But he wasn't as clever as your dad, and one night, when he climbed out the window with his bag of loot over his shoulder, we were waiting for him."

"Why was he called a cat burglar? Did he have a tail and whiskers, like Tabby does?" And then, with the wonderfully mercurial mind of a 10-year-old, "I used to wish I had a tail, when I was a baby like Kate."

"I'm not a baby, Rose!" Kate cried in a wounded voice.

"But you do have a tail," I told her seriously. "It's called a coccyx. It's all that's left of the tails we used to have, ages ago when we were still swinging through the trees." She turned to have a look. "You can't see it," I smiled "– it's under your skin, at the very end of your backbone."

"Uncle Dex, are you having me on?"

"Daddy has a tail," Kate interrupted brightly. "Only it's on his front, and you *can* see it. When he's in the bath. It's called a penis."

"Oh, lovely," said Fiona drily. "Pity your parents aren't here tonight, Brian."

When we finished, I borrowed Brian's apron to do the dishes. Fiona went to give the kids their bath; Brian joined me in the kitchen, and set a cup of coffee on the drainboard at my elbow. "Ta," I said. "By the way, I may have found your motive." I scrubbed energetically at a roasting-pan.

"Are you going to dazzle me with your wisdom, then, or make me guess?"

The random bits of evidence that had stuck in my brain had begun to come together, like the seemingly-unconnected lines on the canvas of a portrait sketch artist I had once stopped to watch in Venice. "I saw Artemis Paul this afternoon. You remember my mate Bernie? Lord Delvemere? Paul said he was being blackmailed. He didn't know who the blackmailer was. But I think I may."

Brian leant forward. "I'm listening."

So I told him about my conversation with Bernie, and his cryptic comment about Suite 455. "I thought he was just telling me Weathersby had been our 'anonymous benefactor,' and later that night, John confirmed he had been. But there was more to it than that. After all, knowing John, generosity on that scale would've been completely out of character. He was legendary for squeezing every pound coin until it screamed. I can't remember the last time he so much as bought a round of drinks."

An incident from our tour of Canada, six years previously, suddenly leapt to mind. One night in Vancouver, five or six of the lads, including John and I, were on our way to a Gastown restaurant for dinner. A grizzled, ancient homeless man had asked us for change. "We can do better than that, can't we lads?" John had said, and, with a wolfish grin, invited the man to join us for dinner. John sat the poor old dosser down at our table, despite the disapproving glares of the staff, and proceeded to order the finest the house could provide, all the while regaling his guest with tales of his rugby prowess and amorous conquests. As we watched in awe, old Aqualung, unable to believe his good fortune, tucked in with a vengeance that left us fearing for his digits.

"John had just finished some sordid story, something about waking up tied to a strange bedstead with alligator clips attached to his scrotum, and ordered a large armagnac. Then he got up and went for a piss.

"We awaited his return. Then waited, and waited some more. But John was already back at the hotel, laughing that hyena laugh of his. In the end, he stuck us with the bill, not only for his own meal, but for the old wino's tab as well. And that was John's idea of a fine joke. On us," I finished.

Brian pondered this moving anecdote. "So your point is...?"

"John wasn't a generous man, except with himself. Look at how he treated Tess and his children. He begrudged them every pence. Why would he suddenly pay for a separate suite to provide a venue for the boys' bad behavior on tour? He'd never done that before."

The light of reason was slowly kindling in John's bloodhound eyes. "You told me he was a man who always had to have the upper hand – an edge of some sort."

"That's right."

"I finally spoke to the man who sold him Finch-Hatton's rifle. Weathersby paid cash."

"£200,000."

"In used hundred-pound notes." Brian tapped his teeth with a pencil, a mannerism he had when the old brain cells were firing at an especially rapid clip. The tapping stopped. "Your friend Weathersby was shearing black sheep."

"I'm inclined to agree. And the Hastewicke Gentlemen were his flock."

"What would you wager that, when I ring the security staff at your hotel in Vegas tomorrow, they tell me they found some recently-filled holes in the walls of suite 455? Holes for fibre-optic vidcams, the latest stuff, sited to cover every angle of the sitting room, the bedroom and the toilet?"

I nodded. "And when we return from tour, John has the boys over, one by one, for a friendly drink. Then he brings out the computer, and treats them to a video replay of their worst indiscretions, complete with editing, soundtrack and popcorn."

"It's diabolical, really clever – what better candidates for blackmail could there be than a bunch of wealthy nobs on rugby tour? I shudder to think what they might have got up to. They'd pay through the nose to keep it quiet."

I knew only too well how true that was, and suddenly felt a bit queasy as the magnitude of John's sacrilege struck home. "Or resort to more primitive means of ensuring his silence. After all, the bond of rugby touring is firmly rooted in mutual sin. If he really did this, some might think John got what he deserved."

"But murder? Come on, Dex – that's a bit harsh, just to keep a bit of slap-and-tickle from the wife."

"Some of us have more to lose than others." Then a sudden thought occurred, and the plate I was washing almost slipped from my grasp. "But John."

"What?"

"What blackmailer, playing for these stakes, would fail to have a backup plan? An insurance policy, if anything should happen to him?"

Brian smiled grimly. "That codicil in his will. The left-luggage key."

I nodded. "Better get a Section 1 warrant."

"I'll get DC Burnett on it first thing tomorrow."

It abruptly hit home just how ugly this could get. And for the first time in a week, I was inexpressibly glad Wicks had pulled me off this case.

7

During the Hastewicke Gentlemen's first tour abroad, to Australia and New Zealand in 1984, we had come up against a brutally proficient club side called Waimeearoa on the North Island. About half of their lads were Pacific Islanders from Samoa and Tonga, magnificent specimens of manhood, tall, heavily-muscled and tattooed, with a well-deserved reputation for warm hospitality off the pitch and ferocious violence on it. They had been looking forward to the chance to rub our generally aristocratic English noses in the rich North Island mud for some weeks, and the large crowd at Waimeearoa stadium obviously shared their enthusiasm, roaring their approval of every crunching tackle and niggling cheap shot.

The game was going splendidly in their favour; the score was 23-6 at half-time. When the match resumed, despite one of

Charlie Chalmers' most inspiring halftime rants, Waimeearoa picked up right where they had left off. With the crowd howling with savage glee, the local lads were pushing for the try that would have clinched it when their fly-half dropped the ball and the ref signaled a scrum.

The two forward packs – eight men each, upwards of 2,000 pounds of prime English and Kiwi beef apiece – came together like coupling railroad-cars, with a tectonic "Oomph!" Just as the scrum-half put the ball in, Winston Tuaasusopo, Waimeearoa's gigantic second row, took advantage of the referee's momentary distraction to deliver a crunching uppercut, between his own prop's legs, that struck our tight-head prop, Harry Barlowe, fairly in the nadgers. Barlowe, bound into the scrum and pushing his guts out, never even saw it coming. He collapsed the scrum, writhing in agony, and as their number 8 picked up the ball, I saw red.

Vince Maitland, our blind-side flanker, made a saving tackle on the number 8, wrapping him up before he could get the pass away. As they squelched into the mud, the ruck – the phalanx of players who converge to control the ball after a tackle – formed and with savage joy I saw Tuaasusopo pick up the ball.

I wasn't the only one who had seen the punch and who had delivered it. As I rocketed toward the massive Samoan, Charlie Chalmers matched me stride for stride, wrapping a meaty arm around my waist. We hurdled the ruck together and drove Tuaasusopo backward into the mud, flat on his back. The ball bounced free but we scarcely noticed. United in vengeful purpose, we methodically stomped him into the mud, using our rugby boots, with their long aluminium studs, to shred his jersey and carve bloody furrows from his ankles to his sternum. I believe he still bears the scars. On the way by, I stumbled and deftly broke his nose with my knee.

Tuaasusopo tottered from the field, nose streaming crimson, and did not return; when play resumed, Waimeearoa found that they had lost their momentum, while we had found ours. In the 80th minute of the match, a cunning kick from George Waters, our tubby but deft and useful little scrum-half, bounced magically along the touch-line and, at the last moment, up into my arms. I plunged over for the score, and we wound up sending the unhappy crowd home at the short end of a 30-26 score.

Afterward, Charlie had thrown an arm around my shoulders and handed me a beer. "This is why I love playing with you, Dex," he said, teeth white in a faceful of mud. "Because you understand, so clearly, that you can never let the bastards win."

II

When I arrived at Hendon on Tuesday morning, Brian had already come and gone. A note on my chair told me that Sir Steven Barnes, Weathersby's solicitor, was in court until this afternoon. Brian would be waiting for him when he returned, hoping to persuade Sir Steven to voluntarily hand over the contents of locker 182; in the meantime, he was cracking the whip over the murder squad's outside inquiries team to gather up all relevant CCTV tapes and canvass results. The note said Brian would meet me at Bernie's later that morning.

Brian and I had agreed to join forces, given the overlap in our two separate investigations. The time had come to ask my teammate some rather searching questions about both Artemis Paul and John Weathersby, an ordeal I was, quite frankly, dreading.

I spent the morning hunched over the computer in my office, adding Artemis Paul's recently-transcribed interview to the growing web of evidence on the case in the Home Office Large Major Enquiry System (HOLMES). As I did so, I marveled, not for the first time, at man's ability to forgive himself his own trespasses. Artemis Paul considered himself a singularly astute and competent businessman, which, in his own callous way, he was. What he chose to ignore was that, in pursuit of his and his family's daily bread, he had ruined countless lives. And then, when the breath of justice at last threatened to collapse his monetary house of cards, he was prepared to murder a policeman to keep it intact a little while longer. To him, that had just been another business decision, like adding a couple of cases to the week's whisky order. I stoically suppressed my loathing, and kept working.

At the appointed hour, I stood once more on Bernie's doorstep in Belgrave Square. Brian was late, which was not unusual. I had just raised my hand to the knocker when the door was opened inward by a shortish, heavy-necked, hard-faced man, who saw me with surprise and, I thought, dismay. He looked familiar; I never forget a face, but I'm crap with names. Then it came to me. "Dean!" I said. "Dean Thatcher! What brings you here, of all places?" For it was Dean who had taken my elbow at Blue Hour, Dean who had guided me to Artemis Paul's inner sanctum, Dean whose manly bundle I had squeezed just before I'd been belted unconscious. "And why haven't you returned my phone calls? We were ever so close, once."

Dean shoved past me. "Fuck off, copper." He started to depart, but instead encountered Brian, blocking the stairs with a brooding expression on his bearded face. His racquet-sized hand closed around Dean's biceps and jerked him back like a pit bull on a leash.

"I believe my partner asked you a question. Would you care to answer it here, in the open air, or at Hendon nick, with the tape recorder turning?"

"I didn't get your messages," he lied sullenly.

"And why are you here?" I asked gently.

"Business," he replied. "Plantagenet – " his pronunciation of the name dripped scorn "– had some business with Mr. Paul."

Dean tried to nonchalant it, but he was starting to look decidedly uncomfortable. "Not anymore," I said. "Artie's no longer in business, and all debts are forgiven. If we find out you've gone freelance, collecting from Paul's clients and pocketing the cash, we'll squash you like a bug."

I stuffed one of my business cards into Dean's breast pocket. "I've still got some questions to ask you about Martin Wallace. You'll be at Hendon at 9 a.m. tomorrow to answer them, or I'll be getting a warrant for your arrest. And Dean – " I got right up in his boat, so there was no mistake about this "– Stay away from Lord Delvemere. And his wife. The only reason I'm not arresting you now is I know it wasn't you who bashed me over the head back at Blue Hour. Leave now, before I change my mind." Then Brian and I shut the door in his face, and I turned my mind to the delicate task at hand.

Normally I'm not at all reluctant to ask questions of a most painfully intimate nature – how did you find out your wife was shagging your neighbour? When did you discover you were a rapist? Didn't your mother ever tell you not to take things that didn't belong to you? – that sort of thing. All part of the job.

But in this case, the sharp blade of my investigatory instincts, honed to whittle away falsehood a lamina at a time, had most decidedly hit a knot. It was one thing to be privy to a thousand shameful secrets as a member of a rugby team. It was quite another to be faced with the prospect of winnowing through those indiscretions in the noonday glare of a criminal investigation. It wasn't right. It wasn't right. But it seemed I had no choice.

When we were shown into his study, Bernie had the look of a man who had just finished a sand castle, and glanced seaward to behold a tidal wave rushing up the beach. Haggard and gulping whisky with a shaking hand, his expression brightened to one of pathetic gratitude when he saw me.

"Bernie," I said. "All right? No damage?"

"No. But that day is coming, if I don't pay Paul soon. Oh, Dex, what have I done?"

I was glad to be able to give my old friend some good news. I explained that Paul had forgiven his debt, and Dean had been warned off. "I don't think you'll see him again," I said. "If you do, just ring Brian or me – any time, day or night. We'll sort it out."

"Thank God. And thank you, Dex – I owe you one."

My discomfort, if it was possible, increased; I fairly squirmed. "No you don't. But Bernie, I have to ask. No, I'll just tell you what we know. It was John, wasn't it? John was blackmailing you. That's why you needed the money."

He looked up at us, thinning hair disheveled, mouth slack with dismay. "Yes. How did you know?"

"It wasn't exactly rocket science, once we put the bits and pieces together. Did you pay him?"

"Who, Weathersby? Yes, a hundred thousand, in hundred-pound notes, cash. He made me sit there while he counted them. Bloody humiliating." Then he heaved a relieved sigh. "At least Jane won't have to find out about this now. Will she?" And he looked up at me with pathetic hope.

I hated to quash it. But events were just moving too bloody fast. "Bernie, I don't even know why John was blackmailing you. If it's not essential to the case we may be able to keep it under wraps. But you need to tell us everything, Bernie, so we can make that judgment."

"No. I... I can't. If you find out on your own, well, I can't help that. But Jane's and my marriage – it couldn't take the strain. Believe me, Dex, it just couldn't take the strain. Dex, please – I'm begging you. We've known each other for a long time. Please let sleeping dogs lie."

I liked Bernie – I always had. And I hated to see him in such a state. But I had to be honest. "I can't promise that, Bernie." I carefully kept the anguish from my voice. "I wish I could, but this is a murder investigation now. A very high-profile murder investigation. John was in the House of Lords, for God's sake! I'll do whatever I can, of course, but under the circumstances, that may be very little."

"A murder investigation." He looked back and forth between Brian and me, and, fresh dismay blooming in his face, seemed to dissolve into his armchair. "And now I'm a suspect, of course."

"It's no longer my investigation, Bernie – I've been taken off the case. I don't know where it will lead. But my best advice to you is to be as cooperative as possible. If you've nothing to hide, you've no worries, mate. Look, Brian's my partner. I trust him with my life, and you can trust him as well. He'll give you a fair shake."

Bernie shook his head stubbornly. "It was nothing criminal – that's all I'm going to tell you. Dex – we've been friends for ages. Please."

"We'll help you all we can. But first you've got to help yourself. Listen, Bernie – Brian has some questions he needs to ask you. Just basic things, about John, and the night he was murdered. I'll leave you to it."

On my way past his chair, I gave Bernie's shoulder a reassuring squeeze. He winced, involuntarily sucking in his breath. "Shoulder trouble, on top of everything else?" I asked.

"It's just scrum shoulder – all those years at hooker. You know how it is for us front-rowers. Had two surgeries, and now the doctor says it's arthritic." I knew that Bernie had had his shoulder scoped six months previously; he had told me, however, that it was feeling much better. I hoped it was. I certainly wasn't.

III

Bernie waved goodbye to Dex's partner, DI Abbott, then returned to his study and poured himself another stiff whisky. It was all he could do to steady his hand enough to stop the strong spirit from slopping over the rim. It had been a hellish morning – first that thug, Dean, with his sneering innuendo and his colon-knotting threats. Then the session with Dex and his very astute partner. DI Brian Abbott had been impeccably gentle and deferential. But he had also made it abundantly clear that he would see through any attempt to obscure the truth.

Bernie thought, for just a moment, what a blessed relief it would be to unburden himself, fully and completely, without restraint. Then his mind jerked back from the thought, like the tendrils of a sea anemone. Unthinkable. Jane – to say nothing of Dex and the other lads on the team – would never understand. His life, so orderly, so privileged, so comfortable, would for all intents and purposes be over. He sensed a grinding doom, like the face of a glacier, approaching, ponderous but inexorable. Somehow, some way, he had to get on top of this, and keep it down. Keep it from crushing all in its path. If only Dex was still on the case – he was a friend. A mate. He would understand.

Bernie's mind reverted, against his will, to the scene that was seared into his memory, the psychological equivalent of the cane-stripes he had occasionally collected at Hastewicke: that terrible night at Weathersby's house. Two weeks before the Charlie Chalmers Memorial, John had invited him 'round for drinks, and, Bernie thought, to discuss the team's plans for next year's tour to Hong Kong. They had spent a few minutes at John's laptop, going over his email correspondence with the various rugby clubs with which fixtures had been proposed. When they were finished, John had casually opened another folder, labeled "Vegas 2013," containing digital images from the Hastewicke Gentlemen's most recent tour.

"Ah. Here's something might interest you." John clicked on a file called "Bernie in Vegas." It was a video, and Bernie had watched its opening frames, showing the sitting-room in Suite 455, unfold with a whisky-befuddled lack of comprehension. Then the full horror of what he was seeing struck home, and he bounded to his feet as if a red-hot needle had suddenly been thrust through the seat of his chair.

"What the bloody hell, John? I appreciate a good joke as much as the next man, but that's not funny!"

"Nor was it intended to be. Sit down, Bernie." John flashed him that maddening white-toothed grin, and poured for them both from the decanter. "We have things to discuss."

Bernie sagged back into his chair, ashen-faced. "You unutterable bastard! You had the suite wired for surveillance! You'll burn in hell for this!"

Weathersby spoke soothingly as the images continued to unfold on the small but crystal-clear screen. "You've been such a bad boy, Bernie. I'd hate to think what Jane would say if she saw – that." The scene had switched to the bedroom; for a moment, John allowed his distaste to show. "But – and here's the crucial bit – she doesn't have to know. It can just be our little secret."

Bernie tried to close his ears to the ecstatic groans and lascivious smacking sounds emanating from the computer. He tried to clear his mind, to come to grips with this world-tilting catastrophe. "What... what do you mean?"

"I mean that, for the right price, I'll wipe this off the hard drive. You can do it yourself, if you like. It will be as if this sordid encounter had never taken place."

"What price?"

"Bernie! So eager! Really, it's a pleasure doing business with someone so keen." He paused for a refreshing sip. "I want £100,000, in cash, no larger than hundred-pound notes, by 5 p.m. Friday."

Bernie had never felt such fury, such utter betrayal. This couldn't be happening! "Or else what?"

John was very serious now. "Or else by 9 o'clock Monday morning, Jane will be in possession of this video. And by 10 o'clock, unless I'm much mistaken, you'll need the services of a very expensive divorce solicitor. I happen to know one – in fact, I'll give you his card, if you like."

"John. Listen to me." Bernie tried to speak calmly, tried to keep the shame and rage from his voice. "I don't have that kind of money just laying about. Everything I have is tied up in my estates – I can't just sell it off! Jane would know! We've a monthly income from our holdings, but by the time everything's paid, there's next to nothing left over! I might be able to raise ten thousand or so, but £100,000? It's out of the question!"

"Pity. I can tell you from personal experience that divorce, for one in our position, is considerably more expensive than that. Think of it as a business proposition, Bernie. A hundred thousand now, or several millions once Jane's barristers finish turning out your pockets. It's up to you, but frankly, you'd be a fool not to take me up on this."

"Why, John? Why me? We've been mates for years." Bernie hated the note of pleading in his voice, but he couldn't stop it. "I'm your son's godfather, for Christ's sake! How could you do this to me?"

"I told you, Bernie." John's toothy grin failed to touch his eyes. "It's business. I need money as much as the next man. More than the next man, truth be told. Either you swim with the sharks, or you're lunch. It's all the same to me. The others will be all the more eager to pay up once they see what happens to you."

"Others?" Bernie was aghast – this couldn't be happening. "There were more?"

"Of course there were more!" Weathersby laughed, a sound like the grating hinges of a long-unopened tomb. "The lads were remarkably unrestrained, but after all, it was Vegas. Sin City, the bloody Yanks call it, and not without reason! So. By 5 p.m. Friday, then! And one other thing."

Weathersby had leaned across the desk, and Bernie could smell the whisky on his breath. "Just a caution – surely unnecessary, in such civilized company. But it's best to be clear about these things. If anything should happen to me – if I should die, under any circumstances, in the next five years, a copy of this file *will* find its way into your wife's hands."

"But... but that's unreasonable, old man! What if you have a car crash, God forbid, or a coronary, or..."

"Then I won't care about you any more, Bernie. And by the way, the same holds true if anyone else on the club, or the police, get so much as an inkling of our little arrangement. So mum's the word! Who knows? You might even want to include me in your nightly prayers."

Back in the present, Bernie fought down the rising panic that threatened to unman him. For better or for worse, John was dead; that was immutable fact, and he'd better get used to it. Whatever arrangements John had made for this contingency were already in motion. There was no way to stop them – unless Dex...? But Dex had told him he was off the case. Well. There was nothing for it. He was a lord, a scion of the English aristocracy. He couldn't disgrace that honorable legacy of power, privilege and dignity – it was unthinkable. He would just have to go down with the ship.

That thought triggered another. And with a ghastly smile, Lord Delvemere reached for the phone.

III

Before I proceed with this fascinating narrative, a rugby physics lesson is in order. When two rugby scrums collide, eight large men, arms wrapped tightly around one another, endeavor to force the other scrum backward, like two massive Cape buffalo bulls locking horns over a particularly large-uddered female. This involves both an initial impact, often of a violent nature, and a subsequent shoving/wrestling match that frequently ends with one or more human bodies contorted in a highly unnatural position.

It is undeniably true that the front row of the scrum – the two props, always among the largest and strongest men on the pitch, with the smaller hooker in between – take the lion's share of the abuse, in their role as shock absorbers and as the interface – the adhesive agent – between the two scrums. Shoulder, neck and elbow injuries are the bane of all front-rowers; if you haven't had at least one major surgery in the course of your career, well, you haven't been trying hard enough, have you?

Bernie was no exception; I knew that, particularly in recent years, he had suffered from chronic pain in both shoulders and an elbow. So his wince, when I squeezed his shoulder, didn't exactly constitute an admission of guilt. Still, it made me wonder.

Whoever had shot John Weathersby would have a contusion on his shoulder from the rifle's donkey-like kick. That I knew, flexing my shoulder with a grimace, from personal experience. Finch-Hatton's massive H&H rifle lacked one modern innovation – a rubber recoil pad. The steel crescent at the butt of the rifle had crushed my shoulder with the force necessary to counteract 5,000 foot-pounds of impact energy, when the bullet found its target. Whoever had absorbed that recoil would still be feeling its effects.

The case against Artemis Paul was now nearly complete; after lunch, I met with a representative of the Crown Prosecuting Service, Terry Chapman, to discuss strategy, evidence, and the roster of charges we would be bringing. Paul had already been arraigned for kidnapping, attempted murder and assault on a police officer; after sampling the fruits of my investigation, Chapman decided to add tax evasion, facilitating prostitution, usury, intimidation and further charges of assault. The Martin Wallace murder investigation would be handled as a separate prosecution.

By the time we added up this grocery-list of offences, Terry thought my off-the-cuff estimate of 15 years in prison, with time off for good behaviour, might have been a bit on the lightish side. Despite the distress this might cause Mrs. Paul and the children, my heart somehow refused to bleed.

I returned to my office, but there was still no sign of Brian. I began to feel the now-familiar prickling of unease whenever I contemplated the murder of John Weathersby. The more I thought about it, the more certain I was that John would have made arrangements to reveal all he knew, should he die before or soon after he had collected his ill-gotten gains. It was simply too obvious an insurance policy for Weathersby to overlook.

The thought of these ticking time-bombs from beyond the grave, waiting to explode in my teammates' faces, made me feel both impotent and furious. Furious with them, for being so unbelievably stupid. And furious with John, for perpetrating such a monstrous betrayal. For the first time in memory, I could summon not an atom of sympathy for a murder victim.

It was nearly four o'clock when Brian finally strode in, waving, to my relief, a sheaf of thick five-by-seven envelopes. "Relax!" he grinned "– you look as anxious as I do, waiting for Fee to come back from dropping the kids at her sister's for our quarterly sex night!"

That gave me pause, despite my worries. "Quarterly? Are you joking?"

"You *are* a bachelor. After 15 years of marriage, don't you think I'm grateful for whatever scraps float my way? Haven't you noticed that my left hand and forearm are twice the size of my right? But you're off-topic. You and your mates owe a debt of gratitude to my improvisational brilliance. If £100,000 was the going rate, these envelopes, whatever's in them, are worth a hundred times their weight in gold."

Sir Steven Barnes, Weathersby's lawyer, had, not surprisingly, been less than cooperative. Brian had politely asked him for the use of the lost-luggage key referred to in Weathersby's will; Sir Steven had merely smiled in sad amusement and, regretfully, declined.

Brian, expecting no more, had merely informed Barnes that a Section 1 warrant was in the works, and that once it arrived, he would be back to take possession of the key. Then, leaving Sir Steven's office, Brian had concealed himself in a convenient alcove down the hall, and waited.

Five minutes later, Sir Steven had come to his office door with a balding, middle-aged man whom Brian recognized as his clerk. After a brief, muttered conversation, the man set off down the hall, with Brian sauntering discreetly behind.

At Euston Station, as expected, Barnes' clerk made a beeline for the left-luggage area. Extracting a key from his pinstriped pocket, he opened a locker, extracted a bundle of padded envelopes, and turned to encounter Brian and DC Goodspeed, warrant cards out.

"We'll take those, thank you very much," said Brian, extracting the bundle from the clerk's suddenly-nerveless fingers.

"You can't do that! That's privileged material!"

Brian raised one bushy eyebrow. "Are you Lord Southampton's solicitor?"

"No, but..."

"Are you in fact a solicitor at all?"

"No, I'm Sir Steven's clerk. But..."

Brian shoved a copy of the Section 1 warrant into the man's nerveless fingers. "In that case, I'm confiscating these envelopes in the Crown's name. They're evidence in a murder investigation."

Now they sat on my desk, mute but ominous. I sorted through the addressees. Lady Jane Plantagenet. Lady Sarah St. John

Barlowe. Catherine Seagrave. All wives of various Hastewicke Gentlemen. The fourth envelope was addressed to Sir Lewis Trilby, chair of the board of directors of the Magwitch Project, Bob Lestrange's charitable foundation. Another envelope was addressed to Cyrian O'Toole, the *Sun's* gleefully malignant society columnist. John had been more vindictive than I had supposed.

As Brian looked on, I unfolded my clasp-knife, pulled a random envelope from the stack – that addressed to Catherine Seagrave – and disemboweled it. A zip drive fell out, labeled "Vegas Tour 2013 – Roger."

"I'll do the honours," said Brian, popping the drive into a USB port.

The first image that appeared was a wide view of the sitting-room of a suite – couch, table, chairs, entertainment system, mini-bar – identical to the one I had occupied in Las Vegas. In the lower left-hand corner of the screen was the door; after a few seconds it opened, and Roger Seagrave, the Hastewicke Gentlemen's greyhound-elegant right wing, entered, with a... companion on his arm. After a few moments of preliminary groping and face-sucking, they made their way to the couch, and... suffice to say that even I, a policeman of more than 20 years' experience, who long ago thought he'd seen it all, obviously hadn't. "Shitting 'ell," was all I could croak.

I can't remember the last time I had last spent such an excruciating 20 minutes. It was about as enjoyable as a prostate exam from Andre the Giant. When the last guttural shriek of passion had died away, the computer screen mercifully went dark, and our eyes returned to their sockets, Brian just looked at me, one eyebrow raised. "I think I know why," I replied to his unspoken question. "But you can never be sure, can you? The heart of man is a fathomless mystery to all but himself."

8

Everything about Las Vegas was exhilarating to Roger Seagrave – the warm sun, the gin-and-tonic-scented desert air, the palm trees, the blissful anonymity, the freedom, the gaudily fantastic hotels, the smell of money in the air. Any pleasure human ingenuity could conceive was for sale here – the "escort services" listings in the Yellow Pages were as thick as a magazine and sorted by fetish, the bars were open 24 hours; there were even video poker machines over some of the urinals. Only the Americans could devise something so grandiose, so repellently vulgar – and so irresistible.

You couldn't help but admire them. Seventy years ago, this vast fairytale city had been nothing more than a shitstop in the endless desert between Los Angeles and Phoenix. Now look at it – a fantastic oasis in the tarantula-infested wasteland, more surreal and grandiose than any mirage, beguiling the mind like a potent drug.

At this moment, however, Seagrave was more concerned with his own survival than with local history. He stood on a lush, sun-warmed rugby pitch on the campus of the University of Nevada, arms outstretched, awaiting the arrival of the rugby ball that floated high above him, tumbling lazily end-over-end, now at its apogee, now beginning its descent.

At pitch level, half a dozen members of the Old Blues – alumni of the University of California at Berkeley and some of the most accomplished rugby players in America – thundered toward him, intent on reaching him just in time to separate him from the ball. As it nestled into his arms, Seagrave hopped deftly to his right, sidestepping his opposite number, the Old Blues right wing. He stepped over an ankle-tackle from another onrushing opponent, then accelerated as smoothly as his 51 years allowed, splitting two more would-be tacklers and leaving them grasping at empty air.

He was in full stride now, gliding up the touch-line, with teammates in support and calling for the ball. With serene detachment, Seagrave saw an Old Blues flanker rocketing toward him; he dummied a pass to Richard Devilliers, the Hastewicke Gentlemen's fullback, on his right wing. The flanker went for the fake, and Seagrave sprinted calmly on, past midfield, toward the 22-meter line, still untouched.

The last line of the Old Blues defense now closed in: the full-back and outside centre, angling him toward the touch-line. At the last possible instant, Seagrave lofted a beautifully-calculated up-and-under kick over the heads of the onrushing tacklers, side-stepped the Old Blues fullback and hared in pursuit of the ball. For just a moment – one brief, blissful moment – he felt 21 again, soaring over the ground, liberated from the weakness and nattering pain that were his constant companions in this, his 51st year. The ball descended, and his perfectly-timed leap brought it to hand and carried him over the try line for the touch-down, his second try of the match.

Seagrave accepted the congratulations of his teammates with barely-concealed elation, the score now 27-14 in the Hastewicke Gentlemen's favour. A few minutes later, the referee blew the familiar three blasts on his whistle, signaling full time. The Hastewicke Gentlemen were through to the final, thanks largely to Roger Seagrave's brilliant play.

As he rummaged through his kit-bag a few minutes later, pulling on sweats to ward off the surprising chill of late afternoon in the high desert, Seagrave encountered the note that had been slipped under the door of his suite the morning before: "An anonymous benefactor wishes it to be known that Suite 455 has been booked through the weekend for the discreet use of any Hastewicke Gentleman..."

The tour manager, Henry Bell, happened to be close at hand. "Well done, Roger," he said "– decent little canter there at the end. Reminded me of old times."

Seagrave smiled sadly. "Some days you feel as though you can outrun time, but he always catches you up in the end. There *is* something about this place, though – makes me feel like a kid again."

"Must be all the sin in the air," Bell observed with a wink.

"Speaking of which –" Roger lowered his voice. "Would suite 455 be... available this evening?"

Bell consulted his iPhone with a conspiratorial grin. "As a matter of fact, it is."

"Good." Seagrave finished puling on his sweats and, accepting Henry Bell's outstretched hand, heaved himself to his feet. He felt his excitement quicken, as a half-formed, long-harbored fantasy suddenly assumed more tangible shape. "Consider it booked, then."

II

An hour later, Seagrave, clad in retina-scorching Hawaiian swim trunks, was soaking up the heat of the glassed-in pool terrace at the Bellagio, headquarters for the Hastewicke Gentlemen during their week's stay. There was an ice-cold Budweiser in his hand, and he contemplated his immediate future with placid contentment. The team had five more days in Las Vegas; after tomorrow's tournament final, they would have 72 responsibility-free hours in which to sample every vice and sordid amusement Vegas had to offer. And Seagrave, with no worries about money, intended to make the most of them.

It was tours like this that kept Roger Seagrave playing rugby, long after most sensible men would have hung up their boots. He loved the chaffing, the camaraderie, the social side of the game; but more than that, he still loved the on-field warfare. Most of all, he loved the element of skill that made the Hastewicke gentlemen so feared in old-boy rugby circles – the precise kicking game, the fluid passing, the near-telepathic backline play that testified to their more than 30 years as teammates.

As for his position on the team, well, Seagrave knew he wasn't one of the dominant personalities – a Charlie Chalmers, a John Weathersby, a Jester Atkinson, whose forceful leadership and quirky senses of humor set the tone for the rest of the lads. He was content to be a back-row boy, a good companion on tour, respected, he hoped, as much for his contributions on the field as his gentle wit off it. Oh, he knew that his meticulous, even finicky, personality raised some eyebrows; he did like things just so, and his habit of carefully folding away his clothes in the bureau, polishing his boots before each match, and dressing elegantly afterward brought him in for a measure of abuse at his teammates' hands – for example, the time they had replaced his custom-formulated toothpaste, delicately flavoured with lemongrass and mint, with Preparation H. Still, a man on rugby tour had to be prepared to suffer the occasional indignity.

Somewhere deep inside, Roger knew he was nearing the end of his playing career, and something at the very core of his being cried out in anguish at the thought. Some day, perhaps soon, a bad fracture, a catastrophic knee injury, a severe concussion, would bring the curtain down on his rugby career. But until that day came, he was determined to play every match as if it was his last.

Seagrave was an analyst in Charlie Chalmers' old stock broker-age firm; his X-ray-like ability to see past the gloss of a company's financial reports and accurately assess its coming performance, coupled with an ear for insider gossip, had made him a partner seven years ago.

Seagrave had been married for 31 years, to Catherine, a gentle, heavyset woman who had grown progressively stouter in the years following the birth of their now-grown daughter Elizabeth. Roger had never complained. But eighteen months ago, Catherine's doctor, alarmed at the growing toll her obes-ity was taking on her circulatory system, ordered her, on pain of early death, to lose 12 stone, and keep it off. To her surprise, and, secretly, Roger's, she had succeeded, and now wore a size 6. But this admirable triumph of will was not without its sur-prising side-effects, at least as far as their marital dynamics were concerned.

The soothing female voice of the hotel operator, crack-ling over the P.A. system, suddenly intruded on his reverie. "Mr... Rhinodong. Mr... Suckah... Rhinodong. Please pick up a white paging telephone." Then, a moment or two later: "Mr. Bollox. Mr. Harry Bollox. Please go to a white paging tel-ephone for a message." And finally: "Lord Ivabiggun. Lord... Ivabiggun. Please pick up a white paging telephone..." Seagrave grinned at George Waters, the Hastewicke scrum-half, who was swimming nearby. "Sounds like one of the boys is getting bored."

Waters turned lazily onto his back, his marshmallow-white paunch floating proudly above the waves. "Bet you a tenner it's Jester Atkinson – you know how he fancies practical jokes."

Seagrave rose stiffly and limped to the nearby white phone, already paying the price for his heroic exertions on the rugby pitch earlier that day. "Yes, this would be Mr. Rhinodong!" he cried irritably, laying on a thick Punjabi accent. "And my Christian name is pronounced 'Sookah!' I tell you now that I do not find my name the slightest bit... oh, hullo, Jester, we thought it might be you. Yes, we're down by the pool – we've a few bottles of the amber nectar on ice. Right, see you soon."

Seagrave returned to his chaise lounge, lowered himself gratefully and bit back a groan of pain. "You win," he laughed. He drained the rest of his longneck, opened another, then relaxed once more. Despite his soreness, he did feel so marvelously relaxed. Then his manhood stirred as he thought of the arrangements he had made for later this evening, and Seagrave was forced to carefully arrange his voluminous trunks to conceal his growing turgidity.

For a moment he thought of Catherine, and felt a not-insubstantial twinge of guilt. If she ever found out about what he'd planned for tonight, she would be absolutely shattered. Seagrave was not a cruel or unsympathetic man; he knew that his wife was both proud and fragile. She would be gutted, completely gutted. He understood her well enough to know that, if she ever discovered how he really felt, her emotional response would degenerate rapidly from pain to bunny-boiling rage. Only chaos would follow, and his well-ordered life would be but a memory of happiness lost. It would be a blow from which she – and their marriage – might never recover.

However, she would never know. He only hoped his planned exertions later this evening wouldn't leave him too drained to perform in tomorrow's final match.

III

Back in the suite he shared with Terry Ross, the Hastewicke Gentlemen fly half, Seagrave patted the last dabs of shaving cream from his face and, making a selection from the carefully-organized toiletries arrayed before him, applied a delicate spritz or two of Ralph Lauren's "Stetson." Then he slipped a pair of Pierre Cardin khakis over his silk Armani briefs, tucked in his flawlessly-pressed Tommy Hilfiger denim dress shirt and tugged on a well-scuffed pair of ostrich-skin cowboy boots. He glanced at his Rolex. His heart rate increased fractionally; almost time to go. He called down to the valet, to ensure that his Nike Tiempo Legend rugby boots would be polished and returned by morning. Then he slipped out the door and down the hall to the elevator.

She is waiting, as he had asked, on the couch near the door to Suite 455. At his approach, she rises gracefully, and he sucks in his breath. She is everything he had hoped, and more. So much more.

The photos on her website fail to do her justice. She stands nearly six feet tall, her hair a silky coil of raven-black cornrow, her skin the color of strong tea with just a touch of milk. Her makeup is tasteful and immaculate; her eyes a luminous brown. Beneath her voluminous, knee-length silk dress, her flesh billows, bounces and jiggles, like the sails of a clipper ship bulging before a gale, from her enormous breasts to the plateau of her endlessly broad, shelflike buttocks. She is ...magnificent.

"Roger?" she asks with a slow, shy smile. Her voice is low and musical. "I'm Rosie. Whole Lotta Rosie."

Seagrave feels himself grow weak in the knees. The truth is that, though slim himself, Roger has always found thin women unappetizingly angular. He loves Catherine, but he had liked her better as she was before she lost weight – soft, wobbly and lavishly proportioned. He had thought her perfect. He has always been attracted to very large women, with faces out of a Rubens canvas and bodies built for sin. There is no explaining it; God knows he has tried. Maybe it is simply their gratitude that appeals to him.

The thought of those acres of soft, undulating flesh, those fathomless, moist and mysterious crevices, in which a man might lose himself and never be found, is almost too much to bear. "Shall we go in?" he asks throatily. Rosie takes his arm, and the scent of gardenias wafts toward him. He almost moans. Instead, he produces the card-key to Suite 455 and opens the door. She is almost too vast for them to fit through the doorway together, but somehow they manage, and he is ever more aware of her mountainous femininity.

Once inside, he kisses her, unable to restrain his need any longer. If he extends his arms fully, and squeezes, he can just touch his fingertips together on the other side of her equator-like waist. The sensation of her yielding mounds of flesh against his member brings him to instant, almost painful, rigidity.

Lotta Rosie notices. With a playful grin, she reaches down and strokes him with her long nails; the pleasure is almost unbearable. "Oooh, Roger – we're gonna be very good friends, I can tell already. You gotta be a whole lotta man to love Whole Lotta Rosie. But first – " she leans forward to whisper in his ear "– business before pleasure. Do you have something for me?"

He has the money ready; she counts it expertly, tucks it into her handbag. "Excellent. And now, Roger." She advances upon him like a tigress; he gives ground toward the couch. "I'm gonna show you what all those white boys with their preying mantis women have been missing."

Rosie engulfs him with her pendulous bulk; the couch-springs scream in protest. "The bigger the cushion, the better the pushin', honey. But then – " the slow grin is back as she hikes up her dress "– you knew that already. Or you wouldn't never have called Rosie."

9

And where was I while these masterpieces of decadence were being created? One of the things I've always enjoyed about rugby, particularly on foreign tour, is getting to know the opposition a bit, once all the on-field action concludes. On the Saturday, I encountered a few members of the Sonoma RUFC, whom we had soundly thrashed earlier that week, in the lobby of the Bellagio. One of them, a second row named Tony DeGraffenreid, turned out to be the sheriff of El Dorado County, California. We found a relatively quiet bar off the Bellagio's cavernous, cacophonous casino, and settled in for a few pints while his mates went off to try their luck at the tables. Our discussion turned naturally to our mutual calling.

I asked him about his most interesting case. Tom narrowed his eyes in concentration, and took a drag on his Camel. "El Dorado

County's mostly pretty rural," he said at last. "The California Gold Rush started there, and Sutter's Mill is in my patrol area. It's still mostly farms and forest, with a piece of greater Sacramento at the west end. Most of my calls are pretty basic – domestic disturbance, car crashes, somebody finds a pot farm tucked away in the trees. It's a pretty interesting job, really; when your patrol area's 100 miles square, you never really know what's going to come your way.

"One night I get a call from this farmer – raises dairy goats and sells the milk to one of the local cheesemakers. Said he'd heard some kinda disturbance in his barn, but when he went down to check, he didn't see anything out of whack. I checked the place out, but there was nothing to see – just a bunch of happy-looking goats and a few tire tracks in the mud outside. I give the guy my card and tell him to call me if it happens again.

"Coupla nights later, I get a call. It's the farmer, yellin' that it's happened again. Only this time, he was ready. He tore out of the house with his shotgun, and fired off a round in the air. Saw some asshole down behind the barn, pulling up his pants. Then the guy jumped into a pickup and hauled ass. But this time, he left something behind – his wallet.

"So I stop by and pick it up, and the next morning, I go to see the guy – driver's license says Joe Slater, some hippy-dippy carpenter, lives up in the hills out of Placerville. And when I show him his wallet, he just crumbles in front of my eyes. Confesses everything, and I mean everything. About how he'd always had this thing for farm animals, since he was a little kid, and about how women had always hurt him, and how there was one pretty little blue-eyed goat he just couldn't get out of his mind... he even shows me the feed-bag he used to keep the fuckin' thing quiet, for Chrissake."

A slow smile crept across Tom's hard-planed face, in anticipation of the story's climax. "I let him talk, and when he finishes, I give him a real hard stare, like this – " he demonstrated "– and I says to him, 'Boy, I just want to know one thing. Was that goat *female*?'" Tom started to laugh, and the tears rolled down his cheeks. "And he says to me, with this horrified look on his face, 'Course she was, Sheriff! Whaddaya think I am, some kinda *pervert*?'"

II

So there was a glimmer of a silver lining, then: thankfully none of my teammates – at least those on Weathersby's blackmail videos – had a taste for barnyard animals in tiny fishnet stockings. I couldn't vouch for Jester Atkinson, of course, whose sexual proclivities were known to be adventurous in the extreme; for whatever reason, he had evidently satisfied them somewhere other than Suite 455.

After viewing the four blackmail videos in sequence, I felt voyeuristic, faintly nauseated, and strangely unable to look Brian in the eye, but also somewhat conflicted. I was relieved to be off the case, spared the responsibility for what now promised to be a hellishly intrusive, sensitive and difficult investigation of my closest mates. On the other hand, it was only too clear where the inquiry was leading: to a likely murder conviction for one of them, and heart-rending personal humiliation and tragedy for all, as their transgressions inevitably became known. All four were my friends, and I could think of a dozen ways I might, as a member of the investigative team, be able to spare them some small measure of discomfort. But that wouldn't be possible now.

There was a rap on the frame of the cubicle. "Wicks wants to see you," said Jade Singleton, the plumpish, pleasant-faced group secretary. Wondering glumly which of my faults would be under discussion this time, I braced myself, knocked and went in.

"Sit down, Reed." He pointed to the single uncomfortable-looking chair before his desk. As before, DCI Oakhurst stood by the window, surveying me with gleeful malevolence. Wicks, on the other hand, looked angry enough to bite the nadgers off a badger. I carefully composed myself in preparation for the impending explosion.

To my surprise, it was Oakhurst who spoke first. "Good news, DI Reed! We're putting you back on the Weathersby case!"

I stared at him blankly for a moment. "Sir? I thought my personal association with the victim and potential suspects was considered a liability."

"We've re-thought that position, and now we want you to ruthlessly exploit that knowledge for our benefit. We expect you and the rest of the squad to bring this case to a swift and successful conclusion. Yes, Peter? You had something to add?"

Wicks merely shook his head, but a flush of magenta was creeping up his scrawny septuagenarian neck, a sure sign that he was ready to go off like a bomb. "You'll be reporting directly to me," Oakhurst continued. "Daily. I want you to begin by giving me a concise profile on each member on the Hastewicke Gentlemen, and every instance of potentially blackmail-worthy behaviour you've ever witnessed on tour."

"But sir..." my horror must have shown, because Oakhurst was suddenly smiling very broadly indeed. "Only four of them were being blackmailed. If there were more, Weathersby's solicitor would've had other thumb drives. He's confirmed that there were only the four."

"We don't know that, DI Reed. We know Weathersby was both greedy and unscrupulous. There could very well have been others."

"If there were, we'll know soon enough." Furious and appalled, I stood to go. "Was there anything else, sir?"

"Sit down, Reed – I'm not finished with you yet. I realize the delicacy of this investigation, and I appreciate the position it puts you in." The cold mirth in his eyes showed just how deeply he appreciated it. "Your familiarity with the suspects could be the key to breaking this case. But I want you to know very clearly that if I discover a single instance of a potentially-relevant fact, however trivial, being suppressed to protect one of your teammates, you will face the severest possible disciplinary action. Is that absolutely clear?"

"As a bell, sir."

"Good. And Reed?"

"Yes, sir?"

"That report – I want it on my desk. By tomorrow afternoon, without fail."

I sat stunned for a moment, trying to come to grips with the enormity of this cataclysm. Wicks glared after Oakhurst's departing bulk, then shut his office door. "Well, DI Reed? What's the matter? Two days ago you were begging to stay on this case. Now you've a face like a slapped arse."

I shot him a look of reproach. "Have you seen the videos, sir?"

"Yes."

"Then you've a sense of what's at stake here. These men are my friends, Detective Superintendent. If the contents of those thumb drives become known outside this office... they're dynamite. They're going to make headlines and things are going to get very ugly, very fast. Public humiliation, divorce, utter ruin. It's all on the table."

"They'll blame you, of course. And if you try to shield them, Oakhurst will have your scrotum for a coin-purse."

"Yes." I could feel the weighty truth of that.

"Dex." Wicks never called me by my Christian name; I glanced up in surprise, to meet his uncharacteristically fatherly gaze. "Don't lose sight of the fact that, no matter how richly he may have deserved it, it's very likely that one of your friends blew John Weathersby's head off with an elephant gun. This isn't the Old West. There's a 98 percent clearance rate on London murders. We catch our murderers here, and lock them up."

I nodded, and he went on. "This case is going to twist you like a pretzel, Reed. You can't possibly bring the requisite objectivity to bear, and it's going to tear you apart. I don't want to see that happen." He looked as though the words were being dragged out of him with red-hot pincers. "You're a good investigator, Dex. But if you knock this one on, I won't be able to protect you from Oakhurst. You're simply going to have to approach this case as if you've never met these people before."

"I appreciate the rugby metaphor. But why, sir?"

"Why what?"

"Why am I back on the case?"

"Oakhurst insisted, and managed to convince Deputy Assistant Commissioner Goddard. Obviously Oakhurst is counting on you giving him grounds for disciplinary action. Just as I am counting on you to bring this case to a quietly successful conclusion."

"Ah."

"There may also have been some pressure from outside the department to re-establish you on this case," Wicks added delicately. "The English aristocracy, while a sad, jug-eared mockery of its former glory, is not wholly without influence. I believe there are some members of the Hastewicke Gentlemen who hope that having one of their own at the centre of the investigation may spare them some embarrassment. Just don't let Oakhurst catch you at it."

"I appreciate that, sir." I rose to go, but his voice stopped me at the door.

"And Dex... perhaps now you also appreciate why I pulled you off this case."

Brian glanced up as I re-entered our cube. "Good news!" I said with false heartiness. "Wicks and Oakhurst have decided that I'm indispensable to the Weathersby case!"

For a moment, Brian just looked at me out of those basset-hound eyes of his, understanding. "You poor bastard," was all he said.

10

"Christ, let me at that toilet! I've just sharted!"

Sir Percival Henry St. John Barlowe, Harry to his mates, cracked the shower door in alarm. Through the billowing steam, he saw his suite-mate, Jester Atkinson, hobble through the door, snatch his trousers to the floor, and leap astride the crapper with a groan of relief. A deafening glissando shook the room, as if someone had attached an industrial air-compressor to a bassoon. It was followed, seconds later, by a stench most foul and ominous – fruity, yet repulsive, with a hint of rotting prawn.

"So fell a blast hath ne're mine ears saluted, nor yet a stench so all-pervading and immortal!" quoted Barlowe, and opening the shower door wider, he turned the showerhead full blast on his unwelcome teammate. "Mark Twain, you graceless twit."

Atkinson stoically endured the deluge, and sat dripping and gurning as he strained to crimp off another length. "I hate it when that happens," he observed sadly.

Harry couldn't help but laugh. You never knew what would happen next when you were on tour with Jester. He was simply unhinged. One minute you might enter the room to discover him at the window, gleefully squirting catsup and mustard at the unsuspecting pedestrians far below. The next, you might catch him applying a thin layer of Atom Balm to your athletic supporter, or humming as he wired a 9-volt battery to the sink taps. His was a mercurial wit that fairly sparked and dazzled, like one of his booby-trapped washbasins, and lesser men could only shake their heads in wonder.

Once, during the Hastewicke Gentlemen's first Australian tour, Harry and Jester had been sitting in the bar of their Sydney hotel with Lord Ewan Ramsay, Hastewicke's towering, dour Scots second-row. The door of the lobby toilet had opened, and a portly Aussie had emerged, his huge beard only slightly less voluminous than the fluffy crinoline dress that sheathed his loins. Its colour, an aggressive mustardy yellow, was particularly ill-suited to his ochre-red complexion; he was more an autumn than a spring. As the three Hastewicke Gentlemen had looked on in wonder, the Aussie had seized the arm of a much smaller bloke dressed in a matching Coleman's-yellow suit and flounced off toward the ballroom. Gazing about the hotel lobby, the three teammates beheld other couples, all men, all dressed in similar his-and-his outfits, all headed in the same direction.

Unable to restrain their curiosity, Harry, Jester and Ramsay had carried their pints over to examine the placard at the ballroom door: "Welcome Pan-Australian Gay Men's Square Dancing Society!" The three had made their way to the gallery above the ballroom, to gaze down upon a scene of exquisite weirdness: dozens of colorfully-dressed male couples, do-se-doing and promenading like the chorus from a production of "Oklahomo!"

For a moment, the three Hastewicke Gentlemen could only stare in wonder. Then Jester had a brainwave. "I say, Ewan. What' your room number?"

Ramsay, his gloomy Calvinistic features twisted into an expression of loathing at the scene below, distractedly fished his key from his pocket. "Ah... 661." He started to tuck the key away, but it was too late; he had already fallen into the trap. With an underhand slap, Jester sent the key spinning through the air. It landed with a tinkle at the feet of one of the dancers, who retrieved the key and, looking upward for its source, encountered Ramsay's eyes, bulging in horror. With a little wave, he tucked the key into his pocket and mouthed the word "Later."

Harry couldn't help but chuckle when he recalled the scene, and its aftermath. Still smiling, he stepped from the shower and began to towel off. Jester, reaching for the toilet-roll, whistled. "Have you seen your back? Lovely set of rake-marks – I think I can see your spine."

Harry had felt the sting of them in the shower; toweling off the fogged-up mirror, he examined them critically: four long, raised, angry-looking welts in the skin over the hard muscles of his lower back, inflicted by the cleats of an opposition number 8 when Harry had deliberately been slow rolling away from the ball in a ruck. He paused for a moment to examine his reflection – six feet tall, 17 stone, his once-luxurious hair now but a fringe, his beard full and sternum-length, with just a trace of grey. Still considerable muscle there, particularly in the chest and arms, thanks to his daily work with hammer and chisel.

"They're beauties all right," Harry said at length "– but they'll heal. Anyway, I'm grateful to have them. It wasn't long ago that I thought my days on rugby tour were gone forever."

II

Harry Barlowe was the only member of the Hastewicke Gentlemen who wasn't drinking on this tour. It had been two years since his last drink, two gloriously productive and fulfilling years. It had taken this long to regain enough of his wife's trust to be allowed to go on rugby tour again. Thinking of all he had lost, and then regained, he didn't miss the booze.

It is an indisputable fact that rugby and beer are intimately entwined. For most players it isn't a serious problem; for those genetically predisposed to alcoholism, however, it can be a dangerous marriage. Both Harry's father and paternal grandfather had been very committed alcoholics; both had died young and badly, after making utter dog's breakfasts of their once-promising lives. Harry had never paused to consider that he might follow in their footsteps. By the time that thought occurred, at the age of 43, he found that he already had.

At first, drink hadn't been a problem for Harry – he could have a few pints with the lads after a match or training-session, and stagger home none the worse for wear. Harry had always been a bit retiring, socially, always secretly afraid he was going to make an ass of himself. After a few pints, his shyness vanished, and he felt one of the lads.

He had begun spending more time at the pub with the boys, sometimes reeling home well-after closing-time. And, of course, weekends and tours were complete piss-ups. Before long, he was drinking every night. When his wife Sarah, home all day with their two young sons, became alarmed at his increasingly habitual insobriety, Harry had obligingly stopped drinking at home. At fairly regular intervals, uneasy at the toll the drink was taking on his work, he would stop drinking entirely, for a few weeks, a month, half a year.

It was easy enough to stop for a time, but he never managed to convince himself it was permanent. One day, he would look down and notice, with some surprise, that he once again had a pint in his hand. An empty pint. Almost before he had realized what was happening, the drinking had begun again.

One dreary November day, Harry emerged from his fog to discover that he had installed a well-stocked drinks cabinet in his sculpting studio. His drinking then assumed a deadly furtiveness; he experimented with various methods of disguising his intake, and felt a thrill of ignoble triumph whenever Sarah seemed not to notice he was intoxicated. When she did notice, he would ignore the desperation in her eyes and lie as he'd never lied before.

The end came on the clear, frosty Christmas night of 2009. Knowing that Sarah's family were coming to dinner, Harry nevertheless managed to consume two bottles of Stolychnia vodka between breakfast and the arrival of their guests. Erroll Flynn had written, in his autobiography, that he preferred vodka because its neutral odor was undetectable on the breath. Flynn was, of course, quite wrong, in this and many things; after all, what can you expect from a man who died at age 50 with a liver the size of a rugby ball?

Christmas dinner was an utter fiasco; even Harry's four-year-old son could tell he was ripped. Despite Sarah's mortified attempts to wrest away the cutlery, Harry had stubbornly insisted on carving. He had nearly lopped off a finger and had bled all over the goose she had laboured for half the day to prepare. At last he had staggered outside for a breath of air, stopped for a piss, and plunged face-first into his wife's prize rose-garden.

There he had lain, near death, until morning's gentle light, and his own uncontrollable shivering, wakened him. Covered with frost and filth, and scourged by rose-thorns, he had reeled, appalled, into the house. The mess from last night's dinner was still on the table. Sarah and the boys were gone. She had left him a note on the bed: "You have ruined our life. Words cannot convey what an unutterable bastard you are. I never want to see you again. My solicitor will be in touch."

It was only then that he realized the truth: that unless he stopped drinking, for good this time, he would die disgraced, alone, and soon. It was as inevitable as the morning mail, as certain as the fact that a ringing phone in the middle of the night heralded bad news. And so he had dried his tears, gone to his studio, poured every drop of booze down the sink, and binned the empties. Then he had checked himself into a very expensive rehab clinic called The Elms.

A month of treatment and many gut-wrenching conversations with Sarah later, he had managed to talk her and the boys back into his life. But she had made it very clear that it was either alcohol, or her; if he ever drank again, they were finished. But he no longer felt the urge to drink; it was as if a great weight of anxiety had been lifted from his soul. He knew, deep down inside, having been mostly sober for the first 25 years of his life, that it was possible to find happiness without alcohol. He threw himself into Alcoholics Anonymous, into work, into fatherhood, into rebuilding his shattered relationship with his wife, cheerfully and without self-pity. At length, to his eternal gratitude, he had succeeded.

And yet he knew from past experience, and from AA, that the threat of relapse was never far away. Indeed, it was at moments like this, when his confidence in his sobriety was greatest, that he actually teetered on the brink of doom.

Sarah hadn't been overly keen on the idea of Harry's joining the Vegas tour. Far from it. For two years she had insisted, with good reason, that he stay away from rugby. But he had seen it as the ultimate test of his sobriety, as well as a way to rein-force his resolve. After all, there are few more pathetic sights than the debauched buffoonery of late Saturday night on rugby tour, viewed through sober eyes.

III

Tonight was a good example. Harry sat in a booth at the Venetian, with a few of the lads: Weathersby, Dex Reed, Atkinson, George Waters, Kevin Gleeson, the Hastewicke Gentlemen's portly inside centre. All except Reed, perhaps, were drunk; Weathersby was giggling, Atkinson was legless, Waters was rat-assed and Gleeson was, in Harry's expert judgment, twat-faced. Their shouts of laughter, and occasional slurred and scandalous choruses of song, rang from the mirrored walls, and only their increasingly generous gratuities ensured a continued flow of drink. Harry placidly sipped soda with lime.

Dex edged closer to make himself heard over the din. "How's it going – the not drinking, I mean?"

"I'm quite happy to be off the stuff, thanks for asking, Dex," Harry replied. "I never would have believed it two years ago, but I'm happier without it."

"Isn't it hard, though? Watching us neck down pints without a care in the world?"

Harry considered. "Situations like this aren't a problem, Dex. I knew there would be drink about on tour, but when you know something's coming, you can prepare yourself – steel your resolve, if you like. It's the thing you don't anticipate that throws you." He looked thoughtfully into his glass. "Besides, everybody knows I don't drink anymore. If I suddenly fell off the wagon, what would you all think of me? I'd just be a pathetic alky, wouldn't I?"

Dex looked at him seriously; perhaps he was a bit ratted after all. "I do admire you, actually – I don't know if I've told you that. But surely you don't care what a bunch of drunken idiots like us think of you, do you?"

At this moment, Kevin Gleeson staggered back from the bar, where he had been chatting up a lush chestnut-haired beauty in a skin-tight bodysuit of scarlet leather. He fell tipsily into the booth, knocking the table in the process; a full row of glasses went over with a crash, and several pints of ice-cold lager rushed toward Atkinson, seated in a captain's chair at the end of the table. The lanky number 8 saw the onrushing flood and struggled, Laccoon-like, to escape, but was defeated by the arms of the chair, and bellowed with shock and fury as the frosty torrent refreshed his groin.

"Good one, Kev," Harry laughed. "How'd you fare with the Michelin Maid?"

"Swimmingly, mate, swimmingly, as one sperm said to another. I asked her whether she had any Irish in her; when she said no, I asked her if she'd like some."

"You didn't! Did she biff you one?"

"Nah. She wants me to call her later – look!" Gleeson flourished a bar napkin, emblazoned with a lipsticked telephone number. He downed half his pint at a quaff, gazed in admiration at his quarry at the bar. "Phwoarg! Look at that camel's hoof! She's hotter than Angelina in a thong!"

"Well done!" Dex glanced up. "But look, Kev – you'd better make your move – she's talking to some bloke the spitting image of Clive Owen!"

Gleeson turned pale in horror. "Christ, you're right – time to turn on the old charm. Harry – you're sober. Do us a favor – " he snatched out his mobile and thrust it into Harry's hands. "Call her for me."

"Call her for you? What do you want me to say?"

"God's bollocks, I don't know... tell her I want to take her for a late dinner at Wolfgang's, then show her the Blarney stones! No, wait! Be subtle! Be suave! Ask her to meet me for dessert!"

"What, a small helping of Irish trifle?"

"This is no joking matter, Dex! Please, Harry – I'm begging you!"

Sighing in amused vexation, Harry flipped open the mobile and punched in the number on the napkin. The things he did for the team. A recorded voice answered on the second ring. "The person you are calling was obviously not interested. For advice on personal hygiene, better grooming, or acceptable ways to approach females, please hold... sorry, all of our operators have better things to do than talk to you." Harry hit "end," then "redial," and wordlessly handed Kevin the phone. The Irishman gave a cry of anguish; when he looked at the bar, both the woman of his dreams and Clive Owen were gone. "Ah, Jaysus," he groaned. "How could she toy with me affections that way?"

Harry shook his head, hiding a grin, then turned back to Dex. "To answer your earlier question, Dex, believe it or not, I do crave your respect. Helps keep me sober, you see. What if, some day, one of you lot decide to go on the wagon? I'd hope you'd come to me – I'd like to help."

It was a noble thought. But when he and a near-comatose Jester Atkinson returned to their suite at the Bellagio, Harry encountered the note: "An anonymous benefactor wishes it to be known that Suite 455 has been booked through the weekend for the discreet use of any Hastewicke Gentleman. Time is available in four-hour blocks. Please book in advance with the tour secretary."

This was a new wrinkle since last he was on tour. But it was nothing to do with him. He was here for the rugby, the companionship, and to reinforce his resolve never to drink again. He tossed the note aside, and went gratefully to bed. Today had been a good day.

The next day was Sunday, when the Hastewicke Gentlemen would play the Old B.A.T.S. – the Bay Area Touring Side, from Oakland – in the tournament final. Harry showered, then pulled on his kit, surreptitiously checking his jock-strap for signs of a foreign substance before snugging it into place. It seemed inert; thankfully, Jester had slept like the snoring dead last night.

Sunday dawned breezily blue, with the smoky scent of Indian summer in the air. The boys arrived at the pitch groaning and shambling; both the three matches they had played on Saturday, and Saturday night in Las Vegas, had taken a grim toll. Still, when the whistle blew, and the kickoff soared skyward from the foot of the B.A.T.S. fly half, they were ready to do business.

The two sides were evenly matched. Harry did his usual efficient work on the pitch – anchoring the scrum, lifting flawlessly in the line-outs, administering the occasional bone-jarring tackle, ripping the ball in the maul, clearing stray opponents from the ruck, sacrificing his body wherever it was needed. He wasn't as mobile as Weathersby, the other Hastewicke prop; he made up for his lack of speed with an artist's eye for the geometry of the game, never wasting a step, always around the ball.

Toward the end of the match, with Hastewicke leading 25-21, there was a scrum about 10 meters out from the Hastewicke try-line. The B.A.T.S. needed a try to win it; Harry heard the B.A.T.S. number 8 call "Blue 87!" He remembered the play from earlier in the game. The B.A.T.S. number 8, a gigantic Kiwi ex-pat named Karl Hammett, picked up the ball; Harry saw Dex Reed and Jester Atkinson launch themselves at Hammett, who, just before impact, dished the ball inside to his number 7. The flanker's eyes widened as he saw a clear path to the goal-line.

But Harry had already torn himself away from the B.A.T.S. loose-head prop; he drove the ball-carrier sideways, into touch, just five meters from the line. The referee consulted his watch, then blew full time. The Hastewicke Gentlemen had won the tournament.

After the match, most of the boys were keen to start the evening's celebration with an excursion to *O*, Cirque de Soleil's erotic underwater extravaganza. Harry begged off – he was suddenly too knackered. He returned to his suite, called Sarah to tell her how it had gone. Then he curled up on the king-sized bed and cried.

Two hours later, he let himself into Suite 455 with the keycard Henry Bell had provided. He set the paper sack on the coffee table, fetched a glass from the bar, added six perfect cubes of ice. He turned on the TV, and poured himself a drink. He stared into its amber depths, mesmerized by the frosty condensation. Fascinated, he watched a droplet of crystalline water slip languidly down the side of the glass, revealing the golden secret within. He licked his lips and shuddered with anticipation as he raised the glass, slowly, like a lover.

The lads would never know. Sarah would never know. Tomorrow he would return to sobriety. But tonight, the whisky tasted like the immortality-conferring blood of some savage god, gulped directly from the vein.

That note. It was a thing he hadn't anticipated.

11

One thing I like about Brian, as a partner, is the way he complements me in the interview process. I'm a bit of a gabbler, and tend to cover a lot of ground, sometimes too eager to move on to the next question before the previous point has been fully explored. Brian mostly listens, occasionally lending an intimidating physical dimension to the proceeding. But his invaluable contribution comes at the end, in the aftermath of my own searching questions, as we're all recovering from the intensity of the interrogation.

I can see him now, leaning on the doorframe of the Hendon lockup, his hand in the air, as if he were attempting to seize the truth before it fluttered, mothlike, out into the high street. "Just one more thing," he says. "How did you come to..." or "Why did you say..." or "Why did she identify..." and, as often as not, his one small, insightful question would become the keystone of the prosecution's case.

He has a rare talent for boiling a thing down to its essence. His abilities were in full flower today, as he laid the case before me. "What do we know so far?" he asked. "We know the deceased was blackmailing at least four of your mates. We can surmise that at least two of them had paid up by the time of the murder, because Weathersby paid £200,000 cash for the rifle that killed him. We know your mate Bernie was one of those who paid. In my view, at least, anyone who had already paid would slide down the list of likely suspects a notch – why kill him *after* you've paid, except for revenge?"

I thought about that. "To get your mates off the hook." Brian nodded slowly, seeing the logic. "One thing bothers me, though – Bernie said John warned him that if anything happened to him, the blackmail videos would be sent out anyway. We have to assume that the others heard the same warning. Of course he'd made copies. Why kill him, and trigger the very disaster you were hoping to avoid?"

"Why indeed?" Brian had his pencil out, tapping his teeth again. "What else do we know? We know what Seagrave, Harry Barlowe, Leicester and Bernie were up to in Vegas; it's right there in living colour." He glared moodily at the five thumb drives on his desk. "I don't know about you, but I'm not sure I'll be able to have sex anytime soon – some of it put me right off."

Brian sighed. "Right. We know that each of them could expect an expensive divorce and, in all likelihood, public humiliation if Weathersby's material ever saw the light of day – more than ample motive for murder, for some. We know that whoever killed Weathersby has a working knowledge of alarm systems, and had to have a certain measure of physical strength to fire that gun. There aren't many women who could've done it. It would also seem that the murderer took Weathersby's MacBook, which presumably contains the master video files. From the violence of the crime, we can surmise that whoever killed Weathersby wanted to make very sure he was dead, although it could be that he just used whatever weapon happened to be to hand."

I nodded. "All four knew about John's collection. They were all familiar with his house – and they were all there on the night of the murder. Is the fingerprint report back yet?"

Brian nodded. "Interestingly enough, nothing had been wiped clean. They found Weathersby's prints, Leicester's, Barlowe's, Seagrave's and Lord Delvemere's at various points around the room, including the rifle. And yours."

I nodded. "Not surprising – we know that's where Weathersby did his business. What about the shell casings?"

"The casing in the gun had a partial of an unidentified thumb and forefinger – might've been the rifle's previous owner. I've sent DI Miller over to take his prints. They did find your prints on one of the shells in the box." He looked at me inquiringly.

"I didn't kill him, if that's what you're wondering – I'm far too pure of heart to be blackmailed." I felt a brief pang at the lie, but soldiered onward. "I handled one of the shells earlier that evening, when John was showing me the gun."

"Ah. The bottom line is that it would appear the killer wore gloves. To continue. Weathersby's financials were a mess – it's pretty clear why he needed the money. He'd been playing the market, and by this time last year, he'd managed to reduce the principal of his inheritance by half. At that point, he rolled everything over into a long-term IRA – safe as houses, but his income was down to £15,000 a month. Not bad for you and me, but for him, with two big houses to maintain, alimony and child support... let's just say there wasn't much mad money left over once all his bills had been paid."

"So he'd been on an austerity budget for the last year. That wouldn't sit easily with a man like John – he hated to deny himself anything. Anyway, it isn't his motive we're concerned with." I looked unhappily at Brian. "Could it have been a burglary gone wrong?"

He considered. "I don't see how. You said the gun was unloaded when he showed it to you earlier in the evening. A burglar would've had to load it before he shot him. He wouldn't've had the time if Weathersby had just walked in on him."

Unhappiness swooped down on me like a buzzard to a shit-wagon, but after all, I had known it would come to this. "What about CCTV?"

"Vesta's on it. I gave him recent photos of the four we know were being blackmailed – Seagrave, Leicester, Barlowe and Plantagenet. The most obvious access point to the communal garden – Montpelier Garden, it's called – and then to Weathersby's French doors is on Rosmead Road. Unfortunately, there's no CCTV camera there, for some inexplicable reason. Vesta's checking to see whether any of our boys might've been caught leaving the crime scene on another camera nearby."

"Right." I pushed back from the table. "Let's get it over with. I'll get the four of them to come in, one at a time."

"We could go see them. Make it easier on them."

I shook my head. "We'll go see Leicester – he lives alone. But I'd prefer to interview the others here. Save them some awkward questions at home. You know – 'Why did Dex and his partner come to see you, dear?' 'Oh, just the usual – I was being blackmailed, and now I'm the subject of a murder inquiry...'"

Brian grinned sourly. "I take your point. Here is fine. D'you want me to make the calls?"

"No, you'll only spook them into fleeing the country. Delicate touch called for, I think."

"Don't say I didn't offer."

III

"You must think me a right bastard, Dex," said Roger Seagrave.

We were seated in one of the interrogation rooms on the third floor of New Scotland Yard; we had just finished watching the blackmail video. The tape recorder was rolling, so there was no mistaking this for a friendly chat. Brian stood in the corner, studying Seagrave dispassionately, as he had done for the past 20 minutes. If Roger was discomfited by his scrutiny, he didn't show it.

What I actually thought was that we cannot help who we are, sexually; we can no more control to whom or what we are attracted than we can control how tall we turn out to be. "Soliciting prostitution isn't illegal in Nevada, Roger," I said mildly.

"It isn't that, although that's bad enough. It's the fact that I do love Catherine, despite how this must look. It might literally kill her if she knew I found her more attractive when she was heavy. Isn't there some way we can keep this from her?"

"I don't know," I replied truthfully. "It will depend on what direction our inquiry leads. I must tell you that it's looking doubtful. It would certainly come out at trial, if it comes to that."

Roger turned pale; beads of sweat suddenly stood out on his elegant forehead. "Trial? Surely you don't think of me as a... a suspect?"

"I've already cautioned you, Roger," I said, as gently as I could " – this is a murder inquiry. Can you tell us what you did on the night of 11 October, after John's party?"

"The night John was killed? Dex, you can't think I killed him! You've known me for decades, for Christ's sake!"

I felt a weight of anguish settle somewhere behind my eyes; this was going to be even more difficult than I had feared. Reminding myself that Oakhurst and Wicks would be reviewing the transcript of this interview, I pressed on. "Right now we're in the interview phase of the inquiry, Roger – we're asking everyone the same questions. Now, what did you do that night?"

"Went home and went to bed, of course. I'd had a skinful at the party – you were there, you know what went on. Catherine and I took a taxi home and went straight to bed – we... we tried to make love, but I just... Christ this is difficult. I slept like the dead, and woke up with a head the size of a pumpkin."

"You never left the house once you got home?"

"No. Not until eight the next morning, when I went to work."

"Catherine can vouch that you were there the whole time?"

"Of course she can! She was sleeping right next to me!"

I moved on. "And what about the blackmail, then? I presume Weathersby made the same demand of you as everyone else? £100,000 in cash, small bills?"

"Yes."

"And had you paid him?"

"Not yet – it was taking me some time to get together. Most of my money's in stocks – I was having to sell a few things, cash smaller cheques, assemble the cash a bit at a time. I was going to pay him this week."

"And did he warn you what he would do if anything happened to him?"

Roger, poor old sod, was sweating freely now. "He did. He said if he died within five years, whatever the cause, or if I went to the police or told any of the other Hastewicke Gentlemen, he would send Catherine the thumb drive. I was going to pay him, Dex, you must believe me! I'd have been mad to kill him! I've been such an ass... I just want all this to go away!"

"And did you? Discuss it with any of the others on the team, I mean."

"No! I had no way of knowing who else he was blackmailing."

Next question; I consulted my notebook. "How much of a hardship was it? Getting the money together, I mean?"

"You mean could I afford to pay him? It was no problem – I've a goodish bit stashed away, for use on tour and the like. The market's been pretty kind to me the last few years. The truth is I'd have paid a lot more than a hundred thousand pounds to keep Catherine from finding out."

"You won't mind if we ask for evidence of that? If we look into your financials?"

"If you think it relevant. Do you really need my permission?"

"No, not really," I said absently. "All right, Roger. Brian, can you think of anything else?"

"No. Although..." He moved away from the wall, came to the table in the centre of the room. "Would you mind unbuttoning your shirt, please?"

"My... shirt? Whatever for?"

"Just to satisfy us on a small point of interest. Do you mind?"

"No, I..." Roger undid his buttons with an air of bewilderment.

"Just show us your shoulder, that's a good lad. Are you right-handed or left-handed?"

"Right. Why?"

"It's something we're checking with everyone we're interviewing. Any tenderness if I squeeze here?"

Roger submitted to this unorthodox examination with poor grace; his shoulder appeared unbruised, but he winced slightly as Brian palpated the muscle. "I say – do be careful, that's my dickey shoulder. You remember, Dex, I separated it in that match against Harlequins last year."

"Right – so you did. Still bothers you, then?"

"Now and again." Roger did up his buttons. His voice had taken on a frosty edge. "Was there anything else, DI Reed?"

"Not just now. We may have more questions for you as our inquiry proceeds."

"Of course. Pity."

"What is?"

"I thought we might rely on you for a little discretion, Dex, that's all. What happens on tour, stays on tour, and all that?"

I thought about that. "John set that rule aside when he black-mailed you – I didn't. And now that someone's killed him, everything is fair game. I don't have a choice, Roger. There's been a murder. It's my job to find his killer, and to see justice done. I won't let anyone, or anything, stand in the way of that."

"Obviously. I'm sure it will be quite a feather in your cap – high-profile case, sensational murder, aristocratic sex scandals. Just do me a favor, will you?"

"What's that?" I asked, stinging from his remarks.

"Try not to trample too many of your teammates underfoot on your way up the ladder. We did trust you once, you know."

12

Early in the Hastewicke Gentlemen's match against the Seattle Rugby Club on the Saturday, Robert Leicester, Lord Palmerston, the Hastewicke outside centre, found himself in a familiar position – with ball in hand, and some hard yards to be made. He shrugged off a tackle from one of the Seattle centres, then stiff-armed another tackler and danced away. A lock hit him at the knees and clung on like a limpet; somehow Leicester retained his balance and kept his powerful legs churning until, abruptly, he broke free.

There was clear green space in front of him now, almost all the way to the try-line. He accelerated to a balls-out sprint, leaving the pitch behind him strewn with tacklers; only the Seattle fullback, Richard Shearer, a crafty ex-pat from Oxfordshire, left to beat. Leicester could hear Dex Reed just to his right, in support and calling insistently for the ball – a two-on-one.

At the 10-meter line, Leicester tried to sell the dummy, but Shearer refused to bite on the fake pass. Leicester prepared for the tackle and, just before impact, offloaded a deft pass to Reed, the hard-working flanker. To his horror, he saw Shearer suddenly change direction, seagull the pass, and take off toward the opposite end of the pitch.

There is no more devastating play in rugby – a sure try for one team turned into a 90-meter score for the other side. Leicester didn't stop to think. He spun about, leaving long furrows in the turf, and sprinted in pursuit. He had to atone for making a pig's breakfast of a sure try.

Shearer was already 10 meters upfield; now he danced easily past a stunned Hastewicke Gentleman defense and burst into the clear. Shearer paused briefly to sidestep a diving John Weathersby, and Leicester gained a yard or two. Shearer saw only the try-line, far ahead. Leicester concentrated on form – arms in, palms open, deep breaths through the mouth. Now he was five yards behind, now four, now three, but the try-line was only 10 meters ahead. He gathered himself for a convulsive leap and, lungs, nearly bursting, caught hold of the hem of Shearer's shorts. They tore with a flatulent rip, but the contact slowed Shearer just enough for Leicester to improve his grip. He leapt onto Shearer's back and bore him to ground just inches from the goal-line.

The ball rolled free; Leicester scooped it up and staggered doggedly back the way he had come, breath labored and gasping now. Once more into the breech, dear friends, once more into the breech...

Afterward, all the lads could talk about had been his saving tackle, which had averted a sure 14-point turnaround. Bob modestly waved off their backslapping praise. "Think nothing of it, think nothing of it – any superhumanly-fit 48-year-old centre could've done it... yes, yes, you're just lucky to have me. Had a better offer from the Harlequins Gentlemen only last week..." But secretly he was happy. To have been the cause of a Hastewicke gentlemen loss... well, that simply wouldn't do. Above all, Bob Leicester hated to lose.

It was his father's doing, he supposed. He could still feel his father's hand close around his skinny preadolescent biceps, still hear that hectoring hiss, laden with loathing and liquor: "Are you just going to take that, you nancy-boy? Are you going to cry now, you big girls-blouse? No son of mine is going to let someone snurge the ball from him like that. Now you get back out there, Bobby, and make that boy sorry he ever saw you, or by God you'll be wearing a dress to school tomorrow!"

Leicester could never think of moments like those – and there had been many – of his father's eyes, bulging and bloodshot in a bloated red face convulsed with rage – without thinking of his death. There wasn't much change of expression before and after the massive coronary had taken him, Leicester reflected – the eyes protruded; the mouth was still open in a final bellow, in mortal agony not unmingled with rage at unfair fate. They had been at their country house for the weekend, his father had just discovered that Bob had decided to offer an extra two weeks maternity leave to the firm's female employees, and Leicester senior was beside himself with rage. He had lashed out with a backhander; Bob had ducked it, and then the old man had abruptly clutched his chest, uttered a strangled, gargling scream, and collapsed to the floor. He kicked for a moment, then froze, limbs drawn up in a fetal position.

Robert had made no move to help. Instead, he had calmly taken a chair, and waited until half an hour had ticked by. Only when he was sure his father was dead did he pick up the phone to ring emergency services. Gazing dispassionately down at the lifeless hulk on the carpet, he had felt only relief, and sudden peace.

His cold, domineering father, Robert Leicester Sr., Lord Palmerston, had made a pile through hostile takeovers of healthy companies, running them into the ground, selling off their assets and downsizing the workforce. It was from him, Bob grudgingly supposed, that he had inherited his own eye for business opportunity.

In his most successful single deal, during Thatcher's gleeful economic jihad of the 1980s, Bob Leicester the elder had bought a controlling interest in a venerable firm of English carmakers, Ocelot. Over two years, he had eliminated more than 2,500 well-paying jobs, shut down three marginally-profitable assembly sites that had provided local employment for more than 50 years, sold off the most profitable subsidiaries to foreign investors. Then, when he had wrung maximum profit from the enterprise, he had sold what remained to a German consortium. Ocelots were still being made, of course. In Dresden, in the former East

Germany. The Leicester firm's profit on the transaction came to nearly £100 million.

Bob's mother had died when he was 15; he had no other siblings. And so it was that, when his father died, Bob accomplished what amounted to a hostile takeover of the family firm. He had ruthlessly done what his father had done to so many other companies: sold every asset and pocketed the cash. Then he had struck out on his own, in a direction that would have left his father speechless with apoplexy had he lived to see it.

Now Bob Leicester was easily the wealthiest and most famous of the Hastewicke Gentlemen, the closest thing the old club had to a genuine celebrity. His firm, Baobob Holdings, Ltd., had parlayed his whale-choking wodge of an inheritance into the largest collection of "green" companies in the world. His holdings included office towers that were marvels of energy efficiency, a subsidiary that was now producing cars powered by liquid air and a network of filling stations to support them, a forest of Scottish windmills producing renewable power, a company hard at work on the next generation of carbon supercapacitors, a gigantic international environmental engineering firm, specializing in cleaning up oil spills and contaminated groundwater, rehabbing historic structures and the like. All very astute, far-seeing ventures, all yielding a gratifying annual income.

When it came to business, Bob Atkinson had one thing his father always lacked: patience. He could simply see farther down the road; once he saw an opportunity and decided to pursue it, he never second-guessed himself. He had the faith and the resources to pour money down a dry hole for years, patiently awaiting the moment when it would blossom forth into profitability. To date, he had seldom tasted disappointment.

He had also put his own philosophy of personnel management into play in his own firm, offering generous compensation and benefits packages to everyone, at every level, in all his companies. As a result, he had been able to attract – and retain – a devoted and highly-motivated workforce. Though nearly as vast as Branson's, the Leicester empire nearly ran itself these days. By and large, that granted Bob a surprising degree of freedom, to play rugby, dabble in film and theatre, and to pour most of the profits from his empire into a network of philanthropic enterprises that rivaled, in scope and complexity, his business holdings.

II

After the last match of the day, the lads hobbled with geriatric delicacy aboard the fleet of limousines waiting to ferry them back to the hotel. It was an article of faith that the Hastewicke Gentlemen always traveled first class, even when it meant subsidizing some of the less-wealthy members of the club. Leicester alighted at the Bellagio, stretched painfully, and slung his kit-bag over his shoulder. All he could think of was the hot bath and massage awaiting him in the suite. He had little use for wealth on a personal level, except for its marvelous power to change lives. But occasionally, the perks of his position were most welcome.

He was halfway to the elevator when he noticed the little girl. She was perhaps four years old, dressed in dirty bell-bottomed jeans and a juice-spotted singlet, clutching a stuffed horse. There were tears on her face as she ran through the lobby on stubby legs, dodging clots of towering grown-ups, falling farther and farther behind. After a moment Leicester spotted her father, striding furiously through the throng with a group of companions, ostentatiously ignoring her terrified whimpers. Occasionally the man would call something encouraging over his shoulder – "Hurry up, or I'll leave you!" or "I'll give you something to cry about when we get home!" Then she dropped her stuffed horse and ran back to get it. Her father had reached the elevator; with a snort of disgust, he pressed the "up" button. She cried out in terror as the door opened and he stepped inside without her.

As the doors began to close, Leicester inserted his body in the gap, held them open until the frantic little girl could rush inside. She held up her arms to her father, a tall blond man with blue eyes the hue of glacial ice. He ignored her. "Can you let the doors go, please?" he asked Leicester – "We're in a hurry."

"Obviously," Leicester observed mildly. "You almost forgot your luggage."

"Luggage." He frowned down at her. "That's about it. Now move. Please."

Leicester stayed where he was. "Why don't you pick her up? She needs comforting."

The blond man glared at him in outrage. "Why don't you butt out?"

"Do you realize the damage you've just done to her? To your daughter. You can never undo it. Hadn't you noticed she's just a child?"

"She's not my daughter – she's my wife's. And you're really starting to annoy me, you Limey prick. Now move, or I'll move you."

But Leicester didn't move. Instead, he made a contemptuous sound. "You're just a bully. I know bullies. Now pick her up and comfort her."

The man hesitated, daunted by the smoldering fury in Leicester's eyes. But he was losing face in front of his companions. He looked at them; they nodded and surged forward, fists flying. Leicester jerked his head to the side; the man's first wild blow glanced off his cheek. The brawl spilled out of the elevator onto the lobby floor; now punches were coming from every direction. Leicester went down beneath the weight of bodies, his kit-bag hampering his movements.

Abruptly his assailants were seized by their collars, jerked to their feet and shoved reeling backwards. Dex Reed, Bernie Plantagenet and Jester Atkinson stood over him, rolling up their sleeves. "A punch-up?" Jester asked brightly. "Haven't had one in ages. Whom should we kill first?" And he turned his mad gaze on the blond man, who took an involuntary step backward.

Security materialized in seconds, a phalanx of burly men in blue coats and earpieces who inserted themselves between the combatants with the ease of long practice. "Gentlemen?" asked their grey-haired supervisor, arriving a second or two later. "What's the trouble here?"

Leicester had risen to his feet. "No trouble. We were just going up to our rooms." He could feel the violence leaked out of the situation like air from a balloon. For just a moment, he caught and held the blond man's gaze. "Remember what I said," he called as the elevator doors began to close. "Get help!"

Dex was looking at him inquiringly. "Tosser. It was the little girl – I couldn't stand to see him..." he shook his head. "Forget it. Thanks, Dex. Jester. Thought I was roadkill for a moment. Dinner's on me tonight."

III

Though he was now, by some calculations, the fourteenth-richest person in the U.K., Bob Leicester had little patience for the trappings of wealth, and pursued a lifestyle that was as simple as his father's had been imperial. He lived alone in a spacious but austerely-furnished flat on the 51st floor of one of his Canary Wharf high-rises, ate simply, drank little, pursued a vigorous daily regimen of running, swimming and weight-lifting, and drove one of his own modest air-powered sedans. Bob believed that the money that flowed from his business empire should itself be put to work, rather than allowed to lay idly about. Over 90 percent of Baobab Holdings' nine-figure annual profit went to fund a network of charitable endeavors so vast that Bob Leicester was now generally recognized as the greatest English philanthropist since Charles Dickens.

In truth, Leicester had a keen admiration for the 19th-century novelist, whose tireless advocacy of the poor and downtrodden, and personal example as a dynamic, hands-on architect of social change, had made him the most revered Englishman of his age. Stocky and energetic, with a luxurious salt-and-pepper goatee, Leicester even resembled Dickens physically.

Like Dickens, Leicester also had a particular sympathy for the working-class youth who were being denied opportunity in an increasingly technological society. The keystone of Leicester's charitable empire was the Magwitch Project, named for the mysterious benefactor of young Pip in *Great Expectations*. The Magwitch Project had centres in every major metropolitan area in the U.K., providing housing, sustenance, counseling and education to thousands of homeless and at-risk children and teenagers.

Like Dickens, Leicester immersed himself in every detail of the project: architecture, curriculum, rules, even the menus served in the cafeterias. When the uniforms worn by the centers" clients proved too drab, he sponsored a competition among the British fashion elite to design smarter ones. He spent as much time as possible at the centres themselves, taking a personal interest in many of his charges. When one of them dropped out and returned to the street, he had been known to plunge personally into the septic maelstrom of Eastcheap or Manchester to convince them to return to the Magwitch Project's benevolent fold. Here, perhaps more than anywhere else, he simply refused to tolerate losing. It was an affront to his competitive nature.

Leicester didn't believe in simply throwing money at problems, or at people – he knew they had to have a goal, a compelling reason to make a permanent life-change. Simply being on the dole wasn't going to do it. He made them learn – bullying, coaxing, cajoling, rewarding – until they began to see the light. The ultimate reward, of course, was lucrative employment with one of his companies, which had an insatiable need for qualified engineers, managers, technicians, workers. His diversified holdings were immune to the usual economic upticks and downturns; employment with one of the Baobab Holdings' subsidiaries was effectively employment for life.

Leicester's sole personal indulgence was rugby. In addition to providing an outlet for his ruthlessly competitive nature and need to push himself to his limits, it left him physically drained and at peace. Oh, he would never be the most popular bloke on the team – he was simply too serious, too tightly-wound, to let go, to allow himself to be seduced unreservedly by the occasionally-terrifying hilarity that was rugby touring. Then, too, there were those on the team who bitterly envied his wealth, his power, his seemingly-inevitable success. But he loved rugby all the same.

He also loved the fact that, particularly when the Hastewicke Gentlemen toured foreign lands, he was completely anonymous. Here, in Las Vegas, no one had the slightest inkling of who he was. Which suited his agenda down to the ground.

Because the truth was that, like Dickens, if the old bugger had been honest with himself, Leicester's philanthropic activities served another, darker purpose: they filled him with a deeply sexual sense of power over those he so energetically labored to save. Old Charlie must have experienced much the same thrill of stern Victorian paternalism, with its undercurrent of quivering sexual dominance, as he inspected the ex-prostitutes of Urania Cottage, his "home for fallen women" in Shepherd's Bush.

Leicester, too, found himself magnetically drawn to the young female clients of the Magwitch Project, whose nubile charms were so apparent, yet as inaccessible to him as the Korolev Crater on the dark side of the moon. How simple it would be to insinuate himself into the intake process for the Magwitch Project, and gratify his darkest desires as a condition for their acceptance into the program! But to lose control in such a way, even once, would be to invite a disaster of nuclear, elephantine proportions. In Britain's rabid, tabloid-fueled news climate, both the reputation and the empire he had labored so long to build would instantly be reduced to dust and twisted girders.

No, he had more self-control than that. But here, in the glorious anonymity of America... ah, that was a different story. No one but his mates even knew he was here. And in Las Vegas, where anything was available for a price...?

Two hours later, there was a knock on the door of Suite 455. Leicester answered it, then paused, looking them up and down. They'd do – lithe, beautiful, and not a day over 16. The taller of the two had hair of glossy blue-black, with the long, muscular legs of a professional tennis player. The smaller one, the blond, had perfect breasts and a sweet, virtuous face, with eyes that twinkled with sin – just the way he'd always imagined Agnes Wickfield in *David Copperfield*.

"Well?" Agnes asked. "Aren't you going to invite us in?"

Wordlessly he stood aside, closed the door after them. The blond girl – Agnes – reached into her purse and pulled out a sheet of paper. She studied it for a moment, then looked up, face shining with carnal amusement. "We're here for the, uh, entrance exam," she smiled.

"Put these on," said Leicester throatily, holding out a pair of Magwitch Project uniforms. He watched, entranced, as they stepped un-self-consciously from their clothes, and slipped the short, flattering dresses over their heads.

And then all of his dreams had come true.

13

I arrived at Hendon early the next morning to put the finishing touches on my report to Oakhurst regarding the historic indiscretions of the Hastewicke Gentlemen on tour. It hadn't been easy to strike the right balance of juicy tabloid innuendo and discretion, but when I laid the report on Oakhurst's desk, I thought I'd done a reasonably deft job of it.

"One thing I've never fully understood," said Brian later as we walked briskly through Green Park, on our way to interview Harry Barlowe at his sculpting studio. "Oakhurst is younger than us, with less service. Remind me again how it is that he's our boss? It can't just be his virtuoso talent for rhinoprocty, although that's obviously been a factor."

"He demonstrated the very leadership competencies management were looking for through those ridiculous team-building exercises he designed." I paused. "And there was Docklands, of course."

"Ah. And he hates your guts for the same reason, naturally. I agree with Wicks that Oakhurst has set you up masterfully on this case. You're going to have to play this one very, very carefully, mate."

I nodded grimly. "Tell me something I don't know, Sherlock." Docklands had been a very nasty business indeed. During the 1990s, I had been assigned to the drugs squad out of Wapping Station. There, in an operation called Docklands, I was wounded in the line of duty – very seriously wounded. Oakhurst had been my partner at the time. Docklands made him my nemesis.

In the fall of 1997, there was an unsolved murder in the East End – a middle-aged man found floating in the Thames with his throat cut. He had cocaine in his system, in very high concentration. His name was Sid Hamilton, and he worked as chief financial officer at a brokerage firm called Central American Trading Partners Ltd. in Docklands.

Right about that time, one of my confidential sources tipped me that a massive shipment of cocaine would be arriving shortly in the East End. I poked around a bit, and discovered that the masterminds of the operation were two young traders who, coincidentally, also worked at Central American Trading Partners. Through a brilliant tap-in and analysis of Central American's computer system, led by Emma Kwan, we discovered that the two of them had used corporate funds to put together a once-in-a-lifetime deal – a cargo container-load of 90 percent pure

Colombian cocaine, which would pass through their hands in a single night, leaving behind a profit of £100 million. They had figured out a way to use wire transfers of corporate funds to take, then replace the money, all within minutes, and make it look like a bank error. The two would then divide their ill-gotten gains and disappear.

Well, that was enough cocaine to supply the entire London metropolitan area for two years. As soon as I'd confirmed the accuracy of the information and identified those behind the deal, I brought Oakhurst in on it. He took it up the food chain, coordinated the details of the raid and press coverage with our supervisors. It was the kind of career-making case that comes along once every 20 years or so, complete with budget-bloating photo-ops of the Chief Superintendent surrounded by mountains of confiscated cocaine.

And so we come to the night of the raid. We ringed the building with an armed strike force; Oakhurst and I had agreed that I would enter the facility, in my role as "buyer," to confirm the stuff was there before the cavalry broke down the doors. "Don't take any chances," Oakhurst told me – "we're all waiting for your signal!"

And so I had gone in – only to emerge 10 minutes later on a stretcher, fighting for my life. Someone had tipped one of the "managing partners" that their "buyer" was an informant – not a copper. They wouldn't cancel the shipment for an informant, you see; they would just kill him, as they already had Sid Hamilton, the company comptroller, who had happened upon their scheme during an unscheduled check on the accounts. When he had confronted them, they had stuck him in the back of the neck with a syringe of product, which they were sampling themselves at the time, then slit his throat and tipped him into the river. So you see the kind of blokes I was dealing with.

Funny, the things that stick in your mind during traumatic events. For me, it was a snatch of conversation: "Damn you, Dex! You should've tipped us off sooner! We might've saved you!" Oakhurst's voice. I knew he had betrayed me then, double-crossed me in order to further his own ambitions, and claim sole credit for a once-in-a-career bust. Obviously he didn't think I'd survive. Fortunately, he was wrong.

It took six months for me to recover sufficiently to resume my duties. By then, Oakhurst had already made Detective Chief Inspector – the youngest in Metropolitan Police history – on the strength of his role in organizing this mammoth drugs bust and for his cool head in saving the life of an over-impetuous fellow officer. What I didn't know was that, in the leadup to the raid, he had done his damndest to cut me out of the picture entirely with our superiors – to them, it was all his sources, his initiative, his hard work, that had led to the massive bust. By the time I left hospital, his version of events – that I had insisted on a daring solo entrance, over his strenuous objections, and that only his prompt action had saved my life and captured the suspects – was more or less set in concrete.

I couldn't prove, of course, that Oakhurst had set me up, so I made no official challenge to his version of events. However,

I made sure that the truth of what had happened that night received a wide airing among the rank-and-file. DCI Wicks, for one, believed me, and, after my recovery, transferred me to Hendon Specialist Crime Directorate, that fascinating catch-basin for the crimes that didn't neatly into the usual categories. Much to Oakhurst's annoyance. It was at Hendon SCD that I had met Brian.

One day, the elevator doors opened, and Oakhurst stepped in. The doors closed, the lift moved downward. We were alone. Oakhurst studiously ignored me; finally I spoke. "It won't be today, and it might not be tomorrow. But I know what you did, and there will come a day, you self-serving bastard, that you'll wish you'd never joined the Metropolitan Police."

Oakhurst merely nodded, an infuriating little smirk twisting his fleshy lips, as if to say, "Fair enough, mate, have a go, then." And that was how we'd left it – until now.

"And now he's got you by the balls," Brian observed cheerfully. "What're we going to do about it, then?"

"There's no 'we,' Brian. This is my fight. And I don't know yet what I'm going to do. But I know what I won't do – I won't cooperate on this report of his. Oh, I'll feed him a few stories, just enough to jolly him along. But I'll resign before I make my mates' behavior on tour a matter of record in this case."

Brian stopped and looked at me very seriously indeed. "That's exactly what he wants you to do, Dex, so that's exactly what you won't do. He wants you to resign, he's begging you to give him grounds for disciplinary action. Don't you see? Then anything you have to say about Oakhurst and Docklands just becomes the ranting of a disgruntled former subordinate. And you're wrong about one other thing. This *is* my business. You're my partner, and you're also my mate. If Oakhurst goes after you, then he's going to have to deal with me as well."

We had arrived at Harry's studio, a sprawling former stable building 'round the corner from the Horse Guards Parade. Harry answered the door covered in fine white dust, his eyes ringed like a raccoon's from the protective goggles that now hung by a strap from around his neck. "Hullo, Dex, come on in – don't mind the mess. You must be DI Abbott." Harry shook hands. "Dex has told me a lot about you." And he ushered us inside.

The studio was a vast open room, brick-walled, with skylights every 10 feet or so dispelling the gloom. A block of white Carrara marble 10 feet on a side dominated the centre of the space, sur-rounded by a snowstorm of fine rock chips; the rough figures of a man astride a great winged horse struggled to escape their stone prison. "My God, Harry, it's immense! I had no idea you worked on such a scale!"

Harry shrugged. "It's my largest yet. Taken me three months just to get this far."

"And how long to finish it?"

"A year." He caressed the rough marble with casual affection, brushing away a few stray chips. "The roughing-out is the easiest bit. It's the detailing and finish-work that really take the time."

"And once you're finished, what then? You have to try to sell it?"

"It's already been sold, to an office block in Spain. All my work's commissions these days. But that's not why you're here." He indicated a sofa and chairs against the far wall. "Sit. Let's talk."

Harry took a bottle of cold water from the fridge, offered the same to us, then opened his and drank deeply. "Look, Dex, I've spoken to some of the other lads. I know why you're here. You've seen the video John took, and you know what a fool I've been. I thought about trying to keep this from Sarah and the kids if possible – that's why I paid John's... fee. I know her. Our marriage will probably be over if she finds out."

"Harry," I began. "This..."

"No, Dex, hear me out. I know you have to find John's killer. And I know we're all suspects – all of us who were being blackmailed. You have to do your job, and that trumps any personal considerations. Even the fact that I didn't kill John probably won't be enough to shield me from the consequences of my own stupidity. All I ask – " and here he looked up, eyes calm "– is that you let me be the one to tell her. That's what AA demands – rigourous honesty and accountability. I have to tell her. I'm just trying to find the guts, you see." And he smiled a heartbreaking, hopeful smile.

I considered. "That's fair enough, Harry. And I'll do everything I can – everything – to protect the privacy of those we interview. I will tell you that this is a very high-profile case, and it's going to take some nasty turns before all is said and done. But I won't drag anyone through the mud unnecessarily."

"That's fair, by God. And now –" for the first time during this interview, Harry smiled. "What d'you want to know?"

II

The interview had lasted an hour; like Seagrave, Harry had stated forthrightly that he and his wife had left the Chalmers Memorial bash at just before 1 a.m. and gone straight home to bed. One item in his favour was the fact that he and Sarah lived in Essex, about an hour's drive from Notting Hill even under the most favorable traffic conditions. Weathersby's housekeeper had stated that the shot rang out at 3:01. Assuming Harry was telling the truth – and my instincts said he was – it would have been almost impossible for Harry to have arrived home, then returned to Penhurst House within that time. Harry had added that raising the money had been no problem; his income was large and fluctuated widely from year to year, depending on his output. Sarah wouldn't have noticed £100,000 more or less.

"Must be nice," Brian grinned on our way back to the office. "Now what's bothering you?"

"Nothing vital." In truth, something had occurred to me, something from the past that I hesitated to raise even with Brian. But he, at least, deserved to hear the truth. "Let me start by saying that I don't think Harry's our boy. But – and this is just between us – back when Harry was drinking, he had... a bit of an unpredictable side."

"Unpredictable how?" Brian stopped to regard me suspiciously.

"Let's just say you didn't want to provoke him. His nickname on tour was 'The Human Hand Grenade' – you never knew when he might go off, and who he might damage when he did. One night in Wellington, about five years ago, I watched him and Weathersby sit down with a bottle of gin apiece. Weathersby used to like to egg Harry on, you see, encourage him to drink, just for the hell of it. Anyway, they had a contest, to see who could finish his bottle the fastest. Harry drank his in 10 minutes flat. Then a few of the boys went out to hit the pubs.

"A couple of hours later, Harry was sitting at the bar when one of the local lads started giving Harry grief about his earring. You saw it, tasteful little gold hoop – only time Harry takes it off is on the pitch. Anyway, this kiwi wouldn't leave it alone. Keeping in mind that Harry's had a bottle of gin and a half-dozen pints, he's quite friendly at first – tells the kid he's an artist, and all artists wear earrings. Then the kid blows smoke in his face and tells him all artists are fags.

"Well, about this time, Charlie Chalmers and I started edging closer – we'd seen Harry in action before. But we were too slow. Before we could react Harry had this kid on the ground, with his hands around his neck. His mates were screaming, glasses shattering – absolute pandemonium. Charlie and I get there, and try to pull him off, but we can't – Harry's unbelievably strong, you saw him. By this time, the kiwi's turned purple, his tongue's sticking out, eyes bulging, it was horrible. Took three of us to pry Harry's hands from around the poor bugger's neck. If we hadn't..." I let the sentence trail away.

"You think he would've killed him."

I shrugged. "I don't know. But I do know that the next morning, Harry didn't remember a thing about it – couldn't figure out how he'd gotten those scratches on his face. I'm just glad he's come to his senses and stopped drinking."

"And you're wondering whether to put that story in your report to Oakhurst?"

"No. I'm not wondering. I won't be including it. But I thought you had the right to know."

"Dex, I told you, you can't...!"

"Look Brian." Even my own partner took an involuntary step back from the fury in my eyes. "I'm not giving that to Oakhurst. Harry didn't kill Weathersby. He wasn't drinking the night of the Chalmers Memorial – he was with his wife. I saw him with my own eyes, spoke to him. He's not the Human Hand Grenade any longer. And anyway, there's no way he could've got to Essex and back to Notting Hill inside of two hours."

To Brian's credit, he accepted my decision – for now, at least. "All right, mate, all right – calm down! But I'm telling you this for your own good. You're not just playing with fire. You're playing with C-4!"

14

Timothy Bernard Plantagenet, Lord Delvemere, was in his element. He sat in the honeyed late afternoon sunshine, drinking in its warmth, in the raucous, palm-fringed beer garden of the Las Vegas Golden Oldies rugby tournament. He had a glass of local ale in his hand, a long Cuban cigar between his teeth. The tournament final had just ended, the Hastewicke Gentlemen had won, and he felt as relaxed and alive as he had in months.

All around him, still in their grass-and-blood-stained rugby kit, stood the triumphant Hastewicke Gentlemen, and the Old B.A.T.S., gracious in defeat, were keeping them well-supplied with beer. Bernie sat between Vince Maitland, the Hastewicke blind-side flanker, and Roy Tasker, the Old B.A.T.S. second row, a Scottish ex-pat whom he and Vince had known and played against for more than 30 years.

"It's all a matter of perspective," Roy was saying. "For example, mah years of rugby experience have taught me to forgive the stamping you gave me at the bottom of that ruck, and even stand you a pint after the game."

"Of course, I wouldn't have put the boots to you if you hadn't been biting my leg," Bernie observed with a smile.

"At least I flossed before the match," Roy replied, eyes twinkling. "Ah, it's grand tae see you lot."

"D'you ever miss the U.K., Roy?" Vince asked.

"Are you kiddin'?" Roy laughed. "San Francisco's a great city. Got a condo lookin' out over the bay, a cracking job, more money than ah can spend, and the women! Did you know that sixty percent of the single men in San Francisco are gay? Sixty percent! And probably twenty percent o'the married men! D'you have any idea how much rampant totty that leaves for me? Ah'm thinkin' of gettin' married just tae ease the strain on my todger."

Vince laughed. "Good idea! You'll live longer."

"At least, it'll *seem* longer," Bernie observed wryly. "But really, Roy, you've got to come on tour with us next time. Think of it – two weeks of rugby and fuck-all in Hong Kong, with tickets for the Sevens. We could use you in the forward pack now that Henry Neville has retired."

"Old Gouger's retired at last, has he? Well, ah'd love tae come – email me the dates and ah'll look at mah schedule." Roy grinned and raised his glass. "Well, here's tae your lovely wife, then, and hopin' she'll let us come along on tour."

"Us?"

"Aye. Ya must know old Vincey here shags her mercilessly whenever you're away..."

There had been so many afternoons like this in the last 30 years, filled with the laughter of friends, genial post-game chaffering, and good ale. Sometimes, Bernie felt he lived a sort of Bertie Wooster life – no financial or job worries to furrow the brow, thanks to a generous inheritance; the lifestyle of a lord; a wife who truly was his best friend; and, thanks to his continued connection with the Hastewicke Gentlemen, the opportunity to see the world with a most congenial set of mates.

If he was Bertie Wooster, then Jane was his Jeeves. The idea of marriage had never really crossed his mind, but one day, there she was – flat on her back in Hyde Park with the wind knocked out of her. He had seen the big gelding shy and throw her, and had run across to see whether she was all right. She was struggling for breath; he had gentled her and made her lie back down with her arms over her head. "You've had the wind knocked out of you. Just relax, your breath will come," he had told her soothingly.

"Are you... a doctor?" she had wheezed when at last she could speak.

"Me? Good lord no." He had laughed at the idea. "I play rugby. This sort of thing happens all the time."

"Are all rugby players trained in first aid, then?" she had asked as he helped her to her feet. "What do you do when, say, someone gets a limb torn off?"

He considered. "Not sure, really – pop it back in the socket and give them a sling, I should think. Did have a mate who ruptured a testicle once – had to have it removed, and replaced with a prosthesis."

"That's horrible!"

"Umm. Of course we offered his doctor an enormous bribe to pop in an extra, so he'd have three, but for some reason he refused. No sense of humour, doctors."

She had laughed, and there was something in her face that he couldn't look away from. There was no denying that she was lovely, breathtakingly so. But there was more to it than that – a sweet earnestness, a guilelessness, an honesty, that made *him* feel as if he'd been thrown from a horse. He realized that he hadn't been this attracted to a woman in years.

And so he had invited her to lunch, and she had accepted, and six months later, they were married. That was nearly 15 years ago. Now Bernie couldn't imagine life without her. When he needed someone to talk to, she was there. When there were problems to be solved, she was a font of practical wisdom. And on those rare occasions when he needed cheering up, her quirky sense of humour never failed to bring him out of his funk. She didn't just compliment him – she completed him. And in return, he treasured her.

God knew she had enough to put up with. At 48, he was still strong, still fit enough. But here of late, the good life seemed to be taking its toll. Drink had softened his once-strong chin and, often, left his startlingly blue eyes peering out between puffy folds of flesh. His hairline had receded like the tide; where once a full and ample crop had sprouted, there now grew only a few sparse tufts. He was growing old, he thought ruefully, while Jane still preserved a preternaturally youthful freshness. If he didn't want to start being mistaken for her father, well – he would simply have to age her before her time.

"Oy! Bernie! There you are, mate, been looking all over for you! Time for the de-bagging ceremony!" Jester Atkinson was beckoning furiously, with Dex Reed in tow. Looking over their shoulders, Bernie could see the captain of the host team, together with the tournament sponsor and his wife, preparing to present the championship trophy to Weathersby, Hastewicke's captain, who looked even more smug than usual. As the assembled throng turned to watch the ceremony, Jester, Dex and Bernie snuck around behind the dignitaries and got themselves into position.

"...showed us that we Americans still have a thing or two to learn about rugby. What more can I say? You really kicked our asses. On behalf of the Starlight Casino, I award the championship trophy."

As Weathersby reached to grasp the prize, the three conspirators suddenly darted in from behind and snatched down his shorts, leaving him naked from the waist down. The crowd roared with laughter as Weathersby, red-faced, yanked them back up again. "Sorry, hadn't planned to give you the full monty. On behalf of the Hastewicke Gentlemen – those of us who *are* gentlemen..."

Laughing at Weathersby's discomfiture, the trio made their way to the bar and ordered three more. "Here's to you, Bernie," said Dex, raising his glass. "For such a mild-mannered sod, you're a holy terror on the pitch. Thought I was a goner until you came hurtling in out of nowhere."

With about 15 minutes to go in the final, and the score knotted at 14-all, The Hastewicke Gentlemen had found themselves in a line-out on the Old B.A.T.S. 22-meter line. A few minutes before, Dex had sorted out the Old B.A.T.S. number 8, who had just used Harry Barlowe's groin for a springboard, with an elbow to the nose. Now, in the lineout, as Dex went up for the ball, an Old B.A.T.S. prop undercut him and sent him crashing heavily to the ground.

Dex, stunned, nevertheless retained possession and tried to present the ball, but the Old B.A.T.S. forwards surged forward to deal him a pummeling. Then a blurred form – Bernie – darted in from the Hastewicke side to drive two opponents backward, clearing just enough space for George Waters, the Hastewicke scrum half, to loft an up-and-under toward the corner. An alert Roger Seagrave had won the footrace to the try-line, and scored to make it 19-14. Meanwhile, Bernie had stood over Dex to ensure that there was no off-the-ball cheap-shotting now that the referee's attention was elsewhere.

"Think nothing of it, Dex. You've done the same for me on many an occasion."

The truth was, thought Bernie, he *needed* rugby. He needed the contact, the violence, the almost post-coital release that rewarded total commitment on the pitch. Yes, he was mild-mannered and even-tempered in everyday life. It was just the way he was made. Couldn't stand upheaval and hurly-burly. But even if he didn't let it show, much of the time, he had more than his share of stress to release. Thank God for rugby – and for Jane.

He didn't think she knew he was gay. Their sex life was vigorous and regular, thanks to his vivid fantasy life. Through the decade and a half of their marriage, he had been scrupulously careful never to let her know who he was really thinking about when they made love.

Michael had been a year older than him at Hastewicke – tall, handsome, witty and modest. Bernie had long recognized that, while he felt comfortable around girls, he was not attracted to them. The sexual side of his being had simply lain dormant – until the first time he saw Michael.

They had remained best friends and lovers through university. Then, one night, as they lay in each others' arms in Bernie's Oxford flat, Michael had made a fateful announcement – a comedy script he'd written had been accepted by an American production company. He was moving to L.A. "Come with me!" Michael had urged him. "You're as free as the air. There's nothing keeping you here!" But there was. The idea of trading in his well-settled and privileged English lifestyle for an uncertain future in a foreign land filled Bernie with dread. All his mates were here, and all his family. It simply wasn't on.

And so Michael had disappeared from his life. Oh, there had been other lovers – all discreet, all brief, all carefully concealed from his mates on the Hastewicke Gentlemen. Then he had married Jane, and become a new man. His family, particularly his sisters, who had begun to wonder, were delighted. But to his despair, he had never forgotten what he and Michael had shared. Eventually, he had found Boris, a young prostitute who bore an uncanny resemblance to the Michael he had known at school. He saw him once a month, but it wasn't the same.

The post-tournament party was winding down. Final beers in hand, kit-bags slung over their shoulders, the Hastewicke Gentlemen made their way to the line of limousines waiting in the parking lot. By the time they reached the Bellagio, rigor mortis had begun to set in; Bernie had already popped several ibuprofen to ease the chronic ache in his shoulder. Crossing the expansive lobby, he noticed Bob Leicester standing in the elevator door in a posture of unmistakable belligerence. Fatigue forgotten, he dropped his bag and, seizing Dex and Jester, he strode over, just in time to see Leicester go down beneath a swarm of attackers. "What the hell...?" said Dex, accelerating to a run.

They had dived into the melee, forming a protective cordon around Leicester and sending his assailants staggering backward. Security had arrived within seconds. "Thanks, lads," Leicester had said "– dinner's on me tonight." Well, he could certainly afford it. Dex and Jester had accepted with pleasure. Bernie had declined with regret. He already had plans for later that evening – plans that had been years in the making.

When he arrived at Suite 455, Bernie paused, self-doubt suddenly paralyzing in its intensity. He hadn't seen Michael in more than 20 years. How could he fail to be disgusted by the ravages time and good living had wrought in Bernie's once-pristine features? Well, there was nothing for it. He was who he was.

Michael had already let himself in with the key Bernie had left at the front desk. When he turned, all of Bernie's misgivings melted like high-desert snow. He saw the same anxiety in Michael's age-softened face.

"Bernie," said Michael. "You look wonderful. It's been so long – I've missed you so terribly." And without another word, he took Bernie's hand and led him to the bedroom.

15

In 1996, the Hastewicke Gentlemen toured Texas by coach: Dallas, then Houston – both armpits of creation – and finally Austin, a lovely little university town on the banks of the Colorado River. One afternoon, as we traversed the blistering desert between Houston and Austin, the air conditioning on the bus failed, at a little town called Carmine, Texas. While the driver arranged for repairs, we passed the time at a biker saloon called Rattlesnake Roy's.

It was a dim, shabby cave of a place, insulated from the rock-blistering heat outside by a foot of adobe and a blissfully-efficient air conditioning system. Snakeskins and stuffed armadillos (one of which mysteriously disappeared during our visit, and reappeared, under equally-unexplained circumstances, in the Hastewicke Gentlemen clubhouse a month later) festooned the walls; rockabilly music blared; the place was inhabited by a colorful and surprisingly friendly mix of sunburned locals and large, bearded, tattooed bikers. They were thoroughly bemused when 25 English rugby players in matching tour polos sauntered through the door.

We shoved some tables together and disposed ourselves near the back of the bar, beneath a large poster of a squinty-eyed George W. Bush in a Stetson hat, with the legend "My heroes have always been cowboys." Jester Atkinson snorted in disgust. "Wasn't he raised in Connecticut?"

One of the bikers – a huge walrus of a man with a bristling Fu Manchu moustache and a sparkling diamond stud in his ear, ambled over to join us. "So," he said amiably – "you boys ain't from around here, are ya?"

"We're from London, actually," Charlie replied "– on rugby tour."

"Rugby! I'll be double-damned! And what brings you to Rattlesnake Roy's?"

"Thirst!" replied Weathersby, signaling impatiently to the waitress. "Oy! How about some service!"

"Shhh!" the biker winced. "That's Large Marge, and today's one of her grumpy days! Whatever ya do, don't piss her off!"

Weathersby looked at him incredulously. "Piss her off? How?"

"Never mind! Yer from the land of good manners! Use 'em, or we'll all suffer! And whatever ya do, don't stare at her growth!"

The biker fairly sprinted back to the bar as our waitress approached. She was six feet tall and grossly obese; for an instant, we all gaped up at her, unable to keep our eyes from the hairy, raspberry-sized wart on the point of her double chin.

"Well?" she demanded in a voice that could cut steel. "You boys gonna order, or just sit there like turds in the bowl?"

"Beer, please my good lady," said Charlie, suddenly recovering his aplomb. "Six pitchers, I think, for starters."

Large Marge grunted. "What about food?"

Charlie snatched up a menu and perused it desperately. "Let's keep it simple – we'll have... the tortilla soup and some of your fine chips and salsa."

She turned to go, then stopped abruptly to fix us with a fish-eyed glare. "Why the hell y'all dressed the same? Ya ain't *Mormons*, are ya?"

"Good God, no," Charlie said with his most winning smile. "We're a rugby club. From England."

"English."

"Yes, that's right."

Her eyes narrowed. "I met a Englishman once. Set right over there at the bar and asked if he could buy me a brew."

"Good lad," Charlie said.

"Said I wuz the hottest-lookin' fox he'd ever seen. Then he leaned over and whispered all the things he wuz gonna do to me when we got back to his hotel."

She paused. We gaped in horrified fascination as the visual images her narrative provoked danced in our heads, and tried desperately not to let our gazes stray to her wart. "And then?" Charlie said, encouragingly.

"And then?" Her voice rose to a sphincter-spasming shriek. "He barfed on his own lap and fell off his barstool! And I've hated you Limey bastards ever since!"

She spun on her heel and stalked toward the bar. A minute or two later, our biker friend scuttled over, eyes bulging in alarm. "Oh, Jesus! What'd ya say to her? I tole ya not ta piss her off!"

Weathersby mopped his face with a napkin. "I thought fat women were supposed to be jolly!"

Large Marge suddenly loomed behind him, three pitchers in each massive fist. "What was that?" she asked sweetly.

Weathersby thought desperately. "I said, 'What a way with women you have, Charlie.'" And he smiled hopefully. For a moment, she regarded us through slitted eyes. Then she thumped down the pitchers, turned without a word and stalked ponderously to the kitchen.

"Come on, Dex," said Charlie bravely, "– time to turn on the old English charm." We arose and made our stealthy way toward the swinging half-door to the kitchen. When we arrived, Charlie peered cautiously through the aperture, then had to bend double to stifle his laughter.

Large Marge stood at the stove, humming. She had removed her voluminous underpants and was in the process of straining our soup through the ancient, yellowed crotch into a large tureen. I looked at Charlie, and we both broke into a helpless fit of choked laughter.

Marge whirled on us with astonishing and menacing grace. "You motherfucking Limeys, I'll..."

But Charlie waved his hands placatingly, still weak with laughter. "No, no, Marge, it's quite all right," he gasped. "I'll even tell you whom to serve!"

An hour later, Large Marge was off shift and sitting at our table, drinking beer straight from the pitcher and laughing until her ample belly shook, as though we were her oldest mates in the world. She was genuinely sorry to see us go. And everyone who'd tried it, including Weathersby, a notoriously finicky eater, assured her the soup was the best they'd ever tasted.

When we returned to the coach, Charlie threw himself down in the seat next to me. We looked at one another, then burst out laughing again. "You see, Dex?" he gasped. "That's the secret to dealing with difficult personalities. Sometimes, to get what you want, you just have to find the right person to throw under the bus."

II

Charlie's wisdom was brought forcefully to mind when I entered my cube early the next morning. I'd hardly sat down when the phone rang, and I heard Oakhurst's unwelcome voice. "DI Reed, can you join me in my office? We need to discuss your... report."

Well, I had known this moment was coming. I made my way upstairs, paused at the door to gather my thoughts, then knocked. "Come," Oakhurst growled.

He looked up from the slim document I had left on his desk as I entered. "So," he said, eyes glinting. "This is your idea of a full and complete catalogue of the potentially-incriminating incidents you've observed in your time with the Hastewicke Gentlemen, is it?"

"To the best of my recollection, yes, sir."

"Well it isn't good enough, is it, DI Reed? You feed me a few feeble anecdotes about indecent exposure, public drunkenness and armadillo theft, and expect me to believe that this is the extent of your insider knowledge, after more than 20 years of international touring? I know what goes on on those bloody tours of yours!"

"Then why don't you write the report? Sir."

"Because I wasn't there, and you were! Now you will re-write this report, and by God you had better refresh your memory before you do, or I'll have you up on a charge of insubordination!"

"Very well, sir, I'll see if anything else springs to mind. I'll have it on your desk by morning." I didn't mind; I had an inexhaustible store of similar, marginally-scandalous anecdotes to pass along. I paused by the door. "And by the way, DCI Oakhurst, you asked for a daily report on the investigation. You'll have the transcript of our Barlowe interview by this afternoon. We're interviewing Lord Palmerston after lunch. Was there anything else, sir?"

"No. Just get out."

After the door closed, Oakhurst sat for a few moments, staring into space. Reed was becoming a problem, one that needed decisive solving.

He didn't fear Reed's ability to damage his career. Too much time had passed since Docklands for a formal complaint to have any chance of success, and in any event, Reed had no proof of what had really happened. Oakhurst had meticulously seen to that.

But the truth of the matter was that he, George Oakhurst, was badly in need of another spectacular success. It had been too long since Docklands had made him the golden boy of the Metropolitan Police Service. Since then, his record on major cases had been mediocre at best. There had been procedural grumblings about several of them; for a fact he was not unwilling to test the bonds of legal restraint when the pressure to clear a case grew intense. There had been a major embarrassment last year; an important case had been dismissed when the lab had failed to find a Yemeni terror suspect's fingerprints on the mobile phone he had supposedly used to place calls to an informant in Leeds. That had been damned careless of him, but there had been no way to obtain the man's prints until he had the suspect in custody.

But now the fates had conspired to place another sensational case in his hands. It had everything – bloody murder, blackmail and sexual scandal involving peers of the realm, the certainty of a hysterical national press response once the facts hit the street. There was even a sporting angle. To top it all off, it also presented the opportunity to rid himself of Dex Reed, finally and forever. If he played his cards right. And there might be other compensations as well.

DCI Oakhurst smiled then, but it was not a warm smile. Oh, yes. He still had cards to play.

III

At my insistence, we went to see Bob Leicester at his penthouse in Canary Wharf, rather than at his office. For a man of his celebrity, the arrival of two Metropolitan Police detectives at his place of work could not fail to provoke comment and speculation. It was one of the little things I could do to keep the investigation of my teammates under the radar for as long as possible.

Copperfields, where Bob lived, was enormous – a 51-story behemoth on the north bank of the Thames, built to the highest standards of energy efficiency. A guard buzzed us through the triple-paned doors; Brian stopped for a word. "I'll catch you up," he said as I headed for the lift.

Bob's flat occupied the entirety of the 51st floor, with panoramic views over the Tower of London, the city and the river. I was astounded at its size – at least 10,000 square feet, sparsely furnished with Stickley couches and chairs, exercise equipment and luminous Persian carpets, each a work of art. Bob was sweating profusely when he opened the door; he had been Stairmastering when I arrived. "Come in, come in," he said. "Let's sit by the fire. Drink?"

"No, thanks," I said. "Spectacular digs."

"Oh, you've not seen it before?"

"No. It's magnificent."

He waved a deprecatory hand. "It's free. I own the building." He went to the bar, poured himself a stiff one, then came and sat beside me and seemed to gather himself. "Right." He sighed. "You're here to ask me about Weathersby."

I nodded. "He was blackmailing you."

"Yes. I assume you've seen the same video he showed me?"

I nodded again, reluctantly. "Yes I have, Bob. And I must tell you that we've sent an inquiry to the Las Vegas police, due to the apparent ages of the girls involved."

He paled. "You haven't."

"We'd no choice, Bob. If they're under 18, it's statutory rape. You'll be prosecuted."

"Dex – please. I'd be ruined!"

I felt my shoulders bowing beneath the familiar yoke of anguish. "I know, Bob, and I'm sorry. But there's nothing I can do. I appreciate your position, but we're well beyond the mates on tour stage now. Anyway, that's a side issue. I must caution you that you do not have to say anything, but it may harm your defense if you do not mention when questioned something that you later rely on in court. Anything you say may be given in evidence. Do you understand these rights?"

Leicester was appalled. "You're cautioning me? Dex – you can't be serious. It's me, Bob Leicester!"

"I know." I struggled for self-control; he had been my mate for over 30 years. "But I don't want there to be any misunderstanding: I'm investigating John's murder. Do you understand your rights as I've explained them to you?"

"Yes."

"And would you like your solicitor present?"

He looked away. "Not at this time."

At this moment, there was a knock on the door. We answered it together, and I introduced Brian. "Sorry I'm late," he said as we re-settled ourselves beside the fire. "Where were we?"

"I was just going to ask – did you pay Weathersby the blackmail?"

Leicester shook his head. "No. I was still weighing my response when I learned John had been killed."

"I assume £100,000 was well within your means?"

"A hundred thousand pounds?" He laughed incredulously. "Was that the going rate? He wanted £500,000 from me."

"Still, I assume that the money was no problem?" Leicester nodded grudgingly. "So why hadn't you paid?"

"I don't like to lose – you know that about me. I was exploring... other options."

I pondered that. "Involving your security staff?"

He shrugged. "I employ some very competent, very skilled, very loyal people. I was exploring the possibility of a covert raid to steal his hard drive. But once John was killed, there didn't seem much point."

"Ah. Because he had cautioned you what would happen if he died."

Bob favoured me with a ghastly smile. "Right as rain, Dex – you always were the clever one. I should have recruited you ages ago. But the truth of the matter is, there was no reason for me to kill him – he had obviously taken precautions. And now all I can do is wait for the other shoe to drop."

I weighed my disapproval of what Leicester had done in Las Vegas against our decades of friendship, then grudgingly told him that Brian had intercepted Weathersby's backup thumb drives before they could be posted. "Thank God! That's the first stroke of luck I've had since all this began! Look, Dex, I'm begging you – if not for me, then for all the kids in my charitable dos. I help a lot of people. It won't help anyone if this Vegas thing becomes public knowledge."

"I appreciate that. I'm facing the same problem with everyone else John was blackmailing. And I'm struggling to keep the lid on – I really am. But sooner or later' it's going to blow."

"Lord Palmerston." Brian quietly interjected his first question of the interview. "What did you do following Weathersby's party?"

"Came straight back here and went to bed, naturally. I didn't leave the party until nearly 1 a.m., and it was a work night."

"Can anyone confirm that?"

Bob shrugged. "The security guard in the lobby can tell you when I came in."

"It's all right, I've already had a word with him – said you got in at 1:32 on the night in question." Brian leant forward, focusing those bloodhound's eyes on Bob's face. "But when I asked, he was also kind enough to show me the security records for the rest of that night. He was somewhat surprised, as was I, to see that someone using your security code left the building via the service entrance at 2:05 a.m., and re-entered at 4:17. We all know you're not a fool. Assuming you don't just leave your alarm code laying about, can you tell us why you went out again that night?"

Leicester sat as still as a wax figure in a stately house tableau, face betraying no emotion whatsoever. Then he spoke, without looking at me. "Do you remember the night of the party, Dex? You ran into me as I left John's office."

"'Dex. Your turn next?'" I quoted, remembering Leicester's words.

He nodded. "He'd shown me the video a couple of weeks before, said that, as a favour to an old friend, he was giving me a special rate – half a million to keep it quiet. That night, the night of the party, he called me to his office. Said he'd been patient long enough, that I had until the Friday to pay him, in cash. If I refused, he assured me that a copy of the video would be delivered to every member of the Magwitch Trust's board of directors by 5 o'clock that night."

"And what did you tell him?"

Leicester shrugged again. "That he'd have his money. What else could I say? It wasn't the money – it means nothing to me. It was the monstrousness of it. When you belong to a rugby team, there's a bond of trust – I don't have to explain that to you, Dex. A rugby tour's one of the few times in life you can truly be yourself, and there isn't one among us who hasn't had a few too many beers and done something brainless. John just thrust that aside as if it meant nothing. He'd crossed a line."

"So what did you do that night?" Brian asked.

"I couldn't sleep. So I slipped out the back way and walked along the Thames for a couple of hours. I do my best thinking when I walk. The idea of just giving in, of paying Weathersby's price – was intolerable. It just wasn't on."

"And did you?" I asked. "Think of an alternative?"

He nodded reluctantly. "I have 23 Magwitch Project centres, dealing with some of the most troubled youth in Britain. I may be an idealist, but I'm also a realist. My security staff's top-notch – some of them ex-Special Branch, ex-SAS. I called my chief of security that night and explained what I had in mind."

"Which was?"

Leicester grimaced, then continued doggedly. "A surgical break-in to steal his hard drive and to install listening devices, followed by 'round-the-clock surveillance on John himself. Money was no object – I didn't care if it cost twice what John was dunning me for. If he moved to send out his backup videos, we'd know ahead of time and take steps to secure them."

"And did any of this actually occur?"

"No," Leicester replied. "By then, John was already dead. There was no point."

"Tell me," said Brian. "Did you happen to meet anyone on this walk of yours? Anyone who could confirm that you were in fact on the Embankment between the hours of 2 and 4 a.m., rather than, say, in Notting Hill?"

My partner was sparing me from having to ask the hard questions of my teammates, and I silently blessed him for it. "No," Leicester replied frostily. "I mean, there were a few... hello, wait a minute – there was one homeless bloke – sprang out of the gorse in Millwall Park and begged a quid from me. I was in such a state I gave him a tenner, I think."

"Can you describe him?"

"Late forties, bald on top, dark beard with a white streak, dirty white anorak, very tall – nearly as tall as you, DI Abbott. He had a Glaswegian accent."

"Right." Brian looked at me, eyebrows raised; we rose to go. "Just one more thing, Lord Palmerston. You're right-handed?" Leicester nodded, perplexed. "Can we have a look at your right shoulder, please?"

Leicester stepped back, suddenly outraged. "Look I've answered your questions. What's my shoulder got to do with anything?"

"It's just to satisfy us on a point of interest. Your shirt, please?"

With a wordless glare for me, Leicester slipped his sweatshirt over his head. There was a fading, yellowish contusion on his right shoulder. "May I ask where you acquired that, sir?"

"It was weeks ago, in one of the matches in Vegas. You remember, Dex. I was on the ground for five minutes or so."

I considered. Bob was a hard, fearless runner and tackler, and there had been two or three occasions when he had taken injury time, but I could recall nothing specific to his shoulder. When I said nothing, Leicester snorted contemptuously. "You know, Dex, when this nightmare began, I thought we could count on you. I really did. But you're not really one of us, are you? In the end, you're still just a scholarship boy."

I stood very still. "Count on me for what, exactly, Bob?"

"Discretion. Understanding. Delicacy. But you see this differently. It's your big chance for glory, isn't it? And nothing is going to stand in your way."

There were a hundred things I wanted to say in response to that. All the petty slights, all the backhanded sneers over my working-class background, from many of my teammates, over all those years, rose suddenly like hot mental bile. But then a thousand acts of kindness, of camaraderie, of friendship, came to soothe the burn. "After all this time, I would have thought you knew me better than that, Bob," was all I said. Brian and I let ourselves out.

A few minutes later, we were in Brian's Ford, heading back to Hendon. "Think he's gaming us?" he asked after a thoughtful silence.

"Don't know," I replied truthfully. "He does have a lot to lose. But I do know one thing."

"What's that?"

"That over the next few days, one of us is going to be spending a great deal of time befriending the homeless in Millwall Park."

16

As a detective, I learnt early on to trust my subconscious. While the conscious mind is a marvelous instrument, able to procure, sort and draw conclusions from mountainous quantities of raw information, it lacks the ability to integrate such a vast, squirming mass into a coherent conclusion. In any investigation, it's the subconscious that does the heavy lifting when it comes to telling us what it all truly means.

We had now interviewed all four major suspects – the victims of John's blackmail – and so far, my subconscious was maddeningly silent. In general, this is a sign that more information is needed. Brian and I agreed that it would be worth our while to interview the other Hastewicke Gentlemen and allekedoos, and to winnow through Weathersby's personal life and business relationships, using financial and phone records, looking for anyone who may have wished him harm.

It was a monumental task, undertaken under crushing pressure to solve the case immediately, if not sooner. Not a day went by that Wicks or Oakhurst, or both, didn't drop by to criticize our lack of tangible progress; both Brian and I grew harassed and testy.

Slowly a matrix took shape on the department's HOLMES system: the complex web of contacts and personal relationships, actions and transactions, the trifles, in Dickens' immortal words, that make the sum of a man's life. We tracked alibis, purchases, payments, phone and email contacts, interview answers. After a week, we seemed no closer to an arrest than we had when we started.

"What we've got so far," Brian sighed, "is sod all, mate. So far as we know, Weathersby wasn't involved with anyone, romantically. All of his ex-girlfriends seemed genuinely happy to see the back of him. He was in debt only to reputable financial entities – there were no Artemis Pauls lurking in the background. There were certainly rival collectors who despised him, but none homicidally so. His ex-wife's alibi checked out, so she's in the clear. Parliament isn't in session, so I don't see a political motivation. If it was a terrorist act, no one's stepped forward to claim the gold star."

Things were less clear when it came to our four primary suspects. All four of their alibis were essentially unverifiable, although Brian had spent some time in Millwall Park in an effort to find the old dosser Leicester claimed to have given money to. Harry Barlowe had a history of violence when drinking, but he hadn't been drunk that night, so far as I or his wife could tell, and lived so far from the murder scene that it would've been nearly impossible, logistically, for him to have gone home, then returned to Notting Hill in time.

"What about firearms residue?" Brian asked. "It only lasts 24 hours on the skin, but much longer in clothing."

"Already thought of that," I said smugly. "FSS have collected every scrap of clothing from our four suspects. They're analyzing it now."

Brian frowned. "None of them seem stupid enough to keep whatever they may have worn that night laying about. Still, can't hurt to check. What about CCTV?"

"Nothing promising thus far, except a case of bug-eyes for young Vesta. He did have quite a good view of a couple having an energetic shag in a car off Lansdowne Road, at least until the windows fogged up. I've given him recent photos of Bernie, Seagrave, Leicester and Barlowe, but so far none of them have turned up on surveillance video after the party broke up. No furtive shapes climbing the garden fence, either – as luck would have it, the camera covering the Rosmead Road entrance to gardens is broken, and there aren't any cameras inside."

My partner shook his massive head in disgust. "Bloody typical. You'd think the world's most extensive CCTV network would make our jobs easier, until you actually have to depend on it. There was one thing, though." He rummaged through the stack of folders on his desk, selected a blue one. "What d'you make of this?"

I perused the file. One line caught my eye. "Forensic found a smudge of a peculiar granitic soil in the carpet near the French doors, typically found in the French Alps near Annecy. Interesting."

"Know whether any of your mates has been to France recently?"

I shook my head, and leaning back in my chair, considered. "All right, Brian." It was time to ask the fundamental question. "You've talked to them all. What do you make of our four prime suspects?"

He ran his fingers through his unruly hair. "Bernie Plantagenet's an unstable wreck, but he seems harmless. Roger Seagrave runs deeper – I don't know what he's capable of. Harry Barlowe was the most open of the four, and the circumstantial evidence is in his favour, but he has a history of violence. Bob Leicester has the most to lose, the most resources to help him to do something about it, and he's ruthless when it comes to losing. None of them has an airtight alibi; they all had enough at stake, potentially, to justify a murder. Yet they all knew that killing Weathersby wouldn't solve their problem, because of his failsafe plan. It doesn't make sense."

I flourished a file. "Well, here's something that might help us – the last month's phone records for all four, plus Weathersby. Let's split them up." I handed Brian his half of the stack, together with a list of the Hastewicke Gentlemen home, office and mobile numbers to compare it to.

By the end of the afternoon, we discovered that a dozen team members had called Weathersby at some point in the preceding month. Only four – Seagrave, Barlowe, Leicester and Bernie Plantagenet – were in contact more than once. And only one of the four called Weathersby on the night of his death, at shortly before 2 a.m. The call lasted four minutes, and not for the first time, I wished British Telecom had the ability to record and archive every call made on its network.

"Why Bernie?" Brian asked as we motored toward Millwall Park. We had agreed to take one more sweep through the park, looking for Bob Leicester's possibly mythical panhandler, before turning the job over to the local constabulary. "Why'd he call Weathersby the night of the murder? He'd already paid. His money was long gone. What would've been the point?"

"Who knows? Bernie was twat-faced by the time I left the party. Maybe he just called to tell Weathersby what he thought of him. Maybe he thought of some pretext, so he could go back to Penhurst House and blow John away, before he could hurt anyone else."

"All right, say that's true – why would Weathersby agree to a rendezvous? What could they possibly have to talk about that was so urgent?"

"I don't know. We'll have to ask Bernie, I suppose. But I have to be honest – I don't see how it could've been Bernie. If they'd arranged to meet, Weathersby would've been waiting for him."

"So?"

By now we'd left the car and were strolling the twilit path through the park toward the Thames. I could see the lights of Copperfields, Leicester's abode, glowing a mile or so to the north.

"You saw the crime scene, Brian. Whoever shot John was waiting for *him*, the gun already loaded."

"We don't know that for sure, Dex – that's just a theory. What if Bernie, or whoever it was, was sitting by the gun and Weathersby turned his back for a moment, or went to the toilet and came back just in time to get a .50 calibre surprise?"

"Fair enough." We paused to admire the lights of Greenwich shimmering on the ponderous flood. "So we're back to square one."

Brian gave a snort of disgust. "We were never on square one. We haven't even started the bloody game! We know it's got to be one of the four, but it could've been any of them, and so far, we've no way to so much as prove or disprove anyone's alibi! I've talked to all the taxi companies, by the way. None of them has any record of a pickup from any of our suspects' houses after 7 p.m. the night of the murder."

At this moment, a shadowy shape detached itself from the landscaping and shambled toward us. "Spare some change?" he asked, holding out a filthy American-style baseball cap.

Glaswegian accent. Tall, balding, bearded. Brian produced a crisp five-pound note. "We can do better than that, but you'll have to earn it."

The old dosser gave him a look of disgust. "Ah may be homeless, but ah'm not that desperate – try Old Compton Street. And anyway, ya'd have tae do a lot better'n five pound."

With a grin, Brian produced his warrant-card. "Get your mind out of the gutter, old-timer – you're not my type either. We seek information."

The homeless man took a dancing step backward. "You're the man! They see me talking tae you, they'll piss in me ears when I'm asleep!"

I was mystified. "Who will?"

"The watchers!. They see all and know all."

Brian was losing patience. "Look. D'you want the fiver or not?"

With a furtive glance around, the grizzled Scotsman moved closer. "All right, all, right – what d'ya want tae know?"

"A week ago. A man was walking along the embankment, late at night. Prosperous-looking bloke in a track suit, about our age, with a goatee, thinning on top. Says he gave you a tenner."

"Ya mean Lord Palmerston?"

Brian was startled. "You know him?"

"Everybody knows him. Walks here a lot! He's a generous man, Lord Palmerston. He was in quite a state, as ah recall. Slipped me a tenner, but he barely knew what he was doin'."

"D'you remember what night that was, and what time?"

"Last Wednesday night, or early Thursday mornin', 'round two or three."

Brian paused. "And how do you remember so exactly?"

"It no every night someone slips me a tenner, is it? And the next day, Man U beat Chelsea."

I pondered this statement while Brian jotted down the homeless Scotsman's vital info. If this story was true, it provided

Leicester, whom I had considered one of our strongest suspects, with a nearly uncrackable alibi for the night in question. Which was only par for the course, I reflected.

II

When I returned to the office early the next morning, Oakhurst, predictably, was not pleased at our lack of progress. He was even less pleased by our activities of the night before. "Stop trying to prove your friends are innocent, and start trying to find out who's guilty, by God!"

I smiled inwardly at his discomfiture. "With all due respect, DCI Oakhurst, you surprise me. To identify the guilty, first we must eliminate the innocent. To do that, we have to try to confirm or disprove Leicester's alibi – that's just basic police procedure."

"Don't lecture me about procedure, Detective Inspector!" He ran a hand over his meaty face. "Do you have anything positive to report?"

Reluctantly I informed him of Bernie's late-night call to Penhurst House on the night of the murder; Oakhurst sat up in his chair. "And where does this Plantagenet live?"

"Belgrave Square," I replied.

"Just a mile or two from the crime scene! Fancy that."

"He does live closer than any of our other suspects, yes. But sir, I've known Bernie Plantagenet for thirty years. He's the most inoffensive soul on the team. He isn't capable of murder."

Oakhurst's eyes gleamed. "I was unaware that you'd become a behavioral psychologist, Detective Inspector. Who really knows what a man's capable of, when extreme pressure is applied?"

I paused, considering. "I suppose you're the expert there. Sir."

Oakhurst laughed that one off. "What about you then, DI Abbott? Do you share DI Reed's confidence in Plantagenet's innocence?"

Brian looked at me uncomfortably. "At this point, we're both keeping an open mind, sir. I must say I agree Plantagenet's the least likely of the four main suspects. For one thing, he was quite drunk the night of the party – it would have been very difficult for him to cope with the alarm, or the weapon." He explained our various theories of the murder, recapping our earlier discussion about the logistics of loading the rifle while Weathersby was in the room, and the various ways that difficulty might have been circumvented.

"So it *could* have been Plantagenet," said Oakhurst, steepling his fingers.

"Technically. It's possible, I suppose." Brian frowned. "But there's one more difficulty. There would've been no reason for Weathersby to agree to a 3 a.m. meeting – what would be the point? He already had Plantagenet's money. What could've been so important? Weathersby would've had to be suspicious. And besides, Plantagenet knew what would happen if Weathersby was killed. Why spring the very trap he'd just paid to avoid?"

Oakhurst shook his head. "You've just told me he was drunk. The courts are littered with cases where normally-reasonable people have committed regrettable acts of violence while intoxicated. I believe DI Reed's judgment is clouded by his friendship with the suspect, and it's influenced your own. Plantagenet clearly had motive for murder. His shoulder was bruised. He called the victim just before the crime occurred. His fingerprints were found at the scene, and on the rifle. And he lived within walking distance of the murder scene. No." As I opened my mouth, he held up his hand. "I don't want to hear it, DI Reed. I warned you what would happen if your close association with the suspects in this case interfered with your investigation. I'm still making up my mind what to do about your clear dereliction of duty. While I do, you will arrest Plantagenet and charge him with murder. Today. This morning."

My eyes filmed with hate, I could only sit in rigid, stunned silence while Brian rose heavily to his feet. "Very well, sir," I heard him say.

For a moment, I dreamed of hurdling Oakhurst' desk. I thought I could crush his windpipe before Brian pulled me off. Instead, I rose to my feet and departed without a word.

Back in our cube, I managed a rueful grin. "Well, that went well."

Brian was pulling on his coat. "For what it's worth, I don't think Bernie's our boy, either. But it's not up to us anymore, is it?"

"Apparently not." I sighed. "Well, let's get it over with."

17

In my third year at Hastewicke, I ran afoul of Harris Wopsley-Armstrong, "Whopper" to his friends, the worst bully in the school. Whopper was a tall, thick-necked seventh-year, with a shock of greasy brown hair and a crop of acne so bounteous it looked as though someone had tap-danced on his face wearing golf spikes. At the start of term, he had transferred to Hastewicke from another school, where, it was whispered, he had committed acts of violence so appalling that only his father's wealth and position had saved him from criminal prosecution.

Predictably, far from moderating his behavior, the incident seemed only to have emboldened him. Immediately upon his arrival at Hastewicke, Whopper instituted a reign of terror among all the younger boys.

His favoured victims were, naturally, anyone he considered his social inferior, which was pretty much everyone. He had a special place in his wizened reptile heart for the scholarship boys, and proceeded to make our lives hell on earth.

Whopper took a skeevy, perhaps sexual pleasure in the anticipation of his atrocities. Once he chose his next victim, he would simply stare at him, sometimes for weeks on end, with a dead, glassy eye and a half-smile that promised nothing but pain. You'd glance up during dinner, and there he'd be, at the next table over, staring unwaveringly. Over the next week or two, you'd see him everywhere – in the halls, in the quad, in the toilets – just staring at you, and smiling that cruel serial-killer smile. I had seen boys piss themselves when they encountered him unexpectedly. Eventually, he would catch his victim in some lonely spot, and beat him until he cried for mercy.

And then one day, he fixed his demented stare on me. At first I ignored it, knowing, as one who had acquired a painful and intimate knowledge of bullies, that to show fear was a fatal mistake. This continued for a week or so, and, familiar as I was with the horrors Whopper had inflicted on his other victims, began to take a toll on my nerves. One Sunday morning, after chapel, I emerged to encounter him, leaning on a pillar, arms folded across his chest, just staring.

He was six inches taller than me and five stone heavier. I took a deep breath and strode across the quad. "If you're trying to frighten me, it isn't working," I lied, trying to suppress the quaver in my voice.

He only grinned more broadly. "Is that a fact? Then why d'you sound like a girl?"

"Look – I'm warning you. Leave me alone, or you'll be sorry you were ever born." And I walked away, in a turmoil of anger and fear.

As I walked back to my house, Charlie Chalmers materialized and fell into step beside me. "Dex! You look like you've just stepped on your own dong!" Since I had taken up rugby two years before, Charlie, the youngest captain of the first XV in school history, had taken me under his wing. Now all my anxiety over my impending confrontation with Whopper came spilling out. Charlie's eyes narrowed. "Wopsley-Armstrong, eh? Yes, I've heard about him. Got kicked out of Eton for shoving a Coke bottle up someone's bum – he's a nasty piece of work."

"Thanks," I said gloomily. "You've given me ever so much to look forward to."

"There's only one way to deal with bullies, Dex," Charlie said seriously. "You've got to stand up to him. With a little help from your friends, of course."

And so it was that, the next day, at dusk, when Whopper followed me to the deserted rugby pitch, intent on violence, four black-clad shapes emerged from the wood bordering the field, carrying cricket bats. The four – Charlie, the two second-rows and a prop from the first XV, proceeded to beat Whopper until he curled into a foetal position and shat himself. When it was over, Charlie leaned close. "We don't like bullies at this school, you cowardly turd. If you put one toe out of line from here on out, God have mercy on you. Not even your daddy will be able to save you."

We walked back to our house together. "Thanks, Charlie," I said.

"Think nothing of it," he said. "If you can't stick up for your teammates, what kind of mate are you?"

II

I had tried to stick up for my mates, to whatever extent I could, as this investigation proceeded. I would continue to do so. And I had taken certain precautions – precautions I thought might pay dividends over the longer haul. But try though I might, I had failed Bernie. I paused, one hand on the knocker. "I'm not sure I can do this," I said to Brian. "It's wrong."

"I know," he said. "But we've no choice. Anyway, the sooner done, the sooner mended." I let the knocker fall.

Apparently, it was the maid's morning off. Jane answered the door. "Dex! What brings you here?"

"We're here on official business, I'm afraid, Lady Delvemere." Brian pushed past me. "Is your husband at home?"

Jane shot me a confused look. "Yes, he's just finishing breakfast. Shall I..."

I closed my eyes in anguish. "Look, Jane, I must see him." I gave Brian a "wait here" signal, and followed Jane into the morning room.

Bernie sat at one end of a long mahogany table, surrounded by orange trees in a glass-walled conservatory, a magnificent but untouched spread of eggs, bacon, kippers and toast before him. He looked up fondly at Jane's approach. Then he saw me.

"Dex! What the hell! Can't a fellow..." He trailed off.

"I'm sorry, Bernie," I said quietly. "But I've been ordered to bring you in."

The blood drained from his already-doughy face. "Dex! You can't be serious!"

Just for a moment, I struggled for my life in a maelstrom of rage, shame and affection. Then, mercifully, the ship righted itself, and I was able to speak normally. "Timothy Bernard Plantagenet, I arrest you for the murder of John Weathersby."

"No!" Jane cried. "You can't think..."

"I'm sorry, Jane," I told her gently. "But I've no choice in this. I must caution you that you do not have to say anything, but it may harm your defense if you do not mention when questioned something that you later rely on in court. Anything you say may be given in evidence. Do you understand these rights?"

Bernie nodded, shoulders slumped, tears streaming down his stubbled cheeks. Jane looked from one to the other of us in horror. "Dex, how can you do this? What possible reason could Bernie have to kill John?"

"I'm sorry, Jane." I moved to support Bernie, who looked ready to collapse. Clearly he had been unable to tell her about the blackmail, or about his activities in Las Vegas. "I can't discuss the case. I will tell you, as a friend, that Bernie needs a barrister – a good one. You'll see to that, won't you?"

She read the anguish in my eyes and reacted. "Yes, of course." She gave Bernie a pat on the cheek and a reassuring smile. "Don't worry, darling. We'll soon sort this out."

"I'm so sorry, Jane," he choked, unable to look at her. "I've really put my foot in it this time."

For a moment she looked at him, uncertain and fearful. I took him gently by the arm. "Don't worry," I told her – "I'll look after him. Ring me when you've chosen a barrister, and I'll make the arrangements." And I led him from the room.

III

After we'd processed Bernie in, I started down to the holding cells to see him comfortably settled in. Brian held back. "Can you manage, or d'you want me to tag along?"

"What's up?" I asked.

"We did agree that we'd interview the rest of your team-mates, just to see if something turned up. I've an appointment with Richard Devilliers in 20 minutes."

I nodded. "Go on – best to leave no stone unturned. Maybe something will turn up. I'll hold the fort here."

After making sure that Bernie had a cell to himself, I returned to my desk and unlocked the drawer where I'd stored the black-mail videos. I wanted to reassure myself that they were still secure, and they were. But as I contemplated the five innocent-seeming zip drives, I found myself wondering who had the most to lose in this case. Barlowe's drinking bout was hardly the stuff of tabloid legend, but would, in all likelihood, cost him his marriage. Seagrave's wild encounter with Whole Lotta Rosie was perhaps more headline-worthy, in the context of a murder investigation, and would also have a similar marital impact. Leicester, though unmarried, had the farthest to fall, from revered philanthropist to pervert – sensational public humiliation and potential loss of a multibillion-pound empire.

And Bernie? He had no career to lose, and a public outing, though potentially embarrassing, simply didn't carry the same poisonous social stigma in these broadminded times. The prospect of losing Jane would be enough to give any man pause, but if I knew her, the revelation that Bernie was a bit confused, sexually, wouldn't be enough to drive her away. She would stick by him, if he wanted her to.

Poor Jane. My premonition about heartache lurking just around the corner had proved devastatingly accurate. I considered our brief but intoxicating time together with a stab of guilt, thinking of the friend I'd betrayed, now sitting alone, fearful and guilt-riddled in turn, in an eight-by-eight cell. But he had had the joy of her, awakening next to her every day for 15 years, while I had never been able to find a woman to compare. If I was honest with myself, I could never regret our time together.

Still, the guilt of it whispered to me, like a snatch of song you can't get out of your head. I wondered to what extent my desire to make amends had clouded my assessment of Bernie's role in this case.

Things would be so much simpler if Bernie were to be convicted of Weathersby's murder. Distressing, of course, for Jane, but I would be there to help her through the trauma.

But even as that ignoble thought occurred, I knew it simply wasn't on. If I'd ever been certain of one thing, as a copper, it was this: Bernie Plantagenet simply didn't have it in him to kill another human being. No matter how much he deserved it. I also knew that I owed it to Jane to rectify this travesty of justice, even if it cost me my job.

IV

The phone rang just as I was preparing to leave for the day. It was Brian, in an ebullient mood. "Meet me at the Red Lion in Parliament Street," he said.

"I'll be there in 10 minutes," I said. "What's up?"

"Tell you when you get there," he said, and rang off.

18

"Your friend Devilliers told me Weathersby tried black-mail at least once before."

Brian leaned back, loosening the tie from around his heavy neck like a reprieved prisoner shrugging out of the hangman's noose. Then he regarded me with a certain smug satisfaction.

"When?" I asked. "On whom?"

"On Chalmers. Just before he died."

"You're joking," I said. But somehow I wasn't quite as sur-prised as I should have been.

"Not about this," said Brian. "Budge up, and let me tell you a story."

It seemed that Devilliers had known of Chalmers' blackmail for more than a decade. However, while Weathersby was alive, Devilliers had kept silent, for fear that Weathersby's information would damage Charlie's old firm, now a thriving concern. With both Charlie and Weathersby dead, however, Devilliers had felt at liberty to relate the following tale.

Charlie had founded Trans-Channel Investments LLC, an investment firm specializing in continental and American stocks and securities, in 1990. However, in the year before he died, in 2004, the firm was fountaining red ink. Charlie's recommendations had enjoyed an unprecedented streak of misfortune, and he had lost several of his most important clients, as well as a goodish chunk of his own investment in the firm. Some change of fortune was in order.

It came in the form of Cedric Ruskin, a former co-worker for whom Charlie had covered up some unspecified past indiscretion. Ruskin now worked as an energy trader for Midlands Power. For the past several years, Midlands had been acquiring utilities and generating resources on the American west coast. They had also been buying long-term options on the energy spot market, betting that the growing demand for power in Silicon Valley, Seattle, Portland and LA would drive energy prices upward.

Midlands now controlled enough generation to tilt the razor-thin power supply balance in its own favour. One night, a pint or two over his usual capacity, Ruskin revealed to Charlie a secret plan to shut down two of Midlands power's largest thermal generating plants in California for "emergency" repairs in late August, at the peak of summer electricity demand. The net effect of this highly illegal scheme was to cause power prices, and the company's earnings, to spike. Charlie, ever alert to his clients' advantage, cashed in, to the tune of a record quarterly dividend. And so his firm was saved.

Somehow – Devilliers had been squidgy on the details – Weathersby had found Charlie out. One night, Weathersby had invited Chalmers 'round for drinks, and shown him copies of certain incriminating documents, documents that, if they found their way into the hands of the regulators, would have meant disaster for Trans-Channel Investments, as well as Charlie's reputation as a financial analyst of rare integrity and success. Weathersby told Charlie that a cash payment of £250,000 would avert this sudden calamity.

Before he could make up his mind how to respond, the distraught Charlie had been killed. Looking back now, I thought I knew how Weathersby had obtained his information. In the spring of 2004, Charlie and Weathersby had been roommates during the Hastewicke Gentlemen's tour of Australia and New Zealand. Weathersby, in his eternal quest for advantage, had obviously ransacked Charlie's papers and computer. I remembered that, on that tour, our last together, Charlie had seemed uncharacteristically preoccupied by business affairs. Charlie was a trusting soul, and this was the price he had paid.

"Interesting," I said to Brian, "but what's the relevance to this investigation? That was a long time ago."

"Maybe nothing. Maybe everything."

"How d'you mean?"

"Charlie was Weathersby's first victim. Plantagenet, Barlowe, Seagrave and Leicester are the most recent. But there's a ten-year gap between them. What if there were others in between? Wouldn't they want to spare their mates what they'd been through?"

"Maybe." I thought back on my own complex relationship with John, on the calculating look in his eyes on the night of his murder, and knew, with absolute clarity, that he had been weighing how much the concealment an affair with a teammate's wife might be worth to someone on a policeman's salary. Obviously he had decided that the potential profit didn't balance the risk that I would simply arrest him on the spot – which I almost certainly would have done. Still, if what Brian was saying was true, how could I have missed the signs?

"Anyway." Brian studied the rich play of light in the depths of his pint. "Something Devilliers said suggested another line of inquiry."

"What?"

Brian made a dismissive gesture. "Probably nothing. I'll let you know if it pans out."

I drained my pint. "I'm not sure I want to know. The farther his case proceeds, the more an ass I feel."

"Speaking of feeling an ass," said Brian, arising, "tonight's sex night, so I shall bid you adieu."

"What, already?" I asked wryly.

"Yes, it's only been two months since our last steamy love-bout. My advice to you, laddy, is to go home and, like me, crawl into bed. You look knackered, and tomorrow's going to be a very long day."

For once, a sensible suggestion. I was suddenly very tired –
tired of it all. "Give my best to Fee," I suggested.

"Well. It'll be *my* best, at any rate," said Brian. And chuckling
to himself, he scuttled for the door.

II

It is truly remarkable the extent to which, in the Bard's immortal
words, a good night's sleep, sore labor's bath, can knit up the ragged sleeve of care. I had taken Brian's advice, gone home to my
flat in the Mews, read a few pages of *Dombey and Son*, and slipped
effortlessly into profoundly restful slumber. I dreamt that I was
22 again, rampaging across the rugby pitch in some exotic foreign
land, and awoke revitalized and ready to cope with Weathersby's
tangled web. A good sluicing in the old shower, some tea and
toast, and I was fairly whistling as I strode the final few blocks to
the office.

I should've known it was too good to last. As I rounded the last
corner, I saw the seething mass of humanity in front of Hendon
nick. At first I thought it was just another demonstration. Then I
noticed the cameras.

"DI Reed! DI Reed! Is it true you've arrested Lord Delvemere?"

"DI Reed! Have you identified the prozzies in Lord
Palmerston's video?"

"DI Reed! Is it true you've used your position to conceal your
teammates' past criminal wrongdoing?"

"DI Reed! Were you being blackmailed as well?"

"DI Reed!"

"DI Reed!"

By the time I had shouldered a none-too-gentle path through the swarm of reporters and paparazzi and gained the relative haven of the security checkpoint inside the vestibule, I was livid with rage. Someone within the department had leaked the blackmail videos to the press. It was a disaster of unimaginable magnitude – for the case, and most especially for my teammates. The hounds of hell were loose now, and had already clamped their ravening jaws around the throats of some of my closest mates. I knew one thing, and one thing only. Whoever had unleashed this apocalyptic shitstorm, whether for financial gain or simply to watch me squirm, would pay, and pay dearly.

The message light on my phone was blinking when I arrived at my desk. I had just finished listening to the last cheery call, from Barlowe ("Dex, you utter prick! How could you do this to me, after you promised to warn me, so I could be the one to tell Sarah? Ah, Dex, she's gone – wouldn't even speak to me! Oh, Christ, what's the use? What's the use of anything?") when Brian arrived, lightning fairly shooting out of his ears.

"Dex! For Christ's sake, how could this have happened? Are the drives still there?"

I unlocked the drawer. "See for yourself."

"How many other copies are there?"

"Two. One for Wicks, and one for Oakhurst."

He paused. "Oakhurst."

"Yes. Said he needed them for his meeting with the Crown prosecutor. But not even he would do something this heinous. He may hate my guts, but he wouldn't put his career on the line just to bugger me. Whoever did this has left the Metropolitan Police Service open to millions in lawsuits. The guv'nors'll go berserk!"

At that moment, my phone rang. "DI Reed, would you step 'round to my office, please?"

I hung up. "Speak of the devil," I said.

"What's he want now?"

"Something I'll enjoy about as much as a fishhook through the ball-sack, I'll wager. But while I'm gone, if you're not too busy, there's something I'd like you to do for me." Brian listened to my request. And then he began to smile.

III

Oakhurst was openly gloating when I arrived. "I don't need to tell you that the events of this morning have put the Metropolitan Police in a very bad light, DI Reed."

"No, sir. You certainly don't."

Wicks was pacing like the pendulum on a metronome, face like woman in third-stage labor whose husband has just told her she looks fat. "A bad light? It makes us look like we've all got shit for brains! My wizened buttocks are black and blue from the bollocking I've just received from the head of SCD! We will discover who leaked those videos, and his or her head will be on a spike before this day is out!"

"With that in mind," I said, "only three copies of the zip drives exist. Mine are still under lock and key. Have you verified that the same is true of yours?"

"Of course!" Wicks barked. "Do you take me for a cretin?"

"Naturally not, sir. What about yours, DCI Oakhurst?"

"They're right here, where I left them last night," he replied, and unlocking a file drawer, demonstrated that this was so. "And now, DI Reed, perhaps you can explain this to me." And he laid a sheet of paper on his desk.

It was a faxed copy of an incident report, from the Wellington, New Zealand police, dated April 12, 1999. My heart sank as I read it. It described a particularly nasty bar fight between local mechanic Andrew Marshall, age 28, and visiting English rugger Harry Barlowe, 35. The police had been inclined to prosecute, but one of Barlowe's teammates, DI Dexter Reed of London's Metropolitan Police Service, had intervened, managing to persuade the dubious local constables that Barlowe had acted in self-defense.

I looked up. "Sir?"

"This incident wasn't in any of your reports." Oakhurst addressed himself to Wicks. "Did I not tell DI Reed, in your presence, that any attempt to conceal information pertinent to the Weathersby investigation would result in the severest possible consequences?"

Wicks frowned. "You did."

"This is a clear violation of departmental procedure. I intend to see that DI Reed answers for it."

"That's at your option, of course. But later. Until we find out who leaked those videos, it's all hands to the pumps."

"Quite. Well, DI Reed? What do you have to say for yourself?"

"The incident report speaks for itself, sir. Barlowe was attacked in a bar, and he defended himself. I was there, helped break up the fight, and gave a statement to the police. They agreed it was self-defense. No criminal charges were filed. It isn't relevant to the Weathersby case."

Oakhurst regarded me incredulously. "It isn't relevant? It says here Barlowe might have killed the man if you hadn't intervened! One of our primary suspects has a documented history of homicidal violence and you don't consider that relevant?"

"He didn't start the fight. He was attacked, and he defended himself. That's hardly what I call a history of homicidal violence. And in any event, I thought you were convinced that Lord Delvemere was the killer. Sir."

"A good investigator keeps an open mind, and isn't afraid to change it when fresh evidence comes to hand! Did it not occur to you, DI Reed, that Barlowe might have felt not only himself, but his family, under attack from Weathersby? If he reacted to some drunken lout in a bar by attempting to choke the life out of him, how would he react to the threat of losing his family at the hands of an unscrupulous teammate?"

I had no answer for that. I rose to depart.

"It must have rankled all these years, DI Reed."

I paused, hand on the knob. "What's that, DCI Oakhurst?"

"Being the lone scholarship boy on a team full of rich nobs. Having your nose rubbed in that lifestyle, but never really being a part of it."

"Is that just a personal observation, sir?" I spoke in a voice carefully neutral, noticing that Wicks had gone very still. "Or do you believe it to have some bearing on the case?"

"Just an observation, detective." And with an airy flutter of his fingers, he shooed me from the room.

IV

Still pondering this enigmatic exchange, I returned to my desk, to find that Brian had left a note: "A promising lead. Meet me for lunch at the Prospect of Whitby in Docklands."

I used the intervening two hours to pursue a promising lead of my own, involving a visit to the exquisite Emma Kwan of the computer crimes lab. When I left, the day seemed brighter, and I hummed as I cabbed it eastward along the Mother Thames.

Brian was waiting when I arrived. An extraordinarily fat bloke, so spherical as to be the same height lying down as standing up, shared his table. "DI Dex Reed – meet Cyrian O'Toole. Old mate of mine."

Everyone in London knew O'Toole; his scandal-raking scribblings were a daily must-read for every social climber in the city. He was the disgraced eldest son of one of the oldest and most conservative families in Britain, whose transgressions at Cambridge had caused his tradition-minded father to cut him off without a farthing. O'Toole, privy to a thousand family and near-family secrets, had embarked on a career as a journalist, and swiftly made himself someone to be feared and cultivated in equal measure. He was, so I had heard, extravagant in his tastes, ambiguous in his sexuality, brilliant, unscrupulous, and deeply insecure.

O'Toole gave a small grimace of distaste as he slipped me a small, moist hand. "Delighted, detective. Now, can we get on?"

"Certainly, certainly." Brian was in high good humour. "I think you know that Cyrian's the society columnist for the *Star*? He was the first to break the Weathersby story."

"Indeed?" I said.

"Yes, well..." O'Toole preened modestly. "It was, between us, quite a coup. Circulation numbers through the roof, my dear chaps! Our rivals shat themselves in fury!"

"You buggered my investigation, and several of my closest friends," I growled.

O'Toole shed his skin of affability like a yearling anaconda, and favoured me with a disdainful glare. "Be serious, detective. Blackmail and murder among the aristocracy? The choicest bits captured on video? Stories like this make journalists' careers." He turned me a knowing wink. "Just like they make policemen's."

"And ruin others."

O'Toole bulbous face flickered through scarlet and into magenta. "Listen, DI Reed. I didn't ruin anyone's career. They did that themselves. It was their..."

"Speaking of ruined careers," said Brian in his best commanding Bobby's voice, "I seem to recall that you were grabbed up for indecent exposure a year or two ago. Something about an 80-year-old granny, I believe?"

"Keep your voice down, for Christ's sake!" O'Toole hissed. "I was just taking a piss in her garden! Anyway, that was never proved!"

"Only because, at the time – " Brian laid a heavy emphasis on the latter word " – one of my colleagues was persuaded not to pursue it. I believe the case file is still open. The statute of limitations is seven years."

"All right, all right, you've made your point," said O'Toole, sweating visibly now. "What d'you want to know?"

"Obviously," I said mildly, "we want to know who sold you the videos."

"I can't tell you that! It was a confidential source!"

"Look, Cyrian. We know it was someone on the inside at Hendon. And they haven't just embarrassed the MPS." For just an instant, I allowed the rage roiling inside me to show in my eyes, fixed with unwavering intensity on his. O'Toole flinched backward involuntarily. "They've embarrassed me personally. And I will show no mercy to anyone who helps them get away with it. None."

O'Toole acknowledged my threat with a flick of a disdainful glance. "I couldn't help you even if I wanted to, DI Reed. I don't know who it was."

"What d'you mean, you don't know?" asked Brian, leaning his massive forearms on the table.

"I don't know because it was an anonymous source!"

"Just tell us what happened," I growled.

"I got a call. Someone who said he worked at New Scotland Yard, and was in the middle of an investigation that would blow the lid off London! He told me about the case and the videos, asked how much we'd pay for copies!"

"And how much did you pay?" I asked curiously.

"A hundred thousand pounds up front, with another £100,000 if the information proved out. He left the zip drives in a blind drop, a rubbish bin near our offices. We made the second payment after we'd reviewed them, and seen they were dynamite."

"How was payment made?"

"Electronic transfer. He gave us an account number, and we gave the order to our bank. Funny thing, though." He narrowed his porcine eyes. "It was actually two different account numbers – one for the first payment, and a different one for the second."

"We'll need those account numbers."

O'Toole shook his head mulishly; a few drops of sweat spattered the tabletop. "I can't. That would tell you who the source was as surely as if I'd given you his name myself."

"So it was a man." Brian leaned backward, a thoughtful look on his face.

"Yes, it was a man! But I've bugger-all idea which man! Now if you'll excuse, me, I've got a very busy day today." He rose.

"Sit down!" Brian roared. "We're not finished! You spoke to this... man, personally?" O'Toole nodded reluctantly. "Would you recognize his voice if you heard it again?"

O'Toole considered. "Possibly. But..."

"No buts. I'll ring you this afternoon with some voice samples for you to listen to. If you recognize one of them, you will tell me."

"But I can't! The *Star*'s policy is absolutely clear – never grass a confidential source! They'd sack me!"

"Not if they don't know you were *our* source," I observed reasonably. "And anyway, you've just told us you don't know your source's name. How can you reveal what you don't know?"

"But if I identify his voice, you'll find him!"

Brian can look very menacing when he wants to. He leant forward, to tower over the suddenly-palsied O'Toole. "On the other hand, if you refuse to help us, you'll also be sacked, when you're prosecuted for waving your willie at someone's helpless granny. And go to prison. Do you know what happens to sexual offenders in prison? Especially those who prey on the elderly?"

O'Toole shook his head mutely; he looked as though his colon was spasming. "Let's just say you'll be biting your pillow from now until Camilla is queen!" Brian hissed. "Now can we count on your cooperation?"

O'Toole trembled like the cornered rodent he was. "All right!" he muttered. "But this is a one-time favour, d'you hear me? And I don't want to hear any more talk about prison!"

"Agreed," said Brian, taking out a pen. "Now, what's your direct line?

19

It was pouring rain as I walked home, the kind of cold, drenching autumnal London downpour that makes you long for firelight, whisky and stew. Arriving home, I accordingly built a cozy blaze in the hearth, poured myself a stiff Bushmill's with a couple of cubes of ice, and hacked up a joint of lamb, some potatoes, leeks, carrots and swedes, and set them to seethe on the hob.

I considered my CD collection. Pink Floyd were too portentous. The Who were too intense. I settled on *Year of the Cat* by Al Stewart – erudite, introspective, melodious. Then, halfway through "On the Border," the doorbell rang.

I was expecting some brave soul from the press. Instead, when I cracked open the door, I saw Jane. Shivering, drenched, and alone.

"Can you forgive a fool?" she asked miserably, water dripping from her nose. "I've been such a fool, Dex"

"You haven't been a fool," I said brusquely. "Come inside, before you catch your death."

She was drenched to the skin and shivering, despite her mac. Before she said another word, I steered her to the bedroom, handed her a towel and some departmental fleece, and closed the door. She emerged a few minutes later, auburn hair slicked back, enveloped in my voluminous training garb. I steered her to the fireside and, in its crackling warmth, placed a large whisky in her hand.

"Now," I said. "What's all this?"

She shook back her wet bangs. "What's all this? Dex, I've just found out that the man I've been married to for a decade and a half is gay! He's been arrested for murder! I don't know who he is anymore!"

"Well," I said, struggling for fairness, "I wouldn't read too much into his arrest. You and I both know he's not guilty – he wouldn't hurt a flea. It's just departmental politics – we're under a lot of pressure. I shouldn't tell you this, but we were ordered to bring Bernie in, against our better judgement."

Jane shivered again, and I moved closer, clumping down next to her where she sat in front of the sofa, and throwing a fraternal arm around her shoulders. "Look, Jane," I said gruffly. "I've been at this game a long time. I don't believe Bernie's guilty. This is a tough time, but in the end, he'll be free."

"Yes," she said, tilting her face toward mine, tears running down her cheeks. "But he doesn't want me."

"How could he not?" I said. "You're the most desirable woman I've ever known." And just to prove it, in spite of my better instincts, I kissed her.

I tasted the salt from her tears, but I felt the urgency of her response. Her body arched against mine as she desperately sought warmth. "You've always been my temptation, Dex," she whispered, clutching my hair. "Now I need you."

I put my hands to her breasts, beneath the thick departmental fleece. But that wasn't enough. I ran my hands underneath, only to tremble at the yielding heat of her warm bare skin. Jane moaned. "That feels wonderful."

Seconds later, our clothes were in a heap on the floor, and she had pulled me atop her, desperate with need. My manhood, hard as a member carved by Michaelangelo, filled her, and it was my turn to groan. It was slow and langourous, like lava moving over a field, then faster, then faster still, blood roaring in our ears, hands clenching, caressing, breath coming in stertorous gasps, and then we were coming, together, inseparable, complete, unstoppable. I think I whimpered gratefully.

Afterward, we lay in each other's arms, utterly spent, content merely to listen to the hissing of the fire in the grate and the November downpour still hammering at the windows. "I shouldn't have done that," I said at length. "You came here for comfort. I've taken advantage of you."

She smiled knowingly. "I came here for a good hard shag, actually. And perhaps for a bit of comfort as well."

I sighed. "Well, it's a bit late for regrets. Hungry?"

"Famished."

I fetched steaming bowls of stew, crusty bread and butter, and a bottle of old Burgundy I'd put aside for a special occasion. This one seemed special enough. We at cross-legged in front of the fire, legs touching, eating ravenously, not saying much, content just to be together.

"So what about Bernie, then?" I asked at length.

"I don't know," she replied helplessly. "I don't know what I feel anymore. It's not his arrest, so much – I don't believe he's capable of violence. But he's been so different these last couple of months – so distraught. He hasn't been himself. Maybe I don't really know him anymore."

"What about his alibi? Do you know for a fact he never left the house once you'd returned from the party?"

Jane looked troubled. "He wasn't in bed when I woke up. I found him down in his study, about half eight the next morning, shaking as he watched the morning news. When he saw the report about John's death, he threw up!"

"And do you still love him?" I asked, keeping my voice casual.

"I... seeing that video was such a ghastly shock, Dex. We have a regular sex life – I truly had no idea he was gay. If he managed to hide that from me for 15 years, what else has he been hiding? Once the trust is gone from a marriage, things are never the same again, are they?"

"You're asking the wrong man – I'm not exactly a relation-ship expert, am I? I suppose you just have to give it time."

"Dex." She touched me gently on the cheek. "Can I spend the night? I can't go back to that empty house. I don't want to be alone tonight."

"Of course. My house is your house."

Her eyes filled with tears. "Thank you, Dex."

II

The rain had stopped by the time Brian picked me up very early the next morning; a pallid moon still chased its own reflection through the newly-washed streets of London. "You look surpris-ingly cheerful this morning," he said, eyeing me suspiciously.

"Yes, well – a clear conscience and a saintly life," I lied. "Where to first?"

We had agreed to spend the early-morning, pre-rush hours driving between Weatherby's house in Notting Hill and the abodes of our four suspects, to get a sense of their relative travel times.

"Might as well start at Bernie's, then – it's on the way," I suggested. Brian obligingly steered a course through the light predawn traffic toward Belgrave Square. I operated the stop-watch as he then drove east on Pont Street, north along Sloane Street, then followed the Kensington Road west along the edge of Kensington Gardens. Brian swung north on Kensington Park

Street to Notting Hill Gate, then north again on Ladbroke Grove to arrive at last at Lansdowne Crescent, then. "Fifteen minutes, 21 seconds," I said. "Ample time to leave Belgrave Square, get here, do the deed at 3 a.m. and return home before Jane awoke." I mentioned Jane's information about finding Bernie in his study at 8:30 the following morning, though I omitted the fact that she had delivered it in the nude.

Seagrave lived on Tavistock Square in Bloomsbury, not far from the British Museum. He had not been in touch since the leak of the blackmail videos, but Catherine had left a voicemail on my mobile. "We've been your friends for years, Dex. For God's sake, how could you let this happen? How could you not have told me?" A raggedly indrawn breath. "You have blighted my life." The drive to their house, mostly along the Bayswater, Marylebone and Euston Roads, took 49 minutes. "That's cutting it very fine, if he and Catherine left Weathersby's at 1," Brian observed.

Next we drove to Canary Wharf and retraced our route from the palatial Copperfield Building to Blenheim Crescent. "Sixty-six minutes," I noted, clicking the watch. "If security have Leicester leaving the building at 2:05 and re-entering at 4:17, that leaves him exactly five minutes to disable the alarm, break into Weathersby's house, signal him to come down, shoot him, and return to his car. That may be cutting it a bit fine, but I suppose it's technically possible. He'd have had to pay off the old dosser in Millwall Park, of course."

Brian snorted dubiously. "If Leicester's responsible, he's far more likely to have recruited some member of his entourage to do the deed. We'll have to do some digging there."

We then looked at the map. Barlowe lived in Essex, near the town of Upminister. "If the fast train to Fenchurch Street was running, that's about 35 minutes, give or take. It's conceivable that a knowledgeable cabbie might get him from Fenchurch Street to Blenheim Crescent in time, but they're a long way apart. Anyway, the train doesn't run after 11. By car, I don't see any way he could get to Notting Hill inside of 90 minutes. I'd say Barlowe's in the clear, if we can satisfy ourselves that he did indeed return home with Sarah that night."

"I'll see if I can reach her," I said. "Since she plans to divorce him, I think it's safe to assume she won't be lying for him."

"Didn't she leave him?" Brian asked. I nodded. "So how d'you know how to reach her?"

I smiled wryly. "By happy coincidence, she called only yesterday, and left her mobile number."

Brian raised his eyebrows sympathetically. "Only yesterday, eh? And how was her mood?"

"Bleak," I said, dialing the number. "And vengeful. Hello, Sarah? Dex Reed."

"Dex. You're the last person I want to talk to. What the hell d'you want?"

"Ah. First of all, to apologize. I can't tell you how badly I feel that you've found out like this."

"Do you want to know how I found out, Dex? I turned on the morning news, as I was fixing the kids breakfast, and there was Harry, big as life, drinking until he vomited and fell off the couch! How could you not have told me?"

"I couldn't tell you, Sarah. It's part of an ongoing murder investigation."

"Oh, yes," she said bitterly. "It was a secret from me – mates on tour and all that. I warned Harry not to go on that tour! 'Oh, no, it'll be a good test for me, love.' Well, he failed the test, didn't he?"

"Everybody makes mistakes, Sarah," I said gently. "This was one of Harry's. I know he's serious about beating the booze. And I know he loves you and the boys. You mean everything to him."

"My father was an alcoholic, did you know that, Dex?" She snorted. "It's probably what attracted me to Harry in the first place, according to my therapist. My own dad beat me, Dex – he beat us all. And I vowed, never again."

"I'm so sorry, Sarah." It was all I could think to say.

"How long have you known?"

"About Harry's drinking? Since a couple of weeks after Weathersby's death, when the blackmail videos came to light. I never saw him drink on the tour."

"I trusted him, Dex. I really did. Now I can never trust him again. Or you! How could you let this happen?" She was crying now. "How could you let the press get hold of this story? I've had to go into hiding just to keep from waking up to reporters on my doorstep, and paparazzi in the hedgerows!"

"I did everything I could to keep all of this confidential, Sarah. And I'm making it my personal mission to punish whoever leaked the videos – you have my word."

There was a pause at the other end of the line. "Funnily enough, Dex, I believe that like nothing else you've said this morning, and I'm grateful. Harry always said you were the protector of the team. Maybe that extends to their families as well. Whoever did that, for whatever pathetic reason, has made the pain and humiliation so much worse than they had to be."

"I know." I hesitated, groping for the right words. "Sarah, I don't want to make things worse, but there's something I have to ask you. We're trying to eliminate Harry as a suspect in Weathersby's murder."

"I don't want to talk about it, Dex! That utter prick! I blame him most of all! He got exactly what he deserved! Isn't there a law that says a wife can't be compelled to give evidence against her husband?"

"Yes there is," I replied. "And I'm inclined to agree about John. I can't compel you to answer. But I know you'll give me an honest answer, despite how you may be feeling about Harry just now. What I need to know is this – on the night of the party, did Harry return home to Upminister with you?"

"Of course he did!" Sarah's voice was incredulous. "We went straight up to bed, for Christ's sake – it was 2:30! Harry fell asleep before I did – he was absolutely knackered from work."

"Thank you, Sarah. I'm sorry to bother you at a time like this, but I'm trying to clear Harry, and find the person responsible for John's death. I hope you understand. And I'm truly sorry about all of this."

I could hear her crying at the other end of the line. "It's... all right, Dex. I'm sorry for the way I've treated you. It's not your fault – I know you couldn't tell me about Harry's drinking. That's between Harry and me. You've always been a good friend. I'm sorry I shrieked at you like a fishwife."

"You didn't, and please let me know if there's anything I can do to help."

"I will, Dex." And she rang off.

"Well?" Brian asked.

"I'm an utter prick, as if you didn't know that already. Also, Harry Barlowe's in the clear."

20

Upon our return to Hendon nick, I stopped by the basement holding cells to check on Bernie. He greeted me apathetically, struggling to arise from the thin mattress on a shelf that was the sole furnishing of the room. I saw that the guards had taken away his belt and shoelaces. "Bernie," I said. "How're you holding up?"

"Well enough, Dex. It's... it's sort of peaceful down here. Gives a fellow time to think."

"Sometimes that can be a good thing," I offered lamely. "Bernie, why'd you call John the night of the murder?"

He screwed up his face, in an effort to remember. "I did, didn't I? I was pretty well twat-faced. I've a vague recollection of telling him what I thought of him – something about being buggered by Hitler in Hell. It wasn't exactly *Blackadder*, when it came to wit."

He looked at me curiously, until I began to feel even more distinctly uncomfortable. "You know, Dex," he said at length, "I never worried about what you'd think. About me being gay. Somehow, I knew it wouldn't bother you."

"It doesn't," I said. "We are who we are. Who the hell am I to judge you? Anyway, you're still the same old Bernie."

"And you're still the same old Dex – watchful, brave and honourable. D'you know why it doesn't bother you that I'm gay?"

"Bernie," I said, "I..."

He waived his hand. "It's because you're so utterly sure of who you are. I never was, myself. You don't feel compelled to judge people, because you can accept the fact that we're none of us perfect."

"Maybe it's because I'm far from perfect myself," I muttered. I took a deep breath. "Bernie, I..."

"Wait, Dex. I must say this. I can't tell you how much better I feel just seeing you here. I've seen your passion for fair play, on the pitch, for over 30 years." There was a shrewd glint in his eye now, something of the Bernie of old. "If you thought I'd killed John, you wouldn't be talking to me like this."

"Let's just say it wasn't my idea to arrest you," I said. "Look, I've got to go. D'you need anything?"

"Something to read, perhaps. And one other thing." I looked up, hand on the door of his cell. "Jane. She must be absolutely gobsmacked by this. You'll look in on her, and give her a cuddle? Tell her I love her, and never meant to hurt her?"

"All right," I managed. "But Bernie, there's something I..."

At this moment, the screw arrived with Bernie's lunch – bangers, mash and boiled cabbage. "Ah – lunch!" said Bernie brightly. "I'm famished! I'll see you later, Dex?"

"Yes," I sighed. "I'll look in when I can."

II

When I stepped off the lift on the fourth floor, Brian was there, an anxious look on his big bearded face. "Dex – there're two blokes from DPS waiting at your desk. They say they need to interview you in private – wouldn't tell me what it's all about."

I was at a loss. The Metropolitan Police's Department of Professional Standards investigated on-the-job misconduct. Suddenly, I tumbled. "Ah, yes," I said. "Yesterday's interview with Oakhurst. He found the incident report on Barlowe's bar fight in New Zealand."

"Ah." Brian grimaced; he hadn't quite forgiven me for that one. "Right. In the meantime..." He held up a digital recorder. "I've got the voice samples we talked about. I'll call O'Toole to see if he can identify which was the voice on the phone."

"Godspeed," I said.

I strode to my cubicle, determined to put this to rest once and for all. The DPS boys were waiting, as Brian had said. One, sable-haired, urbane and sardonic, rested a lean buttock on my desk. The other, tall, younger, roly-poly, with an eccentrically-long goatee, seemed to be in charge. "DI Reed?" he said.

"That's right. How can I help?"

"I'm DI Hackett, from DPS; this is DI Carter. Will you come with us, please?"

"Go with you where?" I asked, genuinely puzzled.

"Downstairs to the interview room – we need to take a statement from you."

"At your service, gentlemen," I said philosophically. "Lead the way."

I slouched confidently in my chair as we settled ourselves into the dreary interview room, a drab grey space redolent of historical pain. I knew what they were going to ask me, and felt serenely prepared.

Hackett pressed "record." "This is DI Bartholomew Hackett of DPS; in the room with me is DI Terence Carter, also of DPS, and DI Dexter Reed of Hendon SCD. It is now..." he looked at his watch, quite a nice one, from where I was sitting "...10:40 a.m. on November 10, 2013. We have advised DI Reed of his right to have his departmental representative, or a solicitor, present." He looked at me expectantly.

"That's correct," I replied. "Now what's this about?"

"DI Reed," said Carter, the worldly, sable-haired one. "Do you recognize this?" He produced a sheet of paper – a copy of a bank statement. I read it over carefully.

"It's a savings account summary, obviously," I replied.

"Whose savings account?" prompted Hackett.

I studied the paper anew, then felt the blood drain from my face. "The account number is mine," I replied, but I've never seen this statement, or these figures, before." The statement showed that £100,000 had been deposited to my account the day before.

"Let the record show that Exhibit H, DI Reed's bank statement, was obtained under court order this morning," said Hackett, whom I was liking less and less by the minute. He seemed very young and disturbingly sure of himself. "Can you tell us why this sum was deposited to your account, DI Reed?"

"Must be bank error. I've never had a hundred thousand together in my life. When was it deposited, and how?"

"Funnily enough," said young snippy, with a curious challenging glint in his eye, "it was deposited just last night. By electronic transfer."

"From what source, DI Hackett?"

By way of answering, he slapped down today's edition of the *Star*. Beneath a three-inch headline – "BOYS WILL BE BOYS!" – the front page featured three lurid full-colour freeze-frames from the blackmail videos: Seagrave locking lips with the lavish Lotta Rosie, a bare-chested Bernie french-kissing his old lover, and Leicester making his tartlets, the Magwitch Project's logo clearly visible on their unzipped unidresses. Cyrian O'Toole's venomous, mocking screed occupied most of the page below the fold.

"Are you telling me the money came from the *Star*?" I asked incredulously.

"Did you think we wouldn't find out, DI Reed?" Hackett hissed. "I thought these men were your mates! How could you do this to them? At least Weathersby had the discretion to keep what he knew to himself!"

The sable-bearded Carter stilled his younger counterpart with a fatherly hand on the shoulder. "That's enough, I think, Bartholomew." As Hackett rose to pace, disgustedly, Carter sat down. He folded his hands and gazed earnestly across the table, like an evangelical about to ask whether I'd accepted Jesus Christ as my personal saviour. "Why don't you give us your version, DI Reed?" he urged. "What's this all about?"

"This is a frame-up – that's what it's all about."

"Are you saying it wasn't you who leaked the videos?"

"Are you daft? I've been friends with these men for more than three decades!"

"So had Weathersby," Carter observed mildly.

I leaned across the table. The numbness of the initial shock of the accusation had worn off, and despite my grinding effort to control it, I was becoming angry. "I'm not Weathersby," I growled. "I've never betrayed a friend's confidence. I never would, unless my duty as a police detective left me no choice. And I'm going to make very sure that whoever betrayed this confidence is very, very sorry."

Carter leaned back. If my vehement denial had nonplussed him, he gave no sign. He steepled his well-manicured fingers.

"Allow me to put forward a theory, detective," he said. "You attended the Hastewicke School as a scholarship boy, surrounded every day of your life by the sons of the wealthy, the privileged and the well-connected. As a member of the Hastewicke Gentlemen, you've gone on rugby tour with these men almost every year, to every corner of the world. You've spent time with them socially. In short, you've had your nose rubbed in a lifestyle to which you, a mere Metropolitan Police Service detective, can never aspire, at least on your current salary."

He reached across the table to tap my hand. "Then Weathersby is murdered, and the blackmail videos that your teammates valued at nearly one million pounds fall into your lap. You're an intelligent man, DI Reed. You saw... an opportunity."

I looked from one DPS man to the other – Hackett triumphant, lip fastidiously curled; Carter fatherly and concerned.

"I see you've been talking to DCI Oakhurst," I said, and saw the shaft strike home. "Perhaps you're familiar with the history of our relationship." That one hit the mark as well. "Mine wasn't the only lap the videos fell into."

"Do you seriously expect us to believe that you've been set up?" Hackett asked incredulously.

"Most competent investigators would consider that possibility," I admitted. "You have your theory of the case, and I have mine. Come and see me this afternoon, gentlemen – I hope to have some alternative evidence you may find interesting. And now, if we're finished...?"

"DI Reed," said Hackett, swelling with importance. "You are on suspension from this moment. You will not communicate with the press, except through the Department of Professional Standards. You will have no further involvement in professional duty until this case is resolved. Do you understand these instructions?"

"You don't have the authority to relieve me of duty," I said contemptuously. "Show me a signed administrative order, and

I'll comply. But for now, I'm in the middle of a murder investigation, and a major departmental scandal has just blown my case to hell. I've got work to do, so if you'll excuse me, gentlemen?" And with that, I returned to my desk.

Brian glanced up apprehensively. "What the hell did they want?"

Rolling my chair over so that our knees touched, I whispered an account of my conversation with DIs Hackett and Carter. "Has O'Toole listened to the voice samples?" I asked.

"Not yet" said Brian worriedly. "He's been dodging my calls."

"Christ!" I swore. "Without his information, I'm bolloxed! Right!" I arose and put on my coat. "Time to pay him a visit."

We found O'Toole in a staff meeting, holding forth in a particularly unctuous voice about his investigative triumph. The assembled *Star* editors and staff were just giving him a standing ovation when Brian and I arrived. Brian, mountainous and menacing, pushed his way to the gossip columnist's side. "Mr. Cyrian O'Toole? Will you come with us, please?"

"Cyrian?" A tall, elegant 50ish cove in a chalk-striped grey suit rose to his feet. "What's this about?"

O'Toole stood whey-faced and paralyzed as Brian seized him by the elbow. "I..." he began.

"We have some questions for Mr. O'Toole, regarding an ongoing investigation," said Brian in his best parade-ground voice. "Come along."

"Let me call in our solicitors," said the grey-suited man. "They can be here in half an hour or less."

Brian paused, aware that the attention of a roomful of journalists was upon him. "Mr. O'Toole is not under arrest – for now," he said. "But if he would prefer to give his statement in the presence of counsel, or even in the presence of the distinguished members of the press – " and here he turned to look O'Toole full in his bulbous face "– the option is his."

O'Toole looked from Brian to his editor, at a loss. Finally he shook his head, and seemed to regain something of his earlier presence. "No," he said bravely, "I will face this alone, for I have nothing to hide. They will never silence me!" And he left the room in our custody, under an escort of applause.

III

"Listen," said O'Toole, when we'd gotten him into the back seat of the car. "I've had second thoughts. I should never have agreed to this. I can't identify a confidential informant. It simply isn't done."

Brian started the car. "Where are you taking me?" the gossip columnist bleated.

"To Hendon nick. We may as well get you processed."

"Processed? For what?"

"For indecent exposure to the elderly, public nuisance and drunk and disorderly – that should do to be getting on with. Dex, why don't you ring Constable Goodspeed to check on that other matter."

I flipped open my phone and hit auto-dial. "Goodspeed. DI Reed. Did you arrange the prisoner transfer we discussed? That's right – Roto-Rooter Maitland. Right, fill him in – we're bringing his new cellmate down. Right, see you in ten. Ta."

"Wait!" O'Toole had turned shocky-pale and sweaty; for a moment, I feared he was on the verge of some sort of spasm. "You can't do this!"

"We can and we will," I said brutally. "You've left us no choice."

"It's really such a simple thing we're asking, Cyrian," Brian observed soothingly.

"All right! Stop the car! Let me hear the bloody tape!"

"You sure?" Brian asked, driving on. "I'd hate for you to compromise your principles."

"Don't push your luck, detective," said O'Toole in a steadier voice. "Regardless of what you may think, I do take my responsibilities as a journalist very seriously indeed."

I forbore comment, and punched "play." A man's voice issued from the speakers, obviously a taped snippet of a phone conversation. "This is sample one," I said.

"...unbelievable, really. Arsenal're playing way over their heads. If they can beat Man U this week..."

O'Toole shook his head. "That's not him."

A second voice came on. "No, I think a change of scenery will do O'Toole a world of good! Soothing green walls, good conversation, an occasional constitutional beating, the regular insertion of ten inches of..."

"Most amusing, DI Reed! No, it wasn't you, either."

We played the third sample. "...you seen the guv'nor's new admin? Cor! I think he gave her the old elbow test – you know, the one where she puts her hands on her shoulders and walks toward the wall, and if her elbows touch before her knockers, she doesn't get the..."

"What terrifically-stimulating conversations you must have around the water cooler," O'Toole observed. "Still, there's something familiar... no, I don't think it was him."

"Sample four," I said.

"...expedited. What the hell are you playing at down there? When you tell me the lab results will be on my desk by the close of business, by God, I expect you to..."

"Stop!" said O'Toole. "It was him."

"You're sure?"

"Positive." A crafty, avaricious gleam came into his eyes. "Who is it?" he asked.

"Sorry," I said. "That's confidential. I'm sure you'll understand."

"But you'll know soon enough, I expect," said Brian. "Here, sign this." He thrust a paper over the seat.

"What the hell is this?" O'Toole asked suspiciously "I, Cyrian O'Toole an employee of the *Star* newspaper, arranged to purchase the Weathersby blackmail videos from the man whose voice I identified as sample number..."

"Four, I growled. "Just fill in the number four and sign it, and your work here is done. You'll be a free man, Cyrian."

For just a moment, I thought the great wanker was going to try to leg it. Then he furiously snatched out a pen and wrote to my direction, "There, bloodsuckers! I've done your reprehensible deed. Your pathetic lives hold no interest for me! Don't ever contact me again!"

Brian opened the passenger door. "Thanks for your cooperation. Now get out."

"Get out? But we're a mile from the office!"

"The walk will do you good," I observed. "Goodbye, Cyrian."

He alighted with poor grace, made a furiously obscene gesture at our rear window, then turned and slouched officeward. I noted with some satisfaction that it had begun to rain. "So," said Brian, driving fast and skillfully through the early-afternoon traffic. "Your hunch was correct."

"Indeed," I said. "Should be an interesting afternoon." Then I opened my mobile and made another call.

21

When we returned to Hendon, a man was waiting by the elevator. He rose when he saw me, face blooming in welcome. It was a warrior's face, all hard planes, scarred, with a broken nose; his thinning grey hair cropped close to his skull. "Dex!" he said. "It's been a long time! What's this about?"

"Docklands," I said, shaking hands. He had a grip like a hydraulic car-crusher. "It's good to see you, Max! Thanks for coming down on short notice!"

"Glad to help," he said.

"DI Brian Abbott, my partner," I said. They shook hands, and I quite enjoyed the look of pained surprise on Brian's face as he retrieved his mangled fingers. "This is Sergeant Max Murdoch, a face from my checkered past."

"Mad Max Murdoch of Firearms Branch?" "Brian asked. "Dex has told me a lot about you, some of it quite complimentary."

"You know," I said as we walked toward our cube, "I think I'm going to quite enjoy this."

Hackett and Carter were, as expected, waiting for me at my desk. Hackett, at least, allowed his pleasure to show. "Ah, DI Reed," he said. "Here's your administrative order. You may review it at your leisure, but as of this moment, you may consider yourself officially on suspension."

"Let's not get ahead of ourselves," I replied evenly. "I believe I told you that you were in error in your view of this case. Before you make a mistake I guarantee you'll regret, I have some evidence you need to hear."

"Do you?" asked Carter, face impassive.

"It doesn't matter," said Hackett nastily. "It's done. You're off the case. Take it from me, detective – no matter how you squirm, your career's over."

Max froze him with a stare the colour of polar ice. "Take it from you. And who the hell are you, boy?"

"DI Bartholomew Hackett of the Department of Professional Standards. And you are?"

"Sergeant Max Murdoch, SO17 Armed Response Branch."

"Ah." It was obvious that even young Hackett had heard of Mad Max Murdoch, a man whose deeds were legend even in the testosterone-gargling world of violent incident response. Perhaps he'd heard about the time Murdoch, armed only with a penknife, had killed three gun-wielding IRA assassins in a safe house. Or the occasion when, handcuffed to a radiator, Murdoch had used his toes to defuse a pound of Semtex only nine seconds before it went off. Or the time he was shot through a lung by an armoured-car robber, but still carried a wounded comrade to safety, zigzagging a hundred yards under fire.

There was also the time he had taken an eager young detective aside, just before a major drugs raid, and told him to be careful. "I've a bad feeling about this," he said, almost invisible in his black camo and boots, a fully automatic Heckler-Koch MP-5 at port arms. "Something doesn't feel right."

"I'll be fine, Max," I said. "You've got my back."

"I do," he said. "It's your front I'm worried about. So I'm going to give you some advice I hope you'll remember: be suspicious. Keep your back to the wall, and at the first hint of trouble, go straight for the ringleader, then sort out the minions."

"What is it, Max?" I asked. My partner, Oakhurst, had disappeared inside the surveillance van; Max and I were alone. "Have you heard something?"

The ice-blue eyes regarded me soberly for a moment. "No. But I think this is too large a quantity of cocaine. These blokes wouldn't do a deal with someone they didn't know very well indeed." I started to speak, but Max held up a hand. "Yes, all right, I know you and Oakhurst have been laying the groundwork for months. But they don't really know you, do they? All I'm saying is, they don't trust you. So don't trust them."

"I won't." I looked at my watch. "It's time. Are you ready?"

Murdoch spoke into a lapel mike, listened to the response on his earpiece. Then he gave me the thumbs-up and melted into the darkness.

I drove the two blocks to the office tower that held the Central American Trading Partners' office/warehouse complex, parked, and walked into the foyer. The building security guard, Vlade, a hulking, neckless Serb, with the sunken eyes of a man whose past deeds kept him up at nights, led the way into the company offices.

Cavendish and Mills, the two masterminds, were awaiting my arrival. Both were in their early thirties, restless and volatile – tonight more so than usual. I suspected that they had been sampling the merchandise. "Search him," said Cavendish, a tall, bookish-looking lad with round spectacles and an Adam's-apple that made him look as though he'd swallowed a golf ball. His partner, Mills, six feet tall and stocky, coldly handsome, looked on impassively, eyes glittering oddly, drumming his fingers on the desk in a mindless, obsessive tattoo.

Drazen patted me down with the dispassionate efficiency of someone special-forces-trained. But he failed to find the tiny transmitter that was broadcasting every word of our conversation to the nearby surveillance van. "He's clean," he grunted.

"Right," said Mills, in a voice fairly creaking with tension. "Let's get this over with. You have the funds?"

"As soon as I verify quality and quantity."

"This way," said Cavendish, opening a side door. He led the way into the warehouse, where a shipping container stood open. I noticed several guards, all armed, posted at strategic points. "Not taking any chances, I see," I said as a warning to Max. "You'll keep your security here until the stuff is loaded aboard my truck?"

"Naturally." We had arrived at the container. It was filled, floor to ceiling, with palletized 50-pound bags of opaque poly, labeled "Quinoa." "The super-grain of the Incas," Mills explained. "This shipment is a little more super than most."

Selecting a bag, he produced a wicked-looking flick knife and inserted it in a bag. It came out coated with fine white powder. I took out a small test kit, dropped in a dram of powder, added a reagent, and held it up to the light. "Eighty percent pure," I said. "Excellent." I went further back into the container, chose another bag at random, and gestured. "This one as well, please."

Grunting in annoyance, Mills again produced his knife. Another sample, same result. "Seen enough?" he asked.

"I think he's seen too much," said Cavendish.

"Too much?" I said lightly, unobtrusively shifting my position so my back was against one of the pallets, and all three men were in my line of sight. "Surely it's just ordinary business sense to check more than one bag."

"It would be," said Mills, "if it wasn't for the call we received an hour before you arrived. You're an informant. A grass!"

"Time to cut the grass," whispered Cavendish, producing a serrated hunting-knife. "Drazen – no guns. Use your knife."

"I like knives best," Drazen grinned, producing a long, slim commando blade that had obviously seen much hard use. "Try to die quietly, English."

I judged Drazen the most dangerous of the three. He came in low, in a crouch. I suddenly lashed out with a foot; my steel-toed boot caught him just below the left kneecap, and he staggered to the side, tears of pain springing to his eyes. As he did so, I put my shoulder into a short vicious overhand punch that caught him squarely on the bridge of the nose; I felt the crunch of breaking bone and down he went, knife clattering to the metal floor of the container.

My unexpected attack, though successful, had left my back exposed. Mills got behind me and I felt the cold sting of his knife at my throat. Desperately I caught the blade with my hand, felt a shock of pain as the keen edge bit deep. I jerked my other elbow into his solar plexus, heard the whoosh of air as the breath left his lungs. As I fought his knife-hand away from my throat, Cavendish danced close. Just as I kicked him solidly in the balls, he sank his knife deep into my belly.

I looked down at the protruding handle in horror and sank to my knees, consciousness fading fast. I was vaguely aware of a spreading coldness, a hubbub of shouted commands, the sound of running boots on concrete, a short burst of automatic-weapons fire followed by a scream of pain. The last thing I heard, before my senses left me, was Oakhurst's voice. "Dex, you damned fool, why didn't you stick to the plan! Oh, dammit, I should have gone in myself! We need an ambulance here now!" Then a roaring sound, like a tornado about to touch down, filled my ears, and I swooped sickeningly into blackness.

Murdoch had come to see me often in hospital during my long and difficult recovery. Two inches to the right and Cavendish's knife would have entered my liver, with almost certainly fatal results. Oakhurst, apparently, had grasped the handle of the knife, intending to pull it from the wound; had he succeeded, internal bleeding would have finished me before medical response could arrive. Murdoch, however, had stopped Oakhurst just in time, seizing his wrist and shoving him roughly away. This did not prevent the grizzled armed response commander from blaming himself for my injuries. "I should have been quicker, Dex," he said one night, face haggard in the harsh fluorescent lighting of the ward. ""I could feel it going pear-shaped. I should've moved sooner."

"Don't be an arse," I croaked. "You couldn't move until they did. One thing does puzzle me, though."

"You wonder who tipped them off," said Murdoch, eyes full of cold rage. "Yes, I wonder that too. I intend to get to the bottom of that, and right smartly."

He never did, though. British Telecom records plainly showed the call in question, but it originated from a phone box three blocks away. We never ascertained who had placed it.

I had my suspicions, of course. In almost any investigation, chances are that, if you can discern who has the most to gain from the crime, you'll find your perpetrator. In this case, the one person who'd made out like a bandit was Detective Inspector – later Detective Chief Inspector – George Oakhurst. However, I'd never been able to prove a damned thing.

Until now. "Right, gentlemen," I said, slipping a thumb drive into the computer's USB port. A recording of a morning news broadcast sprang to life. We watched a brief lead-in from the reporter on-scene outside Hendon nick, and then the opening frames of the Seagrave video filled the screen. I froze the image.

"Note the time/date stamp in the lower left corner of the screen. You will also note the somewhat cryptic code MPSCCD-2. That stands for Metropolitan Police Service Computer Crimes Directorate; two is the copy number – a little precaution Emma Kwan and I dreamt up before she made two copies of the original videos: one for DCI Wicks, and the other for DCI Oakhurst. The original zip drives, still in DI Abbott's and my possession, bear the time/date stamp but no copy number. Wicks' copy, as you'll find, was coded MPSCCD-1."

"All that proves is that whoever copied and sold the videos had access to Oakhurst's office," cried Hackett. "It doesn't prove Oakhurst had anything to do with it."

"True," I admitted. "But this does." And I laid O'Toole's signed statement, identifying sample four as the voice of the man who had sold him the videos, before them.

"This was sample four," said Brian, pressing "play" on his tape recorder. Oakhurst's unmistakable voice filled the cubicle.

"Not to tell you how to do your jobs," Brian rumbled, "but I suspect that if you were to check very carefully into DCI Oakhurst's financials, you'd stand a good chance of finding our missing hundred thousand pounds."

"You're saying DCI Oakhurst leaked the videos himself, and told the Sun to deposit half the money in your account, to frame you?" Hackett asked incredulously.

"Correct."

For a moment, all Hackett and Carter could do was stare at one another, stunned as steers in a slaughterhouse. Then Carter spoke. "If what you say is true," he began, "what's his motivation? Why try to destroy your mates by releasing the videos, and why try to pin it on you?"

I spoke for half an hour, laying out my suspicions about Docklands. Then Murdoch spoke, corroborating many of my hunches and opinions. "I was there," he finished. "I personally stopped DCI Oakhurst from pulling out the knife. At the time, it merely seemed a stupid and dangerously ignorant thing to do. Looking back, knowing what I know now, I think it was more than that. I think Oakhurst was trying to ensure that he wouldn't have to share credit for the success of the operation with DI Reed."

"But you can't prove it."

"I can't prove it, no" Murdoch admitted. "But that's my best professional judgement of the case."

DIs Hackett and Carter rose, glumly silent. "And the administrative order?" Murdoch asked

"Withdrawn. You're back on the job, DI Reed," Carter replied.

"For now," young snippy added defiantly. And whispering furiously to one another, the two DPS men vanished.

"Thank you, Max," I said.

"Anything for a friend, Dex. A pleasure meeting you, DI Abbott." And moving on swift, pantherlike strides, he, too, disappeared.

Brian closed his eyes. "Ah," he said with a malicious grin. "Hear that?"

"Hear what?" I asked.

"The gurgle and swoosh of a once-promising career swirling down the crapper. And the good part is, it's not yours."

"Thanks, Brian. For all your help – couldn't have done it without you."

"Think nothing of it," he said, pulling on his coat.

"Where're you off to?" I asked, pulling a legal pad from my desk.

"Just following up on my interview with Devilliers. You know, that promising lead you didn't want to know about."

"What is it? Now I want to know."

Brian grinned. "I'll ring you if it turns out there's anything to it. First I've got to ask Devilliers a few more questions, about this." He waved a sheaf of papers.

"What're those?"

"Oh, just something I dug up, with some help from someone in computer crime."

"And has he?"

"Who? Has he what?"

"Devilliers. Committed a crime."

"Not that I can prove. Still, there are some surprising aspects to this case. I'll ring you if I get any answers." And off he skived.

I hate it when Brian becomes mysterious – it usually means he's on to something particularly promising, but wants to wait to spring it on me until he's got something solid in hand. I thrust

Brian's flair for the dramatic from my mind and settled in to run through the state of the Weathersby case.

I thumbed through the forensic report on the Penhurst House crime scene. The techs had found Bernie's, Harry Barlowe's, Seagrave's and Leicesters' prints – and mine – in various places around the room. Hardly surprising, since we'd all been there the night of the murder, and that was the room in which Weathersby had transacted his business.

Interestingly, Finch-Hatton's rifle had not been wiped clean. There was a squirming mass of overlapping fingerprints on the stock, the barrels, the trigger and breech – Weathersby's, mine, Bernie's, Leicester's. All were at least partially identifiable. Others – presumably the previous owner's and his friends' – weren't in the SO4 database.

This, and the fact that neither the French doors through which the killer had gained entrance, nor the alarm box he had so expertly circumvented, had been wiped clean, suggested that the murderer had worn gloves. Still, I made a note to check with forensic regarding any unidentified prints.

The forensic report went on to say that the techs' minute examination of the garden beyond the French doors had yielded a single clue – a partial footprint in the narrow strip of flower bed bordering the five-foot-high iron-tipped brick wall that separated Montpelier Garden from the street. It was a logical spot for the killer to have gained entrance and egress – a quiet residential street, with another communal garden over the way. All forensic could tell from the print, blurred by rain and partial to begin with, was that it came from a man's shoe, size 11 or 12.

My phone rang. I was somewhat disappointed to hear Wicks' voice, rather than Oakhurst's. "Step 'round to my office, DI Reed. We've things to discuss."

I tucked my case notes and the various reports – forensic, coroner's, ballistic and investigating officers' – under my arm and strode to Wicks' fourth-floor office,

"Sit down," he said testily as I entered. "I've just heard that DCI Oakhurst has been suspended from the service, pending DPS investigation. You wouldn't know anything about that, would you, Reed?"

I caught him up on the events of earlier that afternoon. As he listened, leaning back in his chair, eyes focused on a framed commendation on the far wall, a grin of malicious pleasure tugged at the corners of his aged-lined mouth. I wondered, not for the first time, just how old Wicks really was. I knew he was a widower and childless. At that moment, I realized, abruptly, just how important the competence and integrity of the Metropolitan Police Service were to him.

Then he noticed my appraising glance, and his appreciative expression morphed into one of severe approbation. "Reed, you cretinous arsewipe! Why didn't you bring this to me?"

"If I may speak candidly, DCI Wicks?"

"Speak!"

"I was reluctant to bring the matter to your attention without proof. Once I had it, things moved too quickly to seek your advice. The DPS boys were waiting at my desk, suspension order in hand."

Wicks was aghast. "Those sheep-felching, pencil-pushers! How dare they threaten to suspend one of my detectives without speaking to me first?"

"If I'm not mistaken, sir, they had DCI Oakhurst's enthusiastic support."

"Yes." He favoured me with a sharky, yellow-toothed grin. "And now the worm has turned. But enough of that – duty before pleasure. Where are we with the Weathersby case?"

I brought him up to speed on the status of the investigation. "It's frustrating," I said at length. "We've at least four suspects with ample motive for murder, but precious little physical evidence. One of the uniformed officers did find a neighbour who happened to be awake at the time of the murder – he'd had a row with his wife and couldn't sleep. His view was partially obscured, but he did see a man hurrying away from the house a minute or so after the shot."

"Description?"

"Tall – more than a foot taller than the wall surrounding the property, which is five foot high. White male, dark overcoat, dark hair. It was too dark to make out anything else."

"Well, that's helpful," Wicks observed acidly. "Come on, DI Reed. There must be one ray of sunshine."

I considered. "DI Abbott is following up a promising lead."

"What is it?"

"Something he discovered when he interviewed Richard Devillers, the Hastewicke Gentlemen fullback and financial advisor."

"You didn't answer my question."

I shrugged apologetically. "He hasn't told me what it is, sir - didn't want to spoil the surprise, at least not until he had the evidence in hand."

Wicks whinnied in disgust. "Communication, DI Reed! I detest mysteries. Do try to keep me up to date."

"I will, sir."

"And Reed?"

"Yes, sir?"

"Don't make a habit of getting your superiors sacked."

II

I was savouring my walk home through the frosty November night, leaves crackling underfoot, thinking of Jane, when my mobile rang. "Reed," I said.

"Dex, it's me."

"Brian! Where are you?" I could tell from the cadence of his voice that he was walking somewhere, not driving.

"I left Devilliers a couple of hours ago, and I've been checking into a few odd bits and pieces. You won't believe what I've found!"

"I could use some good news," I admitted.

"How's this - I think I've solved the case! I know who killed Weathersby!"

I almost dropped the phone. "Steady on, man. It isn't Devilliers?"

"No. But you won't believe it when I tell you – it's a real shocker! Meet me at the Chandos and I'll fill you in."

I could've strangled him. "Tell me now!" I cried.

He chuckled. "All in good time, laddy."

"Brian, you bastard..." I began. Then suddenly, I could hear voices at his end. "Hey, mate, got a light?" said a youngish male voice.

"No," I heard Brian say. "Sod off, I'm on the phone."

"Sod off, is it? I think a lesson in manners is in order, me droogs."

Suddenly, biff! came the unmistakable sound of a blow, followed by an eardrum-shattering clash! as the phone fell to the pavement. From a distance, I heard Brian roar "Back off, you lot! I'm a copper!"

Another voice cried "And we don't give a shite, DCI Abbott!" Then came a veritable hailstorm of impacts – fists and boots thudding into flesh, accompanied by heart-rending cries of pain – Brian's pain. Mocking laughter drifted over the ether.

I stood rigid with shock. "Brian, where are you?" I raved.

"Good one, me droog!" I heard from afar.

"Kick him again, Georgie!"

"Go on, Alex, don't be shy – e's still got a coupla gnashers left!"

"Shit, Dim, 'is mobile's still on!" Then – crunch! And in the eerie suspiration of dead air, like a dying man's last breath, I heard my partner's silent plea for help.

22

They found him in an alley called Denmark Street, just off the Charing Cross Road, not far from Seagrave's house and only steps from his car. He was still alive – barely. At my frantic call to Central Command, every on-duty Metropolitan Police officer in London went into maximum search mode. One of their own was down, and they wouldn't rest until they found him.

It was nearly 20 minutes after our call was so abruptly severed that a uniformed officer noticed a pair of boots protruding from Denmark Street. He found Brian lying in a pool of blood, eyes open, unresponsive – but breathing. His crushed mobile lay on the pavement next to him, along with several of his teeth. An ambulance arrived within five minutes, and Brian was whisked to University Hospital. They were already operating on him when I arrived, volcanic with rage and grief.

The nurses refused me entrance to the operating theatre. As I turned away, I saw the departmental chaplain hurry in, tugging on his cassock and surplice, and my heart turned to ice. Then the door opened again, and I saw Brian's wife, Fee, and summoned all my strength.

She came to me in a staggering rush; for a moment, all we could do was cling to one another. "What happened, Dex, what happened?" she cried into my shoulder. "Who could've done this to my fine boy, my lovely boy?"

I turned her away from the priest, who was preparing to enter the operating room. "I don't know, Fee. I was on the phone with him when it happened. It sounded like kids – four or five of them. It might've been random – I just don't know." But in my heart, I knew it hadn't been a chance encounter. *And we don't give a shit, DI Abbott!*

"Dex." She dried her tears and looked at me soberly now. "He will be all right? It was just a beating. Brian's as tough as they come."

I took her hand, guided her to a couch. "Fee, his skull's fractured. They ruptured his spleen. He's bleeding inside." I fought for control. "I won't lie to you. The nurse told me Brian has a 50 percent chance of living through the night. If they can control the internal bleeding, and the pressure inside his skull, and keep him from convulsing, he has a chance. Fee, I'm so sorry. I should've been there for him. I let him down. I let you down."

"Don't be an ass!" The anger in her voice shocked me out of my self-loathing. "Brian thinks the world of you! How many times have you snatched his fat from the fire? How many times has he told me you're the best partner he's ever had?"

"Thank you, Fee. Believe me, that means a lot..." I had to pause for a moment. "He's not just my partner – he's my mate. I'm going to find out who did this to him – and why."

I felt a hand at my elbow. DCI Wicks was there. "What the hell happened, Dex?" With grave consideration, he included Fee in our conversation. "Fee, I'm so sorry. What do we know?"

"Brian called to say he thought he'd solved Weathersby's murder, but before he could tell me what he'd found, he was attacked." I relayed the conversation I'd overheard.

"Droog?" said Wicks. "Alex, Georgie and Dim? Sounds like *A Clockwork Orange* to me."

"Sir?" I asked, brain fogged by the enormity of the night's events.

"The novel by Anthony Burgess!" Wicks barked. "Made into a movie by Stanley Kubrick. So violent it was banned in the U.K. Still, it's found a cult following. I'll get the word out to the uniforms – shouldn't be too difficult to find those responsible, I shouldn't think."

Wicks pulled out his mobile, sorted through his speed-dial numbers, punched one in. "Ah, DCI Wilkinson – Wicks here. You've heard about DI Abbott? Yes, he's in surgery now – he's pretty battered. DI Reed was on the phone with him when it happened – says there were four or five of them. Called each other droogs. That's right, straight out of *A Clockwork Orange*. Ring any bells? Any gangs that fit the motif? Bowler hats, one false eyelash, that sort of thing? Well, get on it, as a special favour to me. I want these bastards in the net, and right smartly. It was one of our own, Keith." He looked at me. "What did they call each other?"

"Alex, Georgie and Dim."

He relayed the information into the phone. "That's right, Keith – top priority. Thanks, I will." He folded the phone away. "That was Wilkinson in Gang Enforcement. Says he doesn't know anyone offhand who fits the bill, but he's calling everyone in. If anyone can find them, Keith can."

"Thank you, DCI Wicks. Why would anyone... did this have anything to do with the case you've been working?"

"I don't know, Fee," I said truthfully. "But I'm going to find out."

A nurse came then, with some papers for Fee to sign, and I took the opportunity to ring Jane. I got my answering machine. "Jane – if you're there, pick up – it's me."

A brief pause, and I heard her voice. She sounded deliciously sleepy. "Hullo, Dex. Is everything all right? You're so late – I've been worried."

"It's my partner, Brian – he's been attacked. I'm at University Hospital now." I looked around, to make sure Fee wasn't within earshot. "He's not expected to live. Listen, Jane. I don't know what happened yet. But I don't know when I'll be home, and in the meantime, I don't think you should stay there alone. I'd rather you went to your house tonight."

"Dex! You're not in danger?"

"No. But I'd rather err on the side of caution until we get to the bottom of this. You'll do as I ask?"

"Of course, darling. But Dex?"

"Yes?"

"You will be careful?"

"As always." Then the great leap into uncharted territory. "I love you, Jane."

A pause. "I love you, Dex."

Good – that was settled, then. "I'll ring you when I get in," I said.

I rang off and looked at my watch. To my surprise, two hours had passed since I had arrived at the hospital. I went to sit next to Fee, wordlessly took her hand.

A doctor in bloodstained scrubs found us an hour and a half later. "Mrs. Abbott?" he said gently.

"Yes?" said Fee, summoning all her strength. I could feel her trembling, and pulled her close.

"I'm Dr. Sanjee. Your husband's a strong man. A weaker man would have died from the injuries he sustained. But I think he'll live."

"Oh, thank God!" cried Fee, burying her face in my shoulder, and gave way to the mercy of tears.

"He has a lot to live for," I observed.

"Ah. You're DI Reed?" I nodded. "They told me you were here. I'll be honest with you – it was touch and go for awhile. He's lost a lot of blood. His spleen is ruptured, he has four broken ribs, a broken hand, radius and ulna, multiple skull fractures and intercranial swelling. That's what has me worried at the moment – if we can bring the pressure down, and keep him from convulsing, he should be OK. Eventually."

"I desperately need to ask him some questions," I said. "How long before he's conscious?"

Dr. Sanjee regarded me sadly. "He may not regain consciousness."

"What? You just said..."

"I said that if his intercranial pressure comes down, he should be OK, but that's going to take time. How much time, it's impossible to say yet. He may regain function. Some function. Eventually. But he's severely concussed. He's in a coma, DI Reed, and likely will be, for at least a week. You, and Mrs. Abbott, must prepare yourself for the fact that, even if he does recover, he'll never be the same. He won't be able to return to work. He's finished as a policeman."

I ran a weary hand over my face. Fee looked up from my shoulder, soaked with her tears, and searched my face with the utmost compassion. "I'm so sorry, Dex," she said.

"Don't be," I replied, blinking back tears of my own. "Now he can open that restaurant of his."

Fee managed a halting laugh. "Yes. And we'll still expect you every Monday. But now it's going to cost you."

II

Fee and I sat with him until dawn, watching the regular, soothing motion of his ventilator, listening to the encouraging beep! of the heart monitor. His great friendly face was so battered – lips swollen, eyes puffy and blackened, head bandaged, a sutured gash stretching halfway across the forehead that contained the information I so desperately needed.

"You should go home," I said at length. "Talk to the girls, get some sleep."

"You should, too," she yawned. "It's been a long night. Go home to whomever it was you called."

Fee was observant – I'll give her that. She had fixed me up with half a dozen friends over the years, and had never given up on her dream of someday spoiling my offspring. She considered me a catch, for some reason, and she looked at me knowingly now.

"What?" I asked. "She's just a friend."

Fee snorted – giddy from relief and lack of sleep. The nurse had just told us that Brian was doing exceptionally well, considering the severity of his injuries. "Have you shagged her?" she asked.

"None of your business! I don't shag and tell! Now if you'll excuse me, I have to get to the office."

"The office! Dex, you've been up all night!"

"I'll stop at home for a shower and a change of clothes. But there're things to do, Fee."

"Yes." She touched my face gently. "You'll find who did this, Dex?"

Just for a moment, my fury flickered anew. "Oh, yes. And when I do, they're going to be sorry they ever drew breath."

III

Two hours later, much refreshed after a stop at home, I pushed through the revolving doors of Devilliers' firm, Ardenwood Financial Planners, on Bishopsgate Street near the Bank of England. An irreproachably dignified woman of mature years showed me through to his office. "Dex!" Devilliers cried, rising to greet me from behind a solid mahogany desk that looked as though it had been purchased at some former prime minister's yard sale. The view out his windows was of the Tower of London and the Thames; obviously the financial trade winds had blown profitably for Dick in recent years. "I thought I might see you this morning. The attack on your partner's been all over the news! D'you know what happened yet?"

"No," I said, "we don't. It might've just been kids. But it may also be connected to John's murder. What did you and Brian talk about, yesterday?"

"You don't know?"

I shook my head. "No. I was on my way to meet him when he was attacked. He just said he'd seen you, that he was looking into a secondary line of inquiry, something that might relate back to the Weathersby investigation. But he did say that whatever you'd told him might be vital to solving the case. What, specifically, did you discuss?"

Devilliers had been, as I have had previous occasion to mention, Charlie Chalmers' closest mate on the Hastewicke Gentlemen. I had always suspected him of being a little jealous of my own close rapport with Charlie, and my status, to a certain extent, as Charlie's protegé in the forward pack. Now Devilliers regarded me shrewdly. "How unfortunate for you, Dex."

"Unfortunate in what sense?" I asked.

"Because whatever vital inferences DI Abbott may have gathered from our conversation, he didn't confide them to me. I understand he's in a coma?"

"He is," I said shortly. "I need your help."

"I don't know how much help I can be," Devilliers replied. "He was all over the map. Asked me about Seagrave, about Leicester, about Harry Barlowe, and about Bernie. He wanted to know about some of the other blokes on the team as well – George Waters, Gleeson, Jester Atkinson. I handle all of their financials."

"What was the context of the discussion?"

Devilliers sighed heavily. "He wanted to know whether I'd seen or heard anything to indicate that Weathersby had black-mailed anyone else in the years since Charlie."

"And?" It came out sharper than I'd intended; it had been a long and sleepless night.

"Despite my responsibility to protect my clients' confidence, I told him the truth – in the last 10 years, there have been two unusually large and unscheduled payouts from the Hastewicke funds I manage. One for Gleeson, and one for Atkinson. I don't know what they were for – I didn't ask."

"And that's all you discussed? There was nothing else that might've had a bearing on the Weathersby case?"

"No," he replied, regarding me with what seemed to be faint amusement. "You've never invested with me, Dex – I wonder why. I've done very well for our teammates over the years."

"Precious little to invest, compared to the financial heavy-weights on the Hastewicke Gentlemen," I replied.

"Ah," he said, nodding as if I'd just confirmed a long-standing suspicion. "So that's what all this is about."

"All what's about?"

"Your determination to destroy the club," he said with sudden and unexpected bile. "The leaking of the blackmail videos. Your arrest of Bernie. Your relentless prying into the private affairs of everyone on the team."

I managed to master my emotions before speaking. "That does seem spectacularly unfair under the circumstances, Dick. And it's a load of bollocks. Criminal investigations – especially murder inquiries – do require a certain amount of 'relentless prying!' I didn't leak the videos – as a matter of fact, only yesterday I helped find the man who did – he's now facing a criminal investigation. How can you think that, Dick? The last thing I want to do is to destroy the club – the Hastewicke Gentlemen have been one of the greatest sources of pleasure in my life! I've done everything I can to protect the club since this investigation began, to such an extent that I've been threatened with disciplinary action for withholding evidence! And I arrested Bernie because I was ordered to do so – not because I believe he's guilty!"

Devilliers regarded me through slitted eyes. "If you say so, Dex."

"I damned well do say so! But I can't change the facts! And the fact of the matter is, John Weathersby is dead! At least four of our teammates – and now, from what you've just told me, possibly more – had an excellent reason to kill him. My partner, whom I greatly esteem, has been brutally assaulted and may not live, perhaps because he was close to solving this case! Those are facts, Richard! If you think I'm manipulating this situation because I wasn't quite as well-born as the rest of you, you don't know me as well as you think you do!"

I was suddenly very tired. I rose to go. "I'm sorry," I said in a somewhat more moderate tone. "I shouldn't have bellowed at you. It's been a very long and trying night. Please call me if you think of anything else that might be relevant to the attack on DI Abbott, or to the Weathersby case."

"I will, Dex." He shook my hand. "I shouldn't've said what I said, either."

I nodded, and knew the truth I had feared since this case began: that whatever the outcome, my many happy days as a Hastewicke Gentleman were now at an end. I made my way past Devilliers' dignified assistant, and envied her her serenity.

I was strolling back to the car, not really focused on any one particular clue, letting my subconscious sort through the countless details of the Weathersby investigation and hold them up for fit against the attack on Brian, when suddenly it hit me.

Weathersby's alarm system. I had long puzzled over this detail, because so far as I knew, none of our four principal suspects had any aptitude for electronics. But there was one Hastewicke Gentleman who did – who was, in fact, a very successful electronics entrepreneur. Brian had asked Devilliers about him only yesterday: Jester Atkinson.

23

In the early days of the Hastewicke Gentlemen, our unquestioned star player was flanker Dennis Hooper. He was 6'3", 18 stone, with calves as large as my thighs and thighs as thick as my torso. He was a churning, low-to-the-ground monstrosity with ball in hand, and an aggressive, ball-ripping tackler as well. A gentle man off the pitch, when he stepped between the lines, boots on, he became a remorseless, conscienceless maniac, and played the game of rugby with a ferocious disregard for his own – or anyone else's – health. He averaged nearly two tries a game; I once saw him score seven in a match.

We were playing in the final of the 1990 Aspen Rugby Fest against the Chicago Rugby Club when, early in the first half, Hooper, planting his foot to sidestep someone, caught a cleat on a sunken sprinkler-head. With a sickening pop! the ligaments in his right knee snapped like rubber bands. He was carried from the pitch in agony and whisked to hospital. We didn't know it at the time, but Dennis Hooper would never play rugby again.

Though rugby is a brutal game, it is played exclusively on natural grass, and such catastrophic injuries are surprisingly rare. The loss of our most dynamic player threw us into a funk; by early in the second half, we found ourselves down 30-12.

During an injury stoppage, Charlie Chalmers called the forwards into a huddle. "You're all playing like castrated sheep!" he roared. "Quit moping! It's time to elevate your own game! You, John, and you, Harry, and you, Vince! And especially you, Dex! It's time to take personal responsibility – we didn't come 4,000 miles to lose!"

On the very next play, a line-out, Charlie called his own number, skied high in the air to win the ball, then burst through the Chicago line like a rhinoceros with balls aflame. Weathersby and I thundered at Charlie's heels as he bowled over three would-be tacklers, then, at the last instant, fed me with a perfect pass. I drew in the last two Chicago tacklers before slipping the ball to Weathersby, who carried a Chicago player on his back as he touched down the try between the posts.

As we trotted back to halfway to receive the ensuing kick-off, Charlie patted me affectionately on the head. "Always remember, Dex," he told me, ever the teacher. "Whenever things look darkest, that's when your own flame has to burn the brightest."

II

I went straight to Wicks' office. "Come!" he bellowed in response to my knock. "Ah, Reed – how's Brian?"

"No change, which at this point qualifies as good news. His intercranial pressure's still dangerously high. If it doesn't begin to recede soon, they might have to trepan him."

Wicks looked shocked. "Cut a hole in his skull? I thought that went out with the Incas!"

"Apparently it can be quite effective in cases like this, sir. In any event, he's resting as comfortably as possible, for a man with 17 broken bones."

`"Seventeen." DCI Wicks' ancient eyes gleamed with vindictive purpose. "Time to start putting some stick about on that score, I think. Any word from the canvassers, or forensic?"

I held up a pair of files. "Nothing from canvass. Forensic have turned up one or two interesting items from the crime scene. But sir, there's something else, on the Weathersby case. It may be related to the assault on DI Abbott." Quickly and succinctly, I filled him in on my interview with Devilliers.

"Interesting," said Wicks. "So Oakhurst may have been on to something after all – perhaps Weathersby did blackmail some of your other teammates. Ah, well," he said acidly. "Every so often, even a blind sow gets porked." He rose. "Let's talk to the team."

A few minutes later, we stood before the assembled throng in the ready room. "Right," said Wicks. "What's the latest on DI Abbott?"

DI Charleton stood. "We've found no witnesses, sir," she said uncomfortably. "The attack took place in a windowless alleyway, in a business district after business hours. No residences within earshot – whoever attacked DI Abbott chose their ground well. We've put out a Crimestoppers bulletin, asking anyone with information to phone in, but so far, no promising leads."

"Forensic?" Wicks asked.

DI Taylor came forward. "It was a pretty grotty alleyway. But we did find this." He held up a tiny, clear evidence envelope. "A single false eyelash, which would tend to corroborate the *Clockwork Orange* hypothesis. We were able to lift some skin cells and a single human eyelash. No matches so far with our DNA database, but these things take time." He held up another, larger bag, this one containing a bloodied brick. "We also found this. Apparently, it was used to inflict many of DI Abbott's more traumatic injuries."

"Prints?" I asked hopefully.

"Ever try to lift prints from a brick, Dex? Unfortunately, the surface is too rough and porous to lift a clean image."

"Keep on the DNA people, Tom. DIs Morton and Rivers, I want you to liaise with DCI Wilkinson over in Gang Enforcement – see if he's had any luck with the *Clockwork Orange* angle, and give him any help he needs. I want you to find those sadistic bastards and bring them to me. Now, leaving Brian's assault for a moment, DI Reed has some new information on the Weathersby case."

I filled them in on Atkinson – the possibility that he was a previous blackmail victim, that he had the necessary electronics knowledge to disable the alarm, and about his somewhat mercurial temperament.

"Right," said Wicks. "Here's what we'll do. DIs Burnett and Goodspeed, go and see Sir Chester Atkinson. Find out whether he's got an alibi for the night of the murder, for starters, and ask him politely whether he was being blackmailed back in the late '90s. Find out where he lives, what time he left the party the night Weathersby was killed, what time he arrived home, whether anyone can verify that, and whether or not he could've returned to Penhurst House in time to kill Weathersby. That will do to be getting on with."

Chairs scraped, and the various members of the team went about their duties. I took a deep breath. "DCI Wicks," I said. "Lord Delvemere. I don't think he's our boy. We did arrest him, at DCI Oakhurst's insistence, but that was mainly to punish me. Lord Delvemere didn't kill Weathersby. I'd like to release him"

"Why do you say that?" Wicks' parrot eyes regarded me keenly.

I ticked off the points on my fingers. "One, I spent some time with him the night of the murder, and he was too drunk to cope with the logistical difficulties – getting over the fence, disabling the alarm, breaking into the study, loading and firing the rifle with such a high degree of accuracy. Two, he had nothing to gain – he'd already paid Weathersby, and he knew that if Weathersby died, the videos would be sent out anyway. That only leaves revenge for a motive. I've known Delvemere for three decades, drunk and sober. In my opinion, he isn't capable of murder."

"And what if you're wrong?"

"We can confiscate his passport, make him post bail. But I'm not wrong about this."

"All right, DI Reed. I tend to agree, but I'll need to clear his release with the powers that be. I'll let you know. In the meantime, if Delvemere didn't kill Weathersby, who the hell did?"

I sighed. "I don't know – yet. But we're close, sir – the answer is there. But so far, it's just out of reach."

III

Just before he was attacked, Brian had waved a sheaf of papers at me, papers that had some relevance to his upcoming interview with Devilliers, which he had assembled with the help of someone in Computer Crime. I rang Emma Kwan.

"I'm sorry, Dex – I don't know what that was all about," she told me. "I was out of the office on Tuesday. But I'll see if I can find out who Brian was working with."

"Do, please," I said. "I need to know what was on that printout. It's important."

"I'll talk to everyone here. How're you holding up, Dex?"

It was the first time anyone had asked. I was momentarily taken aback. "All right," I replied. "Not so well, to be honest, Em. Equal parts homicidal rage and burning guilt that I wasn't there to help him. I want to find the bastards who did this to

Brian, and Weathersby's killer. I have a sick suspicion the two are connected."

"I'll ring you as soon as I know anything. And, ah, Dex." There was an awkward pause.

"What is it, Em?"

"I was wondering – d'you... would you like to have dinner with me sometime?"

For a moment, I didn't know what to say. The delectable Emma Kwan, as beautiful as she was intelligent. How often had I thought of asking her the same question? But then I thought of Jane. "Em, you've made my day. Can I take a rain check? I'm going to be working late for the foreseeable future."

"Of course, Dex. When you come up for air, we'll talk."

IV

According to the call log for Bob Leicester's mobile, he had called Ian St. Cloud, his chief of security, at 2:07 a.m. on the night of Weathersby's murder. I had met St. Cloud on several occasions. He was ex-SAS, an uncanny dead ringer for Kevin Costner, highly competent in all of the many arcane skills that become second nature to those special forces trained. Suffice to say that, despite the myriad of security challenges associated with a network of 23 facilities serving some of the most troubled youth in Britain, the Magwitch Project had never had a serious problem – no murders, no rapes, no violent assaults. It was a testament to Ian St. Cloud's skill as a problem-solver.

That competence, presumably, explained why Leicester had woken St. Cloud from a sound sleep on the night of Weathersby's murder. I had perused St. Cloud's file in preparation for my interview with him; in addition to top-of-the-line general security expertise, his skill set included clandestine insertion and extraction, computer infiltration, electronic wiretap and surveillance, and all sorts of deadly weapons training. No wonder Bob found him useful.

I found St. Cloud at his desk at the Magwitch Project's offices in Clerkenwell Street. I had called ahead; he waved me to a seat as he coped, via phone, with the latest crisis in the Leicester empire. "No. I've reviewed the case file, and we need to move him! He needs to be as far from her as possible! That's right, Edinburgh! No, don't argue with him – just tell him that's how it's going to be! Right! Ta."

St. Cloud rang off and turned his attention to me. He was handsome, fit, with a chin that might have been carved by Michelangelo and surprisingly warm golden-brown eyes. "Dex!" he said, leaning across his desk to shake hands. "How can I help?"

"Actually, I'd hoped that Lord Palmerston might've had a word with you," I said.

"He did," St. Cloud replied. "He said I was to answer your questions with brutal honesty."

"He called you the night of 11 October," I said. "Late. What did he say?"

"He said he was being blackmailed," St. Cloud replied without hesitation. "Explained the circumstances. Asked me about the probability of success for a surgical strike – go in quietly, take the computer that held the videos, install a few listening devices, get out again, Bob's your uncle. As a follow-up, we would monitor Weathersby's activities – make sure that if he tried to retaliate, we would be in a position to intercept anything he might send out."

"And did you?" I asked. "Go to Weathersby's, and steal the laptop?"

"No," St. Cloud replied. "The operation was set for October 12. There was no way to assemble the team and equipment before then. But by then, Weathersby was already dead."

"And you, and your staff, had nothing to do with that?"

"No." St. Cloud regarded me levelly. "I was home that night, as my wife can attest. Bob's phone call woke her up, and she didn't get back to sleep for a couple of hours. I didn't kill him, Dex, much as he may have deserved it. And as my phone records will show, I didn't call anyone else after Leicester called me."

"Where do you live?" I asked.

"Portland Street, Southwark, near Burgess Park."

Frustratingly far away from Notting Hill and Blenheim Crescent. Par for the course in this case, I reckoned. "Thank you, Ian," I said, rising wearily to my feet. I was suddenly very tired. "I'll call you if there's anything else." But for now I could think of nothing. This case had more dead ends than a pub ashtray.

V

It was late afternoon when DIs Burnett and Goodspeed returned to the squad room. "We saw Atkinson," said Goodspeed, a fit, 40-something detective who looked 10 years younger. "His alibi wasn't that convincing, to be honest."

"What did he say?" I asked.

DI Goodspeed consulted his notebook. "He said he left Weathersby's party about 1:30, then went in search of adventure. He found it, apparently, at a club called Obsessions in Chelsea. Said he met two young women there and managed to talk them back to his flat, which is on the Fulham Road in South Ken. He didn't know their names, and he's never seen them since."

"Sounds like Jester," I said, scrubbing a hand over my face. "What about the blackmail?"

"He was surprisingly forthcoming about that," said DI Burnett, blond and moustached, with a bodybuilder's discomfort in shirt, tie and jacket. "Said Weathersby put the bite on him back in '95. Atkinson was boffing the wife of one of his most important clients, and apparently she had influenced her husband to steer a fair amount of business Atkinson's way. Somehow, Weathersby got it on video. Atkinson paid him £100,000 to hush it up."

"Did he know about the most recent round of blackmails? Seagrave, Lord Delvemere, Lord Palmerston, Harry Barlowe?"

"He said no," DI Burnett replied. "Not surprising, really, since Weathersby told them all he'd ruin their lives if anyone else from the club found out."

"Quite," I said, thinking hard. "Check with the taxi companies – find out if there was a pickup anywhere near Atkinson's house between 1:30 and 2:30 the night of the murder. More important, see if there was a drop-off near Weathersby's house between 2:30 and 3. DI Abbott checked on pickups at or near the four main suspects' houses late that night, but I don't think he asked about drop-offs. Let me know what you find."

"Will do, Dex."

For a few minutes, I just sat, thinking hard. The more I thought about it, the more I suspected that Devilliers might not have been entirely candid with me. There had been a lot left unsaid – items Brian might have discussed with him during their interview but that, with Brian in a coma, I had no way of knowing, and that Devilliers had not volunteered.

I wished, not for the first time, that Brian's memory was more like mine, so that he took a few more notes. His notebook, found in the breast pocket of his jacket the night he was attacked, was essentially a barren, featureless desert enlivened by a few cryptic scrawls. "Delvmr yes, Seagrv probably, Lester doubtful, Barlowe no" probably had to do with driving distance from their houses to the crime scene, and the relative probability that each suspect could make it home, then return to Penhurst House, within the allotted time-frame. But what the hell did "CC to Devilliers' office?" mean? What message or document was being sent to Devilliers, and by whom? There was simply no way to know without talking to Brian.

The normal rules of investigation just didn't apply to this case. None of the four suspects stood to gain more than the others from Weathersby's death. True, Seagrave and Leicester hadn't paid the blackmail money, and so it could be argued that they had more at stake than Bernie or Harry Barlowe. But according to Devilliers, making the required payment would not have imposed significant financial hardship on Seagrave, and it certainly wouldn't have on Leicester. Indeed, all four blackmail victims had substantially more to lose than to gain, financially and in terms of personal reputation, by Weathersby's death. Those who did stand to gain financially – his ex-wife Tess and his children – had alibis for the time Weathersby was killed.

I became aware that my subconscious had at last, ever so quietly, begun to make its opinion known. Tempting though it was to assume that Leicester, Seagrave, Barlowe and Bernie Plantagenet had the most potent reasons to want Weathersby dead, my investigatory instinct was now pointing me in another direction: toward a past blackmail victim who had somehow gotten wind of Weathersby's recent activities, and decided to put a decisive end to them in order to spare his teammates.

Before I left his office, Devilliers had provided me with two documents: single-page account summaries from some time in the past. I looked at them now. In November 2005, in the midst of an unbroken string of regular retirement contributions, Atkinson's account showed a one-time payout of £100,000. He had already admitted being blackmailed by Weathersby. Kevin Gleeson's account showed a similar payout in June 2008.

I rang Gleeson on his mobile and arranged to meet him at the Lamb in Conduit Street, near his office. Kevin was a real estate developer; since the early '90s, he was responsible for the conversion of many of waterfront London's most disreputable warehouses into upscale lofts. I was waiting when he hove into view, looking prosperous and buttoned-down. He went to the bar for a pint, then joined me in my booth.

"Dex!" he said warily. "To what do I owe this honour?"

"It's the Weathersby case, I'm afraid. I need to ask you a few questions."

He nodded. "Ask away."

I consulted my notebook. "In June of 2008 you withdrew £100,000 from your account with Devilliers. May I ask why?"

Just for a moment, the voluble Gleeson looked flustered. "You may," he said slowly. "Dex, you have to understand. That was a crazy time in my life. I was going through... personal difficulties. To be frank, I was in a spot of trouble – one of my female employees made a sexual harassment claim. The money was to make that go away."

"Were you being blackmailed? By Weathersby?"

Kevin looked decidedly uncomfortable. "I think I'd better decline to answer that, until I consult my solicitor."

"Fair enough," I said. "But I will need to know, one way or another."

"Was there anything else?" he asked.

"There was one other thing," I replied, looking him in the eye. "When did you become aware that Weathersby was blackmailing Bernie, Leicester and the others?"

"Saw it on the telly, didn't I? Same as everybody else!"

"None of them talked to you about it? There were no whispers before Weathersby was killed, before the story broke in the press?"

"I had... an inkling. From Seagrave. I'm pretty close to him, as you know, Dex. I knew he was worried about somethin'. I asked him what it was."

"And what did he say?"

"He said it was somethin' that happened in Vegas – he was worried Catherine was going to find out. I tried to buck him up – the sacred rugby oath and all that. But he was worried, all the same."

"The subject of blackmail never arose?"

"Not in so many words. Why d'you want to know, Dex?"

"Because Weathersby's murderer may have been a former victim, someone who wanted to silence him before he could harm his teammates."

"Dex!" Gleeson turned paper-white. "You can't think..."

"I'm not thinking at this point, Kev, and I'm not accusing you of anything. I'm just assembling facts. Have you spoken to Devilliers in the last few days?"

"I did ring him... on the Wednesday, I think." The very day Brian had been attacked.

"What did you discuss?"

"Financial stuff – I want to sell the business and retire next year. There's a lot to talk about."

"You didn't discuss the Weathersby investigation, or DI Abbott's appointment with Devilliers?"

"We might've discussed Weathersby, and he might've mentioned that your partner was coming to see him. It isn't every day one of your teammates is murdered, for Christ's sake!"

"No. It isn't. One last question – you live in Mayfair?"

"You know I do, Dex. Hays Mews, just off Berkeley Square."

"The night of the Chalmers memorial. You went straight home afterwards?"

"And slept like a baby. Why?"

"Can anyone verify that?"

"I'm afraid not." Gleeson looked very uncomfortable now. "You know I live alone, Dex. Why, is it important?"

"Probably not." I sighed wearily. "At this point, it's just par for the course."

24

On Saturday week, the Hastewicke Gentlemen had agreed to play a match against the London Harlequin Gentlemen. Despite our years of close association, this entailed a certain amount of preparation; we had accordingly scheduled training sessions on the Tuesday and Thursday before the match.

Normally I would've been one of the first players to arrive at the training-ground. But the tone of my recent conversations with Devilliers, Seagrave, Gleeson and the others had given me cause to wonder whether I was still *persona grata* with the Hastewicke Gentlemen.

Then there was the blowback from the blackmail video leak. Since their various misdeeds had come to light, Seagrave, Bernie and Harry Barlowe were all facing messy, embarrassing and expensive divorces. Bernie, of course, was still behind bars.

Seagrave's firm were taking an extremely dim view of the adverse publicity they had received as a result of his sudden notoriety, and I'd heard whispers he was being pressured to accept early retirement.

Leicester's was the juiciest case of all, naturally; the press were still running and re-running snippets from his video more than a week after it had first hit the airwaves, and I understood that the unexpurgated "director's cut" was selling briskly via the Internet. The Magwitch Project's board of directors had issued a statement saying that Bob would be relinquishing any active role (carefully avoiding the phrase "hands-on involvement") in the day-to-day operation of the centres, pending the outcome of the investigation into the ages of the girls involved.

I had good news for him there, at least – the Las Vegas PD had identified the two prozzies from the tape and had faxed me their previous. Despite their youthful appearance, both girls were safely over the age of consent, so at least there would be no statutory rape charges to contend with.

After a lengthy internal debate, I came to the depressing conclusion that the Hastewicke Gentlemen were my social life, with the exception of Brian, Fee and Jane, of course. Besides, some fresh air and a good, hard run would do me good. It could be that I wouldn't be made welcome. It could even be that, given the recent misfortunes that had befallen the club, the Hastewicke Gentlemen no longer existed – since no one had bothered to ring me, I had no way of knowing. Fair enough – I'd rather know how things stood sooner, rather than later. And so as I had a thousand times before, I packed my rugby boots, socks, shorts and a practice jersey into a kit-bag.

Jane looked up from her book as I crossed the sitting-room. "You've decided to go?" she asked. "Are you sure that's wise?"

I grinned ruefully. "No. But I could do with a good sweat – feel a bit stale. Anyway, it would be cowardly not to show up. If I don't, they'll just say nasty things about me behind my back."

"What about the Service? Won't they frown on you fraternizing with your suspects?"

"Probably. But I certainly won't be discussing the case with anyone. Anyway, given the state of things, I might be the only one who shows up for training. I just need to find out where things stand – the club's been too much a part of my life for too long to just quit." I kissed her. "In any event, I'll be home early – I'd rather spend time with you."

I was a bit late in arriving at the training-ground; the lights were on and the boys were warming up with a game of touch. It was a cold, dampish evening, with clouds of icy breath ringing everyone's heads and steam beginning to rise from those who had broken a sweat.

After stepping into my kit, I trotted onto the pitch and took up station to the outside of Roger Seagrave. Vince Maitland took the kickoff and raced upfield with his usual élan; he sidestepped Barlowe and passed to Seagrave on the burst. I kept up with him without difficulty, loping along and feeling the old muscles, joints and sinews begin to oil up nicely. Devilliers, on the other side, came up to tackle Seagrave. "With you!" I called. But when

Seagrave saw it was me, the expected pass, which would've led to an easy score, never came. Instead, Seagrave turned the ball back inside to Atkinson, who was immediately touched.

This went on for some time – in 15 minutes of touch rugby, I never once received the ball. The only one who spoke to me was Barlowe, who came to run next to me as the team took a jog around the pitch. "Dex, I wanted to apologize for my tirade the other day, after the videos hit the press. I was... upset. But I shouldn't've taken it out on you."

"No apologies necessary," I replied. "Of course you were upset. You heard we got the bastard who leaked them, that he's lost his job and is facing a criminal inquiry?"

Harry nodded. "Yes. I'm glad you got him. Unfortunately, it came a bit late for me – the horse had already left the barn. Sarah's taken the boys to live with her sister. I heard from her solicitor yesterday."

"Harry, I can't tell you how sorry I am. You must believe me – I did everything I could to keep the videos secret. But in a way it was my fault – Oakhurst, my supervisor, leaked them to get at me. Wanted me out of the Service. I'm sorry, Harry – there's just no accounting for human malice."

"No. And speaking of that..." Harry looked decidedly uncomfortable as we jogged along through the foggy half-darkness. "I overheard some of the boys before training began. There's some talk of... well, of turfing you out. There's no guarantee the Hastewicke Gentlemen will even continue to exist, after recent events. But some of our more influential members seem inclined to blame you for the club's misfortunes. I don't, and I wanted you to know that. As for my own problems, I've no one to blame but myself."

"Thanks, Harry. And I'm truly sorry about Sarah. How's it going with the booze?"

"No problem there. Haven't touched a drop since Vegas."

The lads had pulled up from their jog, and had gathered under one of the lights to stretch – at our time of life, stretching before exertion had become as necessary as breathing. Leicester wasn't present tonight, I saw; nor, obviously, was Bernie. I noticed Seagrave, Gleeson, Devilliers and Vince Maitland standing in a knot to one side, looking my way and engaged in animated discussion. There seemed to be a definite lack of consensus; Vince looked decidedly annoyed, and kept shaking his head mulishly.

After a few moments, Seagrave approached. "Can I have a word, Dex?" he asked.

Wordlessly I arose from my convoluted position and followed him to join the others.

"We've been talking things over," he said uneasily, "and as newly-appointed skipper, I've been asked to speak to you on behalf of the other selectors. We've agreed..."

"*I* haven't!" Vince growled, arms folded, glaring at the other three.

"...that it would be in the best interests of the team if you were to resign from the Hastewicke Gentlemen, effective immediately."

I'd known this was coming; still, it was a nasty shock. I'd thought of little else on the tube over, yet still felt unprepared and unsure what I wanted to say. Vince saved me the trouble. "The best interests of the team!" he snorted. "What a load of bollocks! It's you lot who've cocked up your own lives, and now you want to blame Dex! Dex is the heart and soul of the forward pack! If he goes, I go!"

The rest of the club had gathered 'round, drawn irresistibly by our rising voices and unmistakable postures of belligerence. "What's all this?" Harry Barlowe asked, shouldering forward. "Are you turfing Dex out?"

"He's betrayed the club!" said Devilliers. "It's his fault the videos were leaked!"

Barlowe regarded him balefully. "*His* fault? Dex was doing his job – collecting evidence to find out who murdered one of our teammates. It wasn't Dex on those videos, it was us!" He glared at Seagrave. "I won't punish Dex for my own stupidity. I'll resign my own membership first."

For a moment, there was pandemonium, as a dozen men shouted to make themselves heard – some defending me, others calling for my head. With profound sadness, I saw that the majestic clipper ship that was the Hastewicke Gentlemen, that had sailed so often and so joyfully around the world and back again, had struck a reef and was foundering. I held up a hand for silence.

"Ever since this investigation began, I was afraid it would come to this," I said, and my teammates stopped braying at one another to listen. "And I'm sorry. More sorry than you'll ever know. The best times of my life have been had with you lot – we've grown up together, won together, lost together, seen the world together, been through tough times together, and done a lot of stupid things together. I'm sorry that there was one among us who saw that as a commercial opportunity, rather than as a sacred trust and bond between mates. John Weathersby's the real reason we've reached this moment as a club. But reached it we have. So rather than prolonging the agony, I'll just say, thanks for your friendship, and for all the good times. I resign my membership in the Hastewicke Gentlemen." And without another word, I gathered up my kit, and left them bellowing at one another in the little pool of light.

II

"I'm so sorry, Dex," said Jane later, as we lay abed. "I tried to warn you. It's so much easier to blame you for the club's problems than it is for them to take responsibility themselves."

"I know. I've felt this coming for weeks now. Still, I had to try. And now I know."

After we'd turned out the light, I lay there for awhile, watching a pane of moonlight move almost imperceptibly across the ceiling, head cradled on a forearm, enjoying Jane's warmth and deep, contented breathing in the darkness next to me. I knew that, in the eyes of my teammates, and the world, the fact that she was here with me, while Bernie was in jail, was every bit as reprehensible as anything my teammates had ever done. Perhaps worse.

But the fact was, I didn't care. I loved Jane, loved her with all the intensity it was possible for a middle-aged man, starved of meaningful affection his entire adult life, to feel. Yes, I'd betrayed Bernie, and Bernie was my friend. But Bernie had betrayed Jane first, and wasn't even sure whether or not he wanted to be with her anymore. Too, she was a grown woman, and had the right to decide for herself whether she wanted to be with Bernie, or with me. For tonight, at least, she had chosen me, and for that I was profoundly grateful.

I hadn't noticed falling asleep. But when the phone rang, what seemed only an instant after my last, contented thought, the pane of moonlight had moved halfway across the ceiling. I groped and found the receiver. "Reed," I muttered.

"Dex – it's Fee." I sat up in bed at the panic in her voice. "Can you... it's Brian. He's convulsing. They don't think he's going to..."

"On my way," I said, reaching for the bedside lamp.

III

I hurtled onto the ward just in time to see Dr. Sanjee disappearing into the operating theatre. An outraged-looking nurse blocked my path. "You can't go in there. It's..." I flashed my warrant card and shouldered through the double doors.

Dr. Sanjee shot me a glare from the sink where he was washing up as the nurse, red-faced in fury, seized my arm. "I *said*, you're not allowed..."

"It's all right, Nurse Thompson," said Dr. Sanjee. "You can stay, DI Reed, but on my sufferance only. Give him a mask and gown. Stand over there, DI Reed – out of the way, and don't distract me."

A violent crash drew my attention to the gurney in the centre of the operating theatre. In the spectral glare of the halogen umbrella lights, Brian arched his back, veins bulging from his neck and forehead, eyes closed, thrashing from side to side like a gaffed marlin. One of his great arms had ripped free from its restraint and knocked over an IV trolley, A smallish doctor struggled to control Brian's arm, only to be sent staggering backward. "DI Reed, could you do something about that?" Dr. Sanjee asked calmly.

It took all my weight and strength to return Brian's arm to his side, where an orderly with a Sex Pistols tattoo deftly battened it down with buckled leather straps. "Right," Dr. Sanjee breathed, appearing at my side. He took in the surrounding monitors at a glance. "Atavan, four CCs. A sedative and amnesiant," he said for my benefit. "He won't remember a thing about tonight's events. It also acts as an anti-convulsant. Now lidocaine, five CCs, to bring the intercranial pressure down." He accepted a syringe from the nurse, injected it into the IV port. Brian's seizures became almost imperceptibly less violent. I looked upward at the operating theatre's windows, to behold Fee's pale, death-shocked face, gave her a reassuring thumbs-up.

"Time for the succyncholine – 10 CCs, I think," said Dr. Sanjee. He flicked me a glance, as calm and in control as Churchill during the Blitz. A nurse wiped the sweat from his capacious forehead. "A paralytic – should stop the convulsions – for now at least." As the drug entered his veins, Brian's great form went suddenly rigid, seizures momentarily at an end.

"Right – now we can operate," said Dr. Sanjee cheerfully. A nurse deftly began to shave Brian's head with electric clippers. "There are three membranes protecting the brain, DI Reed," said Dr. Sanjee, rummaging in a tray of instruments "– the meninges, the duramater and the piamater. When the skull is fractured, blood seeps in between these membranes – in the case of DI Abbott, into the akroid space between the duramater and the piamater. This increases intercranial pressure, which causes his convulsions. If we don't relieve it, DI Abbott will continue to convulse until, eventually, he crashes, and we won't be able to bring him back."

"And how will you do that?" I asked in horrified fascination.

"With this," Dr. Sanjee replied, flourishing a pneumatic saw.

The earsplitting dental-chair whine of a high-speed drill fractured the air; there was a gentle pop! like the long cork of an old bottle of claret being drawn. "Ah, that's done it," Dr. Sanjee breathed. "Just catch that in a basin, nurse, thank you – take it to the lab and let's get a cerebrospinal profile. You can relax now, DI Reed – I think he's going to be all right now."

Brian looked peaceful and at ease, despite his forehead sutures and the cast on his arm; the nurses were already bandaging the pound coin-sized hole in his skull. "The next 12 hours will tell the story," said Dr. Sanjee, stripping off his gloves "– if he has no more convulsions, if there is no infection, then he will recover."

"Thank you, doctor," I said. "For fighting for him."

"It was my pleasure," he said "– blokes like you and DI Abbott fight for us every day."

IV

"We've got to stop meeting like this," I told Fee as we sat next to John's bed in the intensive care ward. He still looked terrible, but his colour was better, and he was resting comfortably. He had had no convulsions since the surgery, which was a mildly encouraging sign. The danger in cases like these, so Dr. Sanjee had said, was that the convulsions would continue, with increasing frequency and intensity, until the patient died. There was always the possibility that Brian's intercranial pressure could spike upward again, however, so they were monitoring him closely.

"I know," said Fee, resting her head on my shoulder. "Nothing would give me greater pleasure. But thanks for keeping me company. When you're not here, I talk to him – call him a stupid twat, tell him to get better, tell him how much the girls and I miss him." She wiped her eyes. "It's nice to have someone here who can answer me back."

"Has the doctor spoken to you about what comes after?"

"Once Brian wakes up? Months of rehab, obviously, to get his strength and dexterity back. It's the mental part that's dicey – there's just no way to know what sort of state Brian will be in when he wakes up. There could be whole swaths of his memory gone – he might have to re-learn how to tie his own shoes and dress himself, Dr. Sanjee said. And Brian won't be able to return to the force – you were there when Dr. Sanjee told me that."

I nodded. "I'll miss the big bastard. He's been a champion partner. But it's not worth risking his health. Anyway, I'll still come and beg dinner from you every Monday."

"You're always welcome, Dex. You know that. Perhaps one of these days, you can bring your new girlfriend."

"She's not my girlfriend, Fee. More of an old flame that's flickered back to life."

"Just goes to prove."

"Prove what?"

"That there may be hope for the world yet, if someone as cynical, middle-aged and set in his ruts as you are can find true love."

25

The next morning, after stopping for a word with DCI Wicks, I went to see Bernie down in the holding cells. I told the screw on the door to follow me, then motioned for him to unlock Bernie's cell. "You're free to go, Bernie," I said. "My guv'nor's just okayed it."

He rose slowly to his feet, haggard features painted with relieved disbelief. "I'm no longer under arrest?"

"No. You've been downgraded to a person of interest in the case."

"What does that mean?"

"It means you can't leave the country, at least for the time being. Not until we lock up another suspect or the Metropolitan Police officially determine that it wasn't you."

We were walking out now. "And Jane?" he asked. "You've seen her?"

I nodded. "She's moved out, Bernie. The video was a real shock – she had no idea that you're... gay. Said she'll ring you once you're back home." I didn't mention that I had left her, only that morning, asleep in my bed.

During my walk to work, I had rationalized, coldly and pusillanimously, that there was no point in adding to Bernie's burdens until Jane made up her mind what she was going to do. I knew that was the right decision, at least until she knew her own mind. But I still couldn't look Bernie in the eye.

We stopped by the property desk; I waited as Bernie signed for and pocketed his keys, wallet and watch. Then we walked in silence to the foyer.

"Is she going to... divorce me?" Bernie asked at length.

"I don't know, Bernie. I don't think she knows. But there's no sense borrowing trouble. Just talk to her, mate."

"I will, Dex." We stood in the open air now, traffic breezing by. Bernie turned his face to the wan November sun and breathed in the diesel fumes as if they were the fragrance of the best-kept rose garden in all of England. "Thank you. And thank you for this – you've saved my life, old man. I don't know that I could've stood another week in that cell."

"You're tough, Bernie. You'll get through this."

"Ah, Dex." He smiled sadly. "If only that were true. But thanks awfully, just the same."

II

Afternoon came, and still I toiled over the printouts Brian had requisitioned. Months worth of statements, spreadsheets, performance graphs – Seagrave's, Atkinson's Bernie's, Gleeson's, Weathersby's.

I was damned if I could see what had excited Brian so – with the exception of the previously-noted £100,000 withdrawals from the Atkinson and Gleeson accounts, all five statements showed monthly contributions and steadily-rising net worths. Dick Devilliers, it appeared, really was a financial wiz. Perhaps I did need to put my meager savings in his hands.

My desk phone rang. "DI Reed," I said.

"Dex!" It took me a moment to place the voice – and when I did, excitement and hope set my heart pounding.

"DI Wilkinson," I replied. "What can I do for you?"

"Can you come down to interrogation? There's a few blokes I'd like you to meet."

"You found them?" I asked in a voice hushed with hope.

"We did. Thought you might like to have first crack at the ringleader."

"Keith, I could kiss you," I said. "Be right down."

"Thought you'd be chuffed," he said, and rang off.

DI Wilkinson stood in the hall outside the interrogation rooms, a stocky, balding man in his middle 40s, wearing a departmental training suit with his ID hanging from a chain around his neck. He was keeping a watchful eye on the comings and goings in the hall with the air of a border collie who had just seen his charges into the pen. "Thank you, Keith," I said, and meant it.

"Dex," he said. "We've all been thinking of Brian, and of you. Just make sure you nail these bastards to the wall – they deserve it, many times over."

"How'd you find them?" I asked.

"Made the mistake of achieving celebrity status," he replied serenely. "Got themselves a manager, if you can believe it – thugs for hire. We've got him in custody as well, and he's singing like the next Adele – name's Tony Grant. They'd been operating for several weeks, quite profitably, out of some club in the East End. The Helix. One of our informants grassed them royally – tipped us that their next victim was a music promoter who'd stiffed some house band. We put a detail on him. And just as soon as they swaggered in, we scooped them up."

After providing a few additional details, Wilkinson led the way into the observation lounge. I peered avidly through the one-way glass. A thickset, petulant-looking lad of perhaps 20 years of age sat handcuffed to the metal table, affecting an air of boredom. He had short bristle-blond hair, a fat lip and one glo-riously-swollen eye. "That's Alex," said Wilkinson. "We've got his three mates in separate rooms – some of your colleagues in SCD're giving them a right going-over even as we speak. They're all younger than this one – the youngest is only 16. Alex here looks to be the brains of the bunch."

"He looks a bit... battered," I said happily.

"Well..." Wilkinson looked at his nails. "Had a spot of bother gettin' 'em in the cars, didn't we? Kept bruising their foreheads on the roof."

"Clumsy lads," I said regretfully. "Pity I couldn't've been there to help them in."

"If you had, I suspect we'd've been dropping them off at the morgue, rather than Hendon nick," Wilkinson replied evenly. "Can't say I'd've blamed you – mouthy little pricks. I know how you feel about Brian, Dex."

"Thank you, Keith. I won't forget this."

"You don't owe me, Dex. Brian's one of the good'uns."

III

When I entered the interrogation room, Alex favoured me with a sneer. "Room service, is it? I'll 'ave steak, medium rare, chips and a pint of lager."

I sat down and studied him minutely, from the single gold stud in his left ear to the scabs on his knuckles. He had a pock-marked visage and lips like hovercraft-bladders, twisted into a habitual sneer of cold amusement; there was a nasty, jagged, recently-healed scar extending from his right temple to the bridge of his nose. I looked into his eyes – bloodshot, pale blue, slightly yellowed at the corners. A touch of liver trouble? Drink, perhaps, or pharmaceuticals.

I glanced at his previous, discovered assault with intent to commit bodily harm, burglary, and, interestingly, animal cruelty, in a case involving fighting dogs. I was pleased to see that Alex had recently turned 18, so there was no need for an appropriate adult to witness the interview.

I extended an arm and turned on the recorder. "This interview is taking place on 19 November, 2013, in interview room B at Hendon. Present are DI Dexter Reed of the Metropolitan Police Service Specialist Crime Directorate, Constable Angus McGrath, and Alex Lloyd Watkins, the suspect." I turned to Alex. "DI Wilkinson cautioned you?"

"Yeh."

"And did you understand your rights as he explained them to you?"

Yeh. 'eard 'em before. Know 'em like the back of me 'and."

"Speaking of the back of your hand," I said, "It looks like it's seen some hard use lately. How'd you come by those scabs?"

"'ad some aggro with some sod down the club coup'la nights ago." Alex smiled benignly. "Man's got the right to defend 'imself, don't 'e?"

"Looks painful," I observed.

"You should see the other bloke."

"What club?" I asked.

"The Helix, on Fashion Street."

"Can anyone confirm that?"

"Me droogs."

"Your droogs?" I asked casually.

"Me mates. Georgie, Dim and Fred."

"Ah! Your mates. Well, at least they *were* your mates."

"What d'you mean?" he asked suspiciously, voice betraying the first whiff of uncertainty.

"Because they've just told us you were hired to attack DI Abbott. They say this was all your idea."

He looked at me intently, then laughed. "You're full of shit."

"We've also arrested Tony Grant. Your manager." I made no effort to disguise my satisfaction. "And he's singing like a bloody nightingale."

I laid out the terms of the contract for Alex's benefit, as I had it from Wilkinson. The *Clockwork Orange* boys had been hired to beat Brian to death by a man they had never seen before. He gave no name. The man had initially contacted Grant, their "manager." Grant had arranged the meeting in exchange for a cut of the swag – £2,500 up front, another £2,500 following successful completion of the job.

"We know all about it, Alex. You may as well tell me what happened. I see two choices here. First, you can carry right on messing me about. Or you can try to get out in front of this before the entire weight falls on you. Those are options A and B. Personally, I hope you choose option A."

Alex looked away, grinning once more. "Ah, why not? I just turned 18 yesterday – I was still a minor when we did 'im. Who was 'e, your gay lover?"

"My partner. My mate. A good husband and the dad of two very frightened and miserable little girls. So believe me when I say that your future happiness depends completely on what happens in the next few minutes. Cooperate, and I'll have a word with my mates at Prison Services, and chances are you and your droogs will be reunited behind bars. Hold out on me, and..." I spread my hands. "Belmarsh? Who knows? You may have a harder time making friends."

Alex pursed his sausage-thick lips into a fountain of pink blubber. "Cooperate... how, exactly?"

"Who hired you?"

"'Dunno, do I? Never laid eyes on 'im before."

"What did he look like?"

"Tallish bloke – inch or two taller than you. About your age. Clean-shaven. Posh accent. Gave us a picture of your partner and told us 'e'd be at the Waterloo Building at 2 o'clock. Told us to follow 'im, find a secluded spot, and go postal."

"Hang on!" I said. "The man knew DI Abbott had an appointment at the Waterloo Building at 2 o'clock?"

"Yeh."

"How could he know that?"

"'Ow the fuck do I know? 'E said 'e'd be there, and 'e wos. We waited for 'im, and when 'e came out, we followed 'im. Easy peasy."

"And the man who hired you – you'd recognize him if you say him again, yeah?"

"Oh, I dunno, mate." Alex grinned insolently, a jack-o-lantern's jagged-toothed grin, and I longed to smack it off his face. "Me memory ain't quite what it used to be." He tapped his forehead. "Too many blows to the old melon."

A sudden thought occurred. "Wait here," I said "– won't be a sec."

I went to my cube and stood for a moment, looking at Brian's desk. I wouldn't let them take his things away – not while there was still a chance he might return to the job. His side of the cubicle had already acquired a thin film of dust.

I went to my desk, made a selection from the array of Hastewicke Gentlemen photographs on the wall. Then I returned to the interrogation room and laid the photo before Alex. "Wot's this?" he asked. "The Man-Boy Love Association's annual beach outing? Detective – I never would've suspected such tendencies in you."

It was a picture of the Hastewicke Gentlemen first XV on False Beach in Capetown, from 2001, the cloud-topped bulk of Table Mountain looming over our shoulders. "See anyone you recognize?" I asked.

"I recognize *'im*," said Alex contemptuously. "Mr. Philanthropist! 'Im and 'is bloody Magwitch Centres, lordin' it over us peasants. Well, 'e showed 'is true colours in the end, didn't 'e, detective? And I recognize you as well – you 'aven't aged well, 'ave you, DI Reed?"

"Is the man who hired you to assault DI Abbott in this photograph?" I asked patiently.

Alex leaned back and folded his arms. "Yeh. 'E's there."

I spoke through gritted teeth. "Which one is he, Alex?"

"That's valuable information." He grinned again. "Tell you in the morning, after I've spoken with my legal advisor."

For a moment, I just stared at him, then all my fury at recent events erupted, and I threw my chair aside and went for Alex. Eyes wide in terror, he retreated around the table, and I perceived that while Alex derived great pleasure from inflicting pain, he didn't relish receiving it.

"DI Reed!" Wicks stood at the door; his voice rang across the chamber like one of Hell's bells. "You forget yourself! This isn't *NYPD Blue!*"

With the utmost reluctance, I righted my chair and forced myself back into it. Wicks spoke into the microphone. "Let the record show that Mr. Watkins has invoked his right to counsel. This interview is terminated at 8:21 p.m." And Wicks, with a significant glare my way, pressed the "stop" button on the recorder.

IV

Seething with fury and impatience, I trudged home. Jane was sitting cross-legged before the fire, barefoot, looking ravishing in a soft turtleneck of starlight blue and a pair of old Levis. The kind with the fly buttons, that pop ever so deliciously, effervescent with erotic promise, as you let your fingers do the walking.

She was drinking red wine. Seeing the look on my face as I crested the stairs, she poured me a glass and patted the floor beside her. "Poor Dex," she said "– I don't think I have to ask how your day was. Come sit beside me and tell me all about it."

I shed my coat and did as she bid me, gratefully accepting the proffered glass of wine. It swiftly disappeared as all my anguish came spilling out in a long soliloquy of frustration. "I'm so close, Jane! So close to the truth! If only it was a hundred years ago – I'd have beaten it out of that smug little shit by now."

I slowly became conscious of her luminous eyes, and her hand, gently massaging the kinks from my neck, and suddenly realized how wonderful, how completely, magically incredible, it was to have her here. To have someone to come home to, someone who listened, someone who cared with all her heart how my day had gone. I strategically nestled my head between her breasts, and she stroked my brow in a way that would have melted a lesser man. "Thank you, Jane," I murmured. "Sorry for venting."

"It's my pleasure, Dex," she said, and I felt her warm breath in my hair. "And now there's something I need to say to you." I looked up in alarm, but she pressed me back to her bosom. "Don't worry, it's not like last time. It's just that I've been thinking about things, and I've suddenly realized something. I've been such a hothouse flower, Dex! For 15 years I've been protected, nurtured, kept warm and safe, glassed in with money, never worrying, never threatened – but never growing. Never flowering. These last few weeks with you I've realized how much I've been missing. I've seen you dealing with the attack on Brian, your worry, your tenderness with Fee, and yes! It's terrifying! But it's real life, Dex! I've seen how John's murder, and your situation with the rugby club, has affected you, how you've tried with all your heart to protect them, while still doing your duty to the Service.

Even as they've turned on you one by one. I've seen how the other night at training devastated you, and I'm in awe! You're so full of honour, and so full of life."

She took a deep breath, and reached down to cover my mouth with her hand as I opened it to speak. "And so what I'm saying, Dex, is that I'm tired of cowering in my little patch of ground, watching the world go by outside the glass. To make a very long story short, I'm yours, if you'll have me."

She took her hand away from my mouth then, and I sat up. But before I could respond, the doorbell rang. "Excuse me," I said. "Won't be a sec."

When I opened the door, I beheld a black-haired, fortysomething bloke with a salt-and-pepper goatee, clutching a notebook, whom I'd never laid eyes on before. "Yes?" I asked in my least welcoming tone.

"DI Reed – please don't slam the door. I'm Matthew Teller from the *Express*, and I've heard about your involvement with the Hastewicke Gentlemen and with the Weathersby murder investigation. I'd like to tell your story. It must've been a helluva..."

"No comment," I said, and gently but firmly closed the door in his face.

When I returned to the fireside, I found Jane, arms clasped 'round her knees, staring raptly into the flames. Her eyes, as she turned to me, were lasciviously merry.

"Bloody press," I muttered.

"Occupational hazard for soon-to-be-famous detectives," she observed teasingly. "Bad timing, though – I was just about to say that the sex has been brilliant as well." And she twined her arms about my neck, and kissed me with a greedy, sloppy passion that threatened to suck out my soul.

I detached myself just long enough to utter one breathless sentence. "Yes, I'll have you, please."

She drew back, and regarded me joyfully. "Yes, I think you will." And she slowly peeled off her sweater. She wore nothing underneath.

At that moment, the bell went again. I am, God knows, a mild-mannered and forbearing man, but by interrupting my enjoyment of the bounty before me, young Teller had just risked a violent rupture in the Metropolitan Police Service's occasionally-friendly relationship with the London press. "This could go on all night," I said through gritted teeth. "Don't move. If you hear the sound of blows, don't be alarmed."

I stalked downstairs to the entry and threw open the door. "I *said*, no bloody..." And then I stopped dead, the power of speech knocked clean out of me.

Charlie Chalmers stood on my stoop – Charlie Chalmers, my old friend and rugby mentor, dead these ten long years, but now returned to the living.

And pointing a gun at me – a black, businesslike Glock 17.

He wasn't alone. Bernie Plantagenet, weaving drunk, clutched at the stair-rail for support, looking ready to topple into the hydrangeas at the first breath of wind. "Dex!" he said brightly. "Can you believe it? Iss old Charlie, in the flesh! I was just... just having a quiet drink at home, and there was a ring at the bell, and there he was! I fell off my chair, I really did! He sug... sug-ges... he said we should stop 'round and pay you a visit, and here we are!" He leant forward conspiratorially, enveloping me in a cloud of brandy-fumes. "You wouldn't happen to have anything to drink, would you, old man? I think this calls for a celebration!"

"Hullo, Dex," said Charlie quietly. "It's been a long time. I've missed you." His eyes, and the Glock, pointed at my heart, never wavered. "Shall we go inside?"

Wordlessly I stood aside. Charlie motioned me up the steps first; I gave Bernie a hand. He stumbled and leaned against me, absolutely reeking of alcohol.

Jane, forewarned by our clumsy ascent, was fully dressed once more. "Bernie!" she cried. "And...my God." Her voice sunk to a whisper. "Is it really you, Charlie?"

"In the flesh," he said easily. And then she saw the gun.

26

Charlie motioned with the gun for Jane and I to have a seat on the couch. "Sorry to just pop up like this, Dex. Must be a hell of a shock."

I nodded. "You could say that. Why the gun, Charlie?"

"Just so there's no mistake about tonight's agenda. No need to worry, as long as everyone behaves himself." I felt Jane tremble as his gaze passed over her. "Or herself."

I studied him in the light of the reading lamp beside his chair. The years had changed him little – the same wry expression, the same blond thatch – a bit thinner on top, perhaps. He had the same erect bearing, which emphasized his height – about 6'5" – and sprightly step. He still retained his deceptive slimness and, I could only assume, his yew-like strength.

Charlie was studying me as well, like an Egyptologist trying to puzzle out a particularly obscure hieroglyphic. "You look fit,

Dex," he said at length. "A bit more battered than last I saw you. A bit more... careworn, perhaps."

"It's been a long couple of months," I replied. "First Weathersby, then my partner."

Charlie looked troubled. "Yes. Your partner. Brian, is it? Look, I'm sorry about that, Dex – couldn't be helped. He was a bit cleverer than I reckoned – he'd found me out, you see."

I suddenly felt light-headed. "It was you. I was on the mobile with him – he said he knew who killed John, but he wouldn't tell me who. Then he was attacked."

"John." Charlie's look darkened. "That selfish, greedy bastard. He had no right to live. Not when I was dead to the world, and to everyone I'd ever loved."

"Why don't you tell me about it, Charlie? It might help to talk."

"Why not? We've plenty of time. You always did enjoy a good story, Dex. But first, I think Bernie needs topping up. Pour him a stiff one, and yourself as well."

I went to the drinks cabinet; Charlie watched me alertly as I splashed several inches of whisky into a pair of glasses, took one to where Bernie sat nodding in his chair. "Here, Bern. Cheers."

"Ta, Dex." He peered up at me, trying to focus. "Nice place you've got here. Could you... tell Jane when she's ready to talk, I'm here."

"Drink up, Dex," said Charlie. "All of it, then pour yourself another, and drink that off as well."

Staring into the Glock's unwinking black eye, I had little choice. The strong single-malt made a pool of liquid fire in my empty stomach.

"Where shall I begin?" Charlie mused, as I resumed my seat next to Jane. "Ah, yes – Weathersby. You know he was black-mailing me, just before I died?"

I nodded. "Dick Devilliers told us."

Charlie grimaced. "Careless of him. Weathersby wanted £250,000. I didn't have it. I was mortgaged to the hilt – everything I had was tied up in the firm, and then some. It had been a hell-ish year – we'd lost a lot of dosh. And then Weathersby... bloody tosser. Anyway, one day I hopped aboard my plane to fly to France. Halfway across the Channel, I parachuted out. The plane went into the drink. A French smuggler my brother Ian knew fished me out – paid him a thousand pounds to pick me up. Ian met me on the dock at Le Touquet, drove me to Annecy, where I became Daniel Becket, mild-mannered exporter of wine, cheese and foie gras. Made a refreshing change, actually – Devilliers sent Ian money from my estate every month, so I was never under any pressure to turn a profit. In point of fact, and quite ironically, the export firm's doing very well."

I nodded, feeling a bit woozy from the whisky. "Then Devilliers told you Weathersby was up to his old tricks."

"One afternoon Bernie here came to Dick's office for a consult on his portfolio. He was in a right state – needed to find £120,000 from somewhere, without Jane finding out, to pay off... well, it was that Artemis Paul bastard who tried to kill you, wasn't it?

Saw it in the news. Bernie and Dick had a few drinks, and soon the whole sordid tale came spilling out. Dick made the mistake of putting an abbreviated version into an email to me. Your partner, Brian, found it when he tapped into Dick's computer."

I gave Jane's arm a reassuring squeeze. "Carry on."

Charlie leaned back in his chair; his deep, melodious voice came from the shadows. "Which brings us to the night of John's party. The Charlie Chalmers Memorial." He laughed bitterly. "That's rich. Must've been his way of salving a guilty conscience. I stood in his garden for most of the night, watching you at your revels, longing to pop in and surprise you all. Even saw you and Jane when you came out on the terrace. Heard a bit of your conversation as well – enough to surmise that I'd find her here with you tonight." There was a pause. "Do you have any idea what it's been like for me, Dex? To lose the one thing in the world I truly loved, to be condemned to stand and watch you all, like a ghost?"

I flicked a glance at Jane. "Yes, I think I might. What happened then?"

"I waited until the last of you had gone. Used the intervening time to cut the wires and bypass the alarm – astonishing what you can find on the Internet these days. After the last guest had gone, John went into his study – I could see him working at his computer. When he got up for a piss, I broke the lock on the French doors sat down at his desk, loaded the rifle, and waited. When he came back through the door, I shot him."

"Without a word?" I asked.

"I said, 'Hullo, John. Kangaroo court is now in session. You're guilty as hell.' Then I pulled the trigger. I took his laptop, went back over the wall, walked down to Battersea Bridge and threw it into the Thames."

"Any regrets?" I asked lightly.

"Only that I didn't do it sooner." Charlie regarded me keenly. "You, of all people, understand the impulse, Dex. When someone would cheap-shot one of our teammates, it was always you and I who sorted them out. We're the hard men. Tell me you're not glad John's dead, knowing what you now know."

"I'm not sorry he's dead, to be honest." The whisky was running away with my tongue. "But Charlie, you should've left it to me. I knew something wasn't right about the Vegas tour. I'd've come 'round to John in the end."

Charlie snorted contemptuously. "Would you have? I doubt it. Where were you when I was being blackmailed? Or Jester, or Gleeson?"

"I had no idea. You were my friend, but you never told me, did you? If you'd've come to me, Weathersby would be in jail, we'd've found a way to keep you alive, and none of this would've had to happen. You should've come to me, Charlie! I would have done anything for you! But I'm a copper, not a bloody mind-reader!"

"So what was different this time? Why d'you think you would've tumbled?"

"Because I had Bernie – found out he'd borrowed money from Artemis Paul. I went to see him about it the afternoon of the party. When you killed Weathersby later that same night, then it became a murder investigation. I'd've nailed John, Charlie. But then you made all his victims – our mates – into suspects."

"I wanted to stop him doing to them what he did to me – driving them to desperation!"

"No, you did that yourself, Charlie," I said bitterly. "By killing Weathersby, you triggered the very shitstorm they were hoping to avoid! How could you not know Weathersby had made backup copies of the videos, to be circulated if anything happened to him?"

"I was counting on you to stop that happening, Dex. And you came through magnificently! But then you allowed the videos to slip through your hands! You bloody well knocked them on! How could you have been so bloody careless?"

"Careless? Charlie, when my superiors ordered me to make copies of the videos, I couldn't very well refuse, could I? I took every precaution I could think of – that's how we were able to nail the bastard who leaked them!"

"But by then, the damage was done," he said coldly. "You should've just destroyed them, Dex!"

"Couldn't do that, Charlie. They were the primary evidence in a high-profile murder case! Yes, I'm protective of my team-mates! But even I can't cover up a murder! That's too much to ask, even of me!"

"So what about me, then?" Charlie asked lightly. "Are you going to turn me in?"

I thought about that. Despite my professional responsibility to bring his murderer to justice, no one would ever convince me John hadn't had it coming. And Charlie was officially dead – no one, save Brian, had ever so much as thought of him as a suspect. If it had just been between him and me, if I allowed myself to be guided solely by my own sense of justice, I would've been very tempted to just let Charlie go, as long as Bernie, Seagrave, Barlowe and Leicester weren't prosecuted.

But it wasn't just between Charlie and me – not anymore. He'd crossed that line when he attacked Brian. And now he'd involved Jane and Bernie. Then there was the fact that he was pointing a gun at me, and that I had begun to understand why. Charlie had brought Bernie along tonight for a reason. "Somehow I don't think I'll be given that option," I replied as lightly as I could.

"You didn't answer my question, Dex."

"If I say no, will you leave us in peace, and agree to vanish once again?"

"I can't do that, Dex." Charlie rose, and stood staring into the glowing embers of the fire. "The fact is, I'm very disappointed in you. Thanks to your carelessness, four of the people I care most about in the world are facing personal and professional ruin. And now I find that you've been taking your pleasure with the lovely Jane, even while our old mate Bernie has been locked up, facing prosecution for a crime he didn't commit! I've seen a lot of bad behaviour in 35 years of rugby, Dex. But this really is contemptibly low!"

Bernie stirred feebly. "...'temptably low," he muttered.

Charlie ignored him, fixing me with the same smoldering predatory stare he'd so often used on malefactors on the rugby pitch. "Well? What d'you have to say for yourselves?"

Jane, until now, had huddled silent and trembling beside me. She wasn't trembling any more. "What business is it of yours, Charlie? Are you the moral guardian of the club now? If so, and if half the rumours I've heard are true, you've got your work cut out for you! I didn't know Bernie was gay, Charlie. Do you know what a shock it was when I found out? I've loved Dex for ages! Yes, we had an affair 15 years ago! But since then, I've asked him to respect my marriage, and he's been gentleman enough to agree! When I saw Bernie's video, I came to Dex – even then, he didn't come to me. We're grown-ups, Charlie – all of us. We make our own decisions – you don't make them for us. I love Dex, Charlie! And nothing you can do or say is going to change that!"

It was the wrong tack to take with a man whose years of enforced isolation had created an obsessive and idealized memory of his old mates – as well as a delusional sense of his own rights as judge, jury and executioner. I saw Bernie sit up groggily in his chair, struggling desperately to follow the conversation, as Charlie turned his full attention on Jane.

"Well that's clear enough, then," he said, with sudden decisiveness. "If that's the way things are, perhaps you two lovebirds would be good enough to disrobe, and lie down before the fire."

"What?" I asked dangerously.

"Strip off!" he snarled. "Or I'll shoot you where you sit."

I looked at Jane, mind seething. My MPS training came back to me. Avoid upsetting the man with the gun, play for time, watch alertly for your opportunity. I shrugged, pulled off my tie, and began unbuttoning my shirt. Jane, following my lead, also began slowly to disrobe.

"That's a good girl. Just scatter your clothes passionately on the floor... now lay down by the fire – yes, that's right. Believe me, I take no pleasure in this. Sorry it's come to this, but when a drunken, cuckolded wreck of a man happens on his wife and best friend in a passionate embrace, and you mix in an unregistered, untraceable handgun... well, murder, suicide, it's the stuff of Shakespearean tragedy, isn't it? Goodbye, Jane – and goodbye, Dex, my old friend." And Charlie aimed the gun.

I suddenly lashed out with a foot, to send the lamp crashing to the floor, grabbed Jane and rolled atop her into the precarious shelter of the sofa. At that moment, I heard Bernie suddenly rejoin the damned choir of the living. "That's my WIFE, you bastard!" Then came the sound of two heavy bodies colliding.

I leapt to my feet, to behold Bernie, fighting with maniacal strength for possession of the gun. Charlie, eyes bulging, struggled to force it away from his own torso. Even as I leapt forward to join the battle, a deafening report rattled the windows. Charlie's knees buckled, and he slumped to the floor.

Bernie held the gun loosely at his side. "Charlie!" he cried piteously. "What've I done?" Then his woozy gaze found me, and Jane, where she had struggled to a sitting position. "Oh, God, Jane, what've I done?" he whispered. "I've ruined everything."

"It's all right, Bern," I said. "You had no choice."

He seemed not to hear me, but turned his haunted gaze to Jane. "I'm so ashamed," he said. "I've hurt you so badly! You never deserved it. You deserved a man who was strong, and good, and knew what he wanted to do with his life! For God's sake, you at least deserved a husband who knew what he was! I... I wanted to tell you. I just didn't have the guts."

"It's all right, Bernie," I said, edging closer. "Why don't you give me the gun, now. The police're coming – we don't want any misunderstandings."

"I don't blame you for going to Dex – God knows I've wanted to, sometimes. He's a good man. And you're a rare woman. Forgive me, Jane. You deserved better."

And he raised the gun to his head.

Then Jane was there, walking toward him, nearly naked but calm and unafraid. "Bernie, darling, no," she said. "Don't leave me – not like this. I love you, Bernie. I don't want you to go. It's me who should be asking your forgiveness. Now don't be an ass – this won't solve anything. Give Dex the gun."

"Jane, I..."

Her voice sharpened. "Don't argue, Bernie. You know I'm right. Give Dex the gun."

Like one in a dream, Bernie slowly lowered the Glock until it hung limply at his side. I took it from him carefully as Jane rushed into his arms. "Bernie you ass, you ass! What were you thinking?"

"I... don't know," I heard him murmur dazedly. "Just seemed like the thing to do."

Charlie lay on his back, eyes open, as if unable to believe the unthinkable tragedy that had, at last, overtaken him. I felt his carotid – no pulse. The blackened bullet-hole under his chin and the spreading pool of blood beneath his head told me why. He'd come here tonight to kill me – I knew that. So why was I crying, sobs wracking my weary shoulders, as all the bitter, earth-shaking grief of his loss a decade or more ago came flooding back?

I felt arms around me then, as both Jane and Bernie forgot their own anguish and tried to comfort me. And that's how the uniformed boys found us – three grief-stricken people, two of them half-naked, clinging desperately to one another like lost climbers in an Everest blizzard, with a corpse on the floor and a smoking Glock on the table.

27

The last time I saw Charlie Chalmers, before he vanished from my life in 2004, we'd met for a drink after work, at the Barley Mow in Dorset Street, a cozy old pub with private booths tucked away in various crannies and crevices. Charlie was several pints ahead of me when I arrived, fresh from a particularly sad and disturbing homicide. A pleasant, quiet couple in their 50s, the Healys, had lived for years in a row-house in Nottingham Street, in Marylebone. They'd been married 41 years. Earlier that afternoon, the wife, Beryl, had rung 999 to suggest that it might be a good idea if the police called 'round. When the operator asked why, Beryl had replied calmly, "Because I've killed him." She then provided her address, brushed her hair, touched up her makeup, and waited placidly next to her rapidly-cooling husband for the police.

It seemed that when Mr. Healy had arrived home for his lunch, Beryl had served him a nice curry laced with enough rat poison to kill a hippopotamus. When I asked her why, she had frowned slightly, a pleasant-looking, grandmotherly woman with an impressive bosom, her soft brown hair now running to grey, as if trying to think of a plausible reason. "I couldn't stand the way he belched when he ate," she replied at length.

Charlie had absorbed this tale with gloomy concentration. He looked uncharacteristically harried and out of sorts; I could tell there was something weighing on him. "That's the fascinating thing about relationships, isn't it, Dex?" he'd said when I finished. "You think you know someone, then boom! One day they turn on you. It's like you never really knew them at all! And yet, if you never trust anyone, you'll never be loved in return. And what kind of life is that? Once you're dead, it's like you never existed." He drained his pint, signaled for another. "I hope that, when I'm dead, you, at least, will remember me fondly."

"After all the fines you've given me in kangaroo court? Not bloody likely, mate. Now tell me – what's eating you? You seem a bit gloomy, but perhaps it's just constipation, or impotence."

"That obvious, is it?"

"I'm a policeman, Charlie – I'm paid to notice things. Anything I can do to help?"

For just a moment, he seemed on the verge of spilling it all. Then he managed a sour grin, and clapped me on the shoulder. "Nah, but thanks for asking. You've always been the best of them, d'you know that, Dex? I knew the first time I laid eyes on you that there was something special about you. Remember, in that changing-room at school? You'd just given that stuck-up little turd Lord Westbrook a right walloping. I invited you out for rugby."

I raised my glass. "And started me on the road to perdition. I do have a lot to blame you for, don't I?"

"Let me buy you a drink, to make partial amends," he said, signaling the barman. "Life's an uncertain thing, Dex! Who knows? It could be the last we'll ever have together."

"In that case," I said, "better make it a large one."

And that was the last time I ever saw Charlie Chalmers – until the night, a decade or so later, that he came to kill me.

II

I was dozing fitfully next to Brian's bed, in a chair that apparently had been ordered from Marquis de Sade Hospital Furnishings Ltd., when a croaking voice, like that of Hell's parched doorman, awakened me. "Christ, you look worse than I feel."

"God's balls!" I leapt to my feet. "Brian, you're awake!"

"I just now woke up. Where the hell am I?"

I turned briefly away to hide the tears that suddenly sprang to my eyes. "University Hospital," I managed, after a pause. "How d'you feel?"

"Like shit, mate. My head feels like somebody's drilled a hole in it."

"Funny you should say that."

Brian regarded me speculatively. "They didn't."

"Had to. Seizures. Gave Fee and me quite a turn, I don't mind telling you now."

"What happened to me?"

"You were set upon and beaten within an inch of your bloody life. You don't remember?"

"Last thing I remember is walking down the Charing Cross Road, chatting to you on the mobile, about... what were we talking about?"

"The Weathersby case."

"Right. And after that, it's all a blank until I woke up here. What's the date? How long have I been out?"

"Six days. Today's the 17th of November."

"Six days? JESUS CHRIST!" A pause, and Brian raised his uninjured hand shakily to his brow. "Oooh – shouldn't have done that. Six days! Fancy that. No wonder I'm famished. Who was it attacked me?"

"Four teenaged louts playing at *A Clockwork Orange*. They were paid to thrash you. They're in the clink even as we speak, repenting their sins."

"Paid to attack me." Brian paused to take inventory – bandaged head, stitches in his forehead, right arm in a cast to the armpit, left leg in a cast, broken ribs bound up, assorted abrasions, cuts and contusions. "They earned their money, I'll give them that. I take it they were being paid by the blow. But by whom?"

"D'you remember anything about the conversation we were having when you were attacked?"

Brian frowned painfully. "Is there any water? I'm parched." I found a pitcher, poured a glass and helped him drink. "Thanks, Dex. I remember snatches. Bits and pieces. I remember I'd just been to see... Devilliers. One of the boys in Computer Crime... Graves... had tapped into Devilliers' computer. He found..." Brian trailed off.

"You told me you knew who killed Weathersby – that you'd solved the case. But you wouldn't tell me who it was, you bastard! We were going to meet for a pint so you could tell me all about it."

Brian closed his eyes in an agony of concentration. Then, abruptly, they snapped open. "Chalmers!" he rasped. "It was Chalmers, Dex! I remember now! Graves found an email... Dex, he's alive! Chalmers is alive!"

"Not anymore, Brian." And I filled him in on the events of the last few days.

"Oh, sweet Jesus and Mary," he said when I'd finished. "You poor bastard. He was your mate, wasn't he?"

I nodded, feeling the anguish of it afresh, like heat to a new burn. "Like a brother."

"But he was going to kill you?"

"Oh, yes. And Jane. And Bernie. And make it look like Bernie did it, in a jealous, drunken rage."

"And I'd've been next – a pillow over the face, or an injection of air."

I nodded again. "In all likelihood. Devilliers too, perhaps. Then Charlie's secret would've been safe forever."

"And Jane? How did she happen to be there?"

I told him about Jane and I. I wanted no secrets between us. Not anymore.

"Well," he said, not quite knowing what to say. "I'm shocked and appalled, in case Fee asks. Just between you and I, having seen her, I don't think I could've resisted her wiles either. Is this going to be a permanent arrangement, then?"

"I hope so," I replied. "I'd like it to be, but it's up to her. I'm meeting her in half an hour – guess I'll find out then. And now..." I went to the bedside phone, punched in a number, and held the receiver to Brian's ear, "there's someone you need to talk to more than me."

"Hullo, gorgeous," Brian croaked. "Send the kids away and drop your knickers – I'm coming home!" I pretended not to notice the tears running in rivers into his beard.

III

Jane had asked me to meet her in the bar at the Park Hotel – the very place our affair had begun so many years ago. I hadn't seen her since that terrible night in my flat, though we had spoken often and affectionately on the phone. She was sipping a gimlet when I arrived; she rose and kissed me softly. "Hullo, Dex," she smiled. "I like to come here sometimes, you see. To think about that thrilling night 15 years ago, when we first..." she trailed off.

I felt an awkwardness between us, a constraint that hadn't been there two nights ago. Then, talking to her had seemed the easiest and most natural thing in the world. Now I sensed a wariness in her, saw something in her warm brown eyes that gave me pause. "How's Bernie?" I asked at length.

"Oh, you know. On the mend. At times he seems the Bernie of old. But it's going to take time. All of the press coverage isn't helping."

"And how's Jane?" I asked quietly, taking her hand.

"Muddled, Dex, to be honest." She gave me a tremulous smile. "I love you – I'm clear on that. But you saw Bernie the other night. He was going to... Dex, I just don't know what to do anymore."

I'd be the first to tell you that I'm a mess, romantically – unable to commit unreservedly, distant, wary, emotionally stunted. But now, for once in my life, I knew I had to consign caution to the crapper. I took Jane's other hand, and pulled her 'round to look me in the face.

"I'll tell you what to do, then. All my life I've done good deeds for other people – opening doors for old ladies, punching sadistic bastards on the rugby pitch, putting criminals in prison. And what's it got me? It seems to me that, here lately, every time I do someone a good turn, fate gives me a swift kick in the googlies. Fair enough, I'm a big boy, I can take it. But I'm through doing the honourable thing. I've always been honest with you, Jane. So I'm going to tell you the God's honest truth – I love you. I love you, beyond dreaming and hope. I love the way the morning sun looks on your face, and strikes sparks from your hair. I love the sounds you make while you're sleeping. I love coming home and smelling your perfume, and the delicious anticipation of knowing you'll be waiting there for me. I love the way you reach out absently and caress me while we're reading, or watching the telly, or talking. I love your tender heart, even though I know it's the reason I'm going to lose you again." I paused, for there were tears in her eyes now. "I am going to lose you, aren't I?"

She threw her arms around my neck, sobbing like Eve as the gates of paradise closed behind her, hot tears soaking my shirt. I just held her, and stroked her lovely curly hair, knowing in my too-weary heart that it was, in all likelihood, for the very last time. Finally she drew back, that heartbreak face red, tear-tracked and swollen. All she could do was nod mutely.

"Why?" I asked. "I've waited so long for you, Jane. Can't you find a little pity for me as well?"

"You're the strong one, Dex! You saw what Bernie did the other night. His brother has disowned him – saw the report on the news and called to say he never wanted to see Bernie again. He's the only family Bernie's got! If I leave him now, he'll be all alone! I'm afraid he'll kill himself – maybe not with a bullet to the head, but more slowly, with drink! I just can't have that on my conscience. I've got to get him settled first. Then I can come back to you."

"Jane," I said, as gently as I could. "If someone's going to kill themselves with drink, there's nothing you can do. They have to want to live!"

"I know," she said, looking me fiercely in the eye. "I know that's true, Dex! But I can't give him another reason to want to die."

There was a weighty sense of finality about that. Still, I had to try. I had to. "I need you too," I said. "For 15 years I've been waiting for you to come to your senses. I know it's pathetic, but since the night we met here, in this bar, I've never loved anyone but you. I'm begging you. Don't go."

She kissed me then, tenderly, and with such emotion, that I dared to dream, for one brief moment, that hope, true love and passion had triumphed over guilt, and fate, and the clinging arms of weary obligation. And then she put her hands on my biceps, and pushed herself away.

"I'm so sorry, Dex. I just can't leave him. Not now." And then fell the heaviest blow of all. "We're going to New Zealand. To get away from the paparazzi – they've been so horrible."

"New Zealand," I murmured, like a man in a dream.

She rose. "I'll call you when I get settled. And some day, some day soon..."

I rose too. "You'll love New Zealand. It's green, and quiet, With lots of exotic flowers. You'll be right at home, there. Goodbye, my love." And then I left, before I could wound her further.

28

And so the Hastewicke Gentlemen, the only rugby club I'd ever known, were no more. And Jane was gone as well, far away and over the sea, never to return. I contemplated a future without either of the great loves of my life, and realized, with sudden chilling clarity, what a cold and monochromatic place the world could be.

The long night, alone in my flat, loomed before me. I started to ring Brian, out of ancient habit, then remembered and clicked off the phone. Instead I stirred up a bite to eat. But the food tasted like jersey-fabric; I should know. I went to my bookshelves, took down *The Pickwick Papers*, but even the droll adventures of Sam Weller, Mr. Snodgrass, Mr. Winkle and the Fat Boy failed to cheer me.

I suddenly remembered it was music night at my local pub, the Old White Beare. Perhaps a pint, and an hour or so of the old dulcet strains, would set me right. I slipped on a leather jacket and wandered down.

The Beare was crowded tonight; I squeezed in at the bar and ordered Sam Smith's from the oak. The comforting hiss of the hand-pump was barely audible over the raucous growl of an old Pogues tune, emanating from the tiny bandstand in the corner. Celtic tonight, it would appear. The song ended, and most of the band left the stage. A single musician remained, seated on a stool, head bowed over his instrument. Suddenly the haunting moan of the Uilleann bagpipes, so much sweeter than their Highland counterparts, wafted over the room, keening of unsustainable grief and bitter loss, in perfect harmony with my own bleak mood.

Then the piper raised his head, eyes closed, lost in his wordless tale of heart-squeezing melancholy. It was Mick Ryan, Artemis Paul's onetime leg-breaker, the bellows strapped to his arm, playing the pipes with great concentration. Then his eyes opened, and he noticed me, and nodded. When the tune mourned eerily to a close, the band took a break, and he wandered over.

"Great tune. Stood the hairs up on the back of my neck."

"Thanks. It's one I wrote. Is that for me?" He indicated the second pint at my elbow. I nodded. "Cheers. It's thirsty work."

"I've heard the Irish pipes are the most difficult instrument to learn in all of music. Is that true?"

Mick shrugged. "I've practiced every day for the past 20 years. Another 20, and I might scratch the surface of what they can give me."

Mick set down his pint, shot me a speculative glance. He opened his mouth, then closed it again, as if unsure how to proceed. "Listen, I just wanted to tell you somethin'. I'm not gay."

"I know. Never thought you were. Never thought it mattered. We are what we are, and we do what we have to do to survive."

He gave a satisfied nod; that cleared that up, then. "So. Ya still playin'?"

"What, rugby? Not lately." And, with nothing better to do, I wasted fifteen minutes of his time, and told him the whole sordid tale. "And so the Hastewicke Gentlemen are now but a memory. I know one thing for sure. If I ever play again, I'll be a lot better-behaved on tour."

"Nah." He grinned. "Ya won't. That's the glory of the game, isn't it? It's all about trust. After all, if you can't trust your rugby mates, who *can* you trust?"

Mick signaled the publican for two more of the same. "Why not join us, then?"

"Who? The band?"

"Christ no – I've heard ya sing at drink-ups. The London Celtic Gentlemen, o'course. Our open-side flanker's just about ready to hang it up – got two bad knees and a hietal hernia. Not worth a damn on the pitch, really, but we keep him around for his fine tenor voice. You should hear him sing 'The Balls of O'Leary.' Bring tears to your eyes, it would."

"Open side, you say." I said, and suddenly, just a pixel at a time, some of the old colour crept back into the world. "I've always played blind-side."

"That's my position," he grinned. "But we'd have a hell of a pack, with you on the other side. Graeme, the hooker, used to play for Wasps, and Tynan was a second-row at Bath in the '90s. Anyway, think about it – we practice Tuesdays and Thursdays in Spitalfields. Whitechapel Road – ya can't miss it." And with a nod, he returned to his music.

The London Celtic. It had a comfortable ring to it. Then I thought of Jane, wherever she was, and drank a silent toast. And then I turned to go. On. To go on. And knew Mick Ryan had just saved me, once again.

THE END